“Do you k

to kiss you, Julie

She shook her head because she did not know but wanted to…desperately.

“Since I was fifteen years old.” The warmth of Trea’s breath inched closer to her lips.

“That’s a very long wait. I think you ought to do it… now.”

The warmth, the possessive pressure of his lips coming down upon hers, was half a heartbeat from a miracle. For as long as he claimed to have dreamed of this moment, so had she. His grip on her waist was firm, his fingers warm, tender as they inched up her back in a possessive advance. Muscular arms circled her ribs, drew her in.

With heartbeat pressed against heartbeat, Trea Culverson changed her world.

Life might appear normal once he released her lips, but she would never be. In time she might have recovered from a kiss given by the fifteen-year-old boy, but not the man. No, she would never recover from him.

And if he didn’t feel the same way?

She could not let herself think it. Right now, in this moment, they were not simply meeting mouth to mouth, but soul to soul.

Author Note

Does it seem to you like the year has gone by in a blink? No sooner have we taken down the Christmas tree and here we are putting up a new one? For me, this is a very good thing since I love Christmas. December overflows with pretty decorations, extra-yummy food, lovely music, good will toward men...and Christmas stories!

Thank you so much for picking up a copy of *A Texas Christmas Reunion*! I hope Juliette and Trea's romance will add to your Yuletide cheer. Juliette as a schoolgirl was fresh and eager for life. Were you like her? Perhaps in hopeless infatuation with a handsome boy, one you were even too nervous to even say hello to? Maybe you daydreamed about holding hands with him, wondered what it would be like to slow dance with him...or *kiss* him? I imagine that for most of us life moved on and that boy became a fading dream.

But what if one day you turned a corner and there he was? What if the grown-up you was given a second chance at unrequited love? It happened to Juliette! Come along through the pages and live that second chance with her. Naturally, her path is not straight or easy, but it does lead her to the place she always dreamed of being.

It is my wish and prayer that the holiday finds you surrounded by loved ones and filled with the joy that is unique to Christmas.

CAROL ARENS

A Texas Christmas Reunion

Recycling programs for this product may not exist in your area.

ISBN-13: 978-1-335-05183-7

A Texas Christmas Reunion

This edition published by arrangement with Harlequin Books S.A.

For questions and comments about the quality of this book, please contact us at CustomerService@Harlequin.com.

Printed in U.S.A.

Carol Arens delights in tossing fictional characters into hot water, watching them steam and then giving them a happily-ever-after. When she is not writing, she enjoys spending time with her family, beach camping or lounging about a mountain cabin. At home, she enjoys playing with her grandchildren and gardening. During rare spare moments, you will find her snuggled up with a good book. Carol enjoys hearing from readers at carolarens@yahoo.com or on Facebook.

Books by Carol Arens

Harlequin Historical

Dreaming of a Western Christmas
"Snowbound with the Cowboy"
Western Christmas Proposals
"The Sheriff's Christmas Proposal"
The Cowboy's Cinderella
Western Christmas Brides
"A Kiss from the Cowboy"
The Rancher's Inconvenient Bride
A Ranch to Call Home
A Texas Christmas Reunion

The Walker Twins

Wed to the Montana Cowboy
Wed to the Texas Outlaw

Visit the Author Profile page
at Harlequin.com for more titles.

To Lauren Iaccino,

Your loving heart and spunky spirit
reflect Heaven's sparkle.

Chapter One

If not for the fact that Juliette Lindor had a baby riding her hip, she would have been tempted to march across the street and disrupt the robbery taking place at Beaumont Spur Savings and Loan.

Goodness knew Sheriff Hank would not be running to the rescue of the townsfolk's money. No doubt the half-hearted lawman was having a fine high time with his cousins, who were at this very moment incarcerated in his jail.

"For pity's sake," she muttered, witnessing the crime through the front window of her restaurant.

Apparently the bank was destined to be robbed today. According to town gossip, which there was plenty of, the sheriff's Underwood cousins would have held it up had they not been arrested last night for previous crimes. Beaumont Spur's lawman was not so unworthy as to set his relatives free, but neither was he dedicated to holding up every jot and title of the law.

Moments ago, the robber committing the current crime while wearing a ragged coat and a half-crushed hat had glanced every which way except heavenward before he slithered into the bank.

Straining to listen, Juliette heard shouting but thankfully no gunshots.

The thief backed out the door and nearly tumbled into a horse trough. Righting his balance, he dashed across a mound of melting snow that glittered in the midmorning sunshine. On the run, he glanced up and down Main Street, a leather bag tucked under his arm.

Juliette rushed to the front door of the café and shoved the bolt into place. If the criminal was looking for a hiding place, he would not find it in her establishment.

She would forbid him entrance for the muddy state of his boots alone, set aside the fact that he was a low-down lawbreaker.

The single customer in her restaurant looked up from his soup.

"It's the bank again," she explained, catching and kissing the small fist grabbing for the front of her blouse.

The gray-bearded gentleman shook his head but continued to spoon soup into his mouth. "Been ten months since the last holdup. I reckon that's something. Still, this town isn't what it used to be."

No truer words, as far as Juliette was concerned. She dearly missed the sweet Beaumont she had been born and raised in. "Levi, do you remember when we all used to gather about the spring in the town square on Sunday afternoons?"

"Those were good days. My Martha used to make the sweetest cherry pies for everyone. You were only a little thing but you might remember."

She'd been eight years old when Martha Silver died, but she still recalled the flavor of sweet cherries on her tongue and the indulgent gaze of the woman smiling down at her.

"Anyone get hurt this time?"

Juliette walked back to the window and moved the curtain aside. "Mr. Bones is chasing the thief, so I imagine he wasn't armed."

"That's a mercy. Don't begrudge the banker his business, but we did just fine without a bank for years before the rail spur came to town. I'm keeping my cash in the safe at the mercantile. Can't recall Leif being robbed in all the time he's been open."

Nor could Juliette. Of course, Leif Ericman was a giant of a man who had taken to wearing a sidearm since the arrival of the rail spur. For all that Leif had a wicked scowl, he was known for his kindness. A robber, a stranger to Beaumont Spur, would not know it, though.

"I'm finished." Levi slapped his spoon on the tablecloth.

"Would you like a piece of cake before you go?"

"What I mean is, I'm finished with Beaumont Spur. I'm moving on to a place the railroad hasn't corrupted."

"Levi! You can't. You've lived here since—oh, since forever!"

He sighed, nodded. "Since before you were a glimmer in your parents' smiles. I brought my bride here because it was a good, peaceful place to settle. Sure isn't that anymore. I'm not the only one talking about leaving."

Yes, she knew that. A whole group of families were considering the move together.

But Levi Silver? It couldn't be!

In spite of what it had become over the past few years, Juliette loved her town. It broke her heart to see it falling to ruin. Even children were dashing about during school hours without proper discipline because the schoolteacher had quit suddenly in October and the new one had not yet arrived.

What this town needed was a reliable sheriff and a strict schoolmaster.

A hotel without fleas wouldn't hurt, either. It was her firm opinion that a gracious inn would attract a better sort of clientele than the saloons did. The town might then thrive, and new families would move here to replace the ones who were leaving.

Baby Lena curled her fat little fist around the ribbon tied in Juliette's braid. She drew it to her mouth and sucked on the yellow satin.

"Here comes Mr. Bones back again. From here it looks like he's grinning. He's got a leather bag tucked under his arm. He must have caught the robber, then."

"Looks like your money is safe until the next time, Juliette." Levi stood up, then dug about in his pants pocket. Withdrawing some coins, he stacked them neatly on the table. "If I were you I'd keep my cash under the bed or in the mercantile safe, like I do."

Stashing money under her big lonely bed was the least safe place she could think of. Strangers were not the only ones hoping to snatch unsecured funds.

Crossing the room, Levi joined her at the window and peered out. He cupped the curve of Lena's dark, curly-haired head in his bony hand, his fingers gnarled with age and years of hard work.

"A widow like you." He shook his head then kissed

Lena's chubby fingers. Turning, he walked toward the door, slid the bolt free. "With the responsibilities you've taken on—you shouldn't be here. Go someplace safe and find a good man to marry."

"I've had a good man."

Steven Lindor had been reliable in every way a husband could be. What was left of his body was buried in the cemetery outside of town, alongside Thomas Warren Lindor's equally broken body.

"I still say he and his brother never should have taken a job with the railroad."

Looking back, no one would deny that. But at the time, Steven and Thomas had both been newlyweds and could not turn down the generous pay the railroad offered.

Even the fact that both men had babies on the way had not kept them from going. No—she believed it had actually propelled their decisions.

Her husband and her brother-in-law had perished.

But she had not.

Yes, she had wept, pounded her fist against her pillow and railed against fate. But in the end she had given birth to a beautiful baby girl.

In the instant she'd heard her newborn's cry, hope for the future bloomed in a way Juliette could never have imagined.

"Take care walking home, Levi. The boardwalk will be slippery."

"Been walking these streets more than half my life, missy, don't reckon I'll lose my balance now. See you at dinnertime."

Juliette watched him go then closed the door, relieved to see that he did test each step as he proceeded down the boardwalk.

In the distance, the train whistle blew. She heard the rumble of the big engine as it pushed the train back toward Smith's Ridge.

If only—oh, never mind.

Wishing that the railroad had picked some other town in which to set down its spur was as useful as wishing there was something she could do to restore Beaumont to the hometown she loved. The place where neighbors smiled at one another when they passed on the boardwalk, where one laid down one's head at night in blissful slumber without the racket of saloons to disturb the peace of the evening.

A flash of yellow caught her eye. A hatbox with a fluffy yellow bow sat on one of the tables.

Oh, no! A customer—Miss Quinn her name was—must have left it behind. The woman had been distracted with joy over boarding the train and going home to marry the handsome man she was engaged to.

There was nothing to do but store the hatbox away in the event that Miss Quinn returned for it one day.

Reaching for it, Juliette saw an envelope tucked between the box lid and the bow. Curiously, Juliette's name was written on the delicate parchment.

Before she had a chance to wonder about it, she heard a baby's strident cry coming from the small room behind the kitchen.

"Sounds like your brother is hungry, Miss Lena."

"If you can't keep that boy content, you shouldn't be running a business. Family comes first for a woman." Her father-in-law's grumble reached the dining room from the kitchen.

Thankfully there were no customers present to hear his lament.

Truly, did the man not understand that she would rather be at home tending her husband and their child?

Circumstances had sent her life another way. She could smile at the future or weep over the past.

She chose to smile.

Juliette sat down at a table in the back of the dining room and draped a shawl over her left shoulder. Tenderly she tucked the end under Joe's small padded bottom.

There was rarely a time when she put him to her breast that she did not think of Lillian. For all that she smiled while she cooed to Joe and tickled his fat little belly, she felt a tug of sadness that it was Juliette feeding him and not his mother.

"Your mama was beautiful, Joe—just like you are. And she loved you so very much."

Truly, no one could have looked forward to a child's birth with more joy than Steven's brother and his wife had.

Juliette knew this because they had shared a wedding day and a home. Lillian had only been one month along in her pregnancy with Joe when Juliette conceived Lena.

Their large home had nearly vibrated with happiness over anticipation of the babies' arrival. But there was worry, as well. Her husband and her brother-in-law were determined that their children would be born to the best of everything money could buy. The trouble was, at that point in their young lives, they'd been far from able to provide a pair of silver spoons.

So the men had left their pregnant wives behind and gone away to California…to make a living working for the Southern Pacific Railroad.

During the wee hours of a January morning in the mountains at Tehachapi, the rear cars of the train they'd been on had detached, rolled back down the grade, crashed and burned. Life as Juliette knew it had perished along with Steven and Thomas.

Lillian lost her will to live. Try as Juliette might to get her sister-in-law to look toward the future for her child's sake, she could not draw Lillian out of her despondency. After Joe's birth she grew even more morose. She wouldn't eat or take the fresh air, choosing instead to sit in her darkened room and weep.

Until the chilly night she'd crept quietly out of the house to crouch in the rain. Juliette didn't know how long her sister-in-law had been in the yard shivering. She only discovered Lillian was out there when Joe began to cry.

That had been the first time she took her nephew to her own breast. The poor baby was hungry and his mother refused him. As Lillian sat in front of the fire, shaking with cold, a distant look in her eyes, Juliette had known she'd set her sights on death.

For a week she had tried to get Lillian to eat, to smile at sweet baby Joe, to do anything but stare blankly into space. In the end, her sister-in-law caught a fever and was gone within three days.

"But I love you, Joe." Juliette stroked his soft round head. "I'm yours forever."

Juliette was more grateful for this unexpected son than she could say. He was her sweet little miracle in the ashes of what had been her life.

Smiling down at him, she was rewarded with the endearing sigh babies made when they nursed.

"What do you suppose this note has to say, sweet boy?"

Reaching for the hatbox, she could not even imagine.

The bell on the front door jangled. A young woman blew inside along with a gust of cold wind.

"Hello, Nannie," Juliette said with a smile for her customer. "Just give me a moment. Coffee? Pastry?"

"Oh, I've no time to eat! I've found out a tasty bit of news that simply has to be shared." Nannie's small, closely set blue eyes glittered in apparent delight with what she was about to impart. "You know, Juliette, you'll ruin your figure nursing both those babies."

"I suppose that's a risk I'll have to take if Lena and Joe are to survive."

Nannie Breene tipped her head to one side, frowning. Unless Juliette missed her guess, the girl would have spent no less than an hour and a half this morning arranging her blond hair in flirtatious curls about her face.

"I'm sure you know best, of course. But wouldn't a wet nurse do as well?"

"A wet nurse in Beaumont Spur?" Juliette would not hire one even if there had been a woman wanting the job. Love and cuddles went into the feeding as much as life-sustaining food did. "Someday you'll—"

Nannie cut her off with a crisp snap of her fingers.

"My news!" Her small eyes flashed in clear anticipation of Juliette's coming reaction. "You won't believe this!"

Nannie sat down in a chair across from Juliette, anchored her elbows on the table then stretched her neck forward, leading with her dainty, pointed chin.

"It's hardly news that the bank has been robbed," Juliette pointed out. "Can I get you some tea—a cookie?"

"How can I even think of it? Not knowing what I know—and it certainly is not something as common as the bank being robbed."

For all that Nannie was bursting to repeat her news, she was apparently waiting for Juliette to drag it from her.

Very well. "What is your news? It must be something urgent."

"Oh, it is!" Nannie leaned farther forward and whispered, "Trea Culverson is returning to Beaumont Spur."

It was after midnight when Juliette wrapped a blanket about her shoulders and stepped onto the back porch of her small house. She stared up at the moon. It was full and bright. Not even halfway up the sky, it looked huge and close, almost as if she could reach out and touch it.

Her day had not ended when she bade the last customer good-night then put the Closed sign on the restaurant door. She'd wrapped the babies against the late November chill, tucked them in the pram then bundled her father-in-law up in a heavy coat.

As he normally did, Warren Lindor had insisted on being led to The Saucy Goose. As she always did, she pushed the pram with one arm and dragged the old man home by the coat sleeve.

Luckily, home was only a block away from her café.

By the time she fed the babies, tucked them into bed, gave Warren a snack and settled him into his room, and then baked the pastries for the next morning, it was late. Her neighbors had doused their lamps hours ago.

Perhaps she ought to do the same, but now was her

time. No matter the weather, it was her custom to stand on her porch and listen to the quiet whispers of deep night. The sounds changed with the seasons, but her sense of peace in the moment did not.

In the beginning, when she'd first discovered this precious time, she had stood in this spot gazing up at the deep sky, often weeping while she held the image of Steven close.

But it had been a year since he went away to work for the railroad. She still thought of him. She always would, of course. But she did not do it as frequently now, and when she did it was with smiles more often than tears.

She had been blessed beyond reason with a daughter and a son. Oh, she might have been crippled by grief and loneliness, but because of the babies she carried a song in her heart.

After selling the big house she had shared with Steven and his family, she had been able to purchase her restaurant and this cozy cottage.

Each morning she had a purpose in waking, breathing, smiling at the new day and wondering what it would bring.

If the gossip was correct, it would soon bring the return of the prodigal son.

Although, unlike the prodigal, there would be no loving father's arms open in welcome. For Trea there would be no fatted calf given in celebration.

Everyone in town, except a dozen girls with fluttering hearts, had been glad to see the last of him.

And Juliette? She had not been happy to see him go. It had broken her young heart.

Even after all these years, she remembered his expression in the instant he'd fled.

The reflection of flames consuming the livery that night had cast his face in a red-orange grimace. To many people his silence, his failure to declare his innocence while he risked his life leading horse after horse to safety, was the same as an admission of guilt that he'd set the fire.

That was not what Juliette believed. To her way of thinking, Trea would never have done anything to endanger an animal.

Was she the only one to have noted that every able-bodied man standing and witnessing the destruction had done so from across the street, leaving the rescue of the animals to a seventeen-year-old?

While it was true that Trea had always been the town bad boy—a hellion born of one—unlike his father, he was never mean-spirited.

More often than not his crimes involved kissing the girls in town. As far as Juliette could tell, none of them considered it a crime at all.

It did, however, cement his reputation as the black sheep begotten of a black sheep. Whenever a minor crime of any kind was committed, it was assumed that Trea was the perpetrator.

Juliette had valid reason to believe he was not the wicked child they had cast him as. Perhaps, in part, due to the fact that he had never kissed her. She might be the one girl in Beaumont who had never had her heart broken by him.

Which didn't mean that she had not envied those girls and spent dreamy moments wondering about Trea's kisses. How many nights had she lain awake in her bed imagining what it would be like to feel his lips, hear sweet whispers of affection, and all the while brooding over which of her friends might be finding out right that moment?

And now, if the gossip proved true, Trea Culverson was coming home.

Even though she was a woman grown, a widow with children, her heart beat a little faster, even her belly tickled.

She knew it was silly. Years had passed. Trea was no longer the daring, forbidden boy who'd taken her breath away.

He was a man grown. Heaven only knew who he had grown to be.

Chapter Two

It was half past midnight when Trea Culverson dragged the grease-splattered apron off over his head for the last time. He folded it in a neat square then set it on top of the laundry pile.

The saloon washerwoman would have it cleaned by morning for the new cook.

Grease coated his hair, his arms and even the creases of his eyes. If he never fried another chicken it would be a fine thing.

Opening the door of the huge iron stove, he checked the fire to make sure it was small enough to leave unguarded.

With a last look about the place that had employed him for the past several years, he bade it farewell.

The job was far from his ideal occupation, but it had earned him the money to pursue the one that was. At last, his training was finished and he was ready to begin the career he had been working so hard toward.

Stepping outside, he pulled the door closed behind him. The moon looked like a glowing ball suspended partway between the horizon and the North Star. The full of the moon always struck him as a magical sight.

The door hadn't clicked closed before he heard, "Trea! Wait!"

"Good night, Mags," he said to the woman stepping out onto the porch.

Cold moonlight shone down on her face, revealing the creep of middle age that she fought so hard to hide.

"You were leaving without a goodbye kiss?"

"Not much for goodbyes." Since he'd never even kissed the woman hello, it would have been awkward to kiss her goodbye.

"I'll miss you, Trea." The waitress lifted one shoulder. The strap of her gown slipped. "We all will—but… well, I thought maybe you wouldn't want to sleep at the livery on your last night? It's warmer in my room."

She touched his cheek with soft fingers.

There had been a time when he'd have sought this woman, kissed and bedded her within an hour of meeting her, but that would have been a long time ago.

"You're too fine a lady for a greasy fellow like me." He caught her hand, lowered it, but squeezed softly as he let go. "I can't afford a moment of your time, Mags."

"As if I'd charge you." She went up on her toes, kissed his cheek. "Be on your way, then, you handsome young thing. I hope you find what you are looking for back in your hometown."

"Reckon I'll know once I get there."

"Safe travels," she said with a half smile, then she went back inside and closed the door behind her.

He hadn't lied when he told her he could not afford her time. Couldn't afford the bath he was headed for, either, but only soap and hot water would scrub the grease off his skin and hair.

Truth be told, he'd have bathed in the stream in order

to save money if it weren't nearly frozen over. But he also needed a shave. He'd neglected the condition of his chin for far too long.

He walked uphill toward the bathhouse. Luckily the facility was owned by the saloon and would be open for another two hours, plenty of time for the soaking he would need.

Warmth filled his lungs as soon as he walked in out of the cold. Humid air wrapped around him.

He paid the fee to a sleepy-looking woman sitting near the front door, and within ten minutes he was behind a screen, submerged in water that was, if not completely clean, at least good and hot.

With his eyes closed he felt the kiss of steam curling about his neck and face. For him this visit was a luxury. In pursuit of his goal, he'd rarely indulged in anything that was not food, basic clothing or shelter.

Because he'd been living in a shed attached to the livery, he'd been able to put aside a fair amount of money. Last month he'd purchased a house in Beaumont Spur, sight unseen. He hoped it was all the previous owner claimed it to be. With so many decent folks leaving town, he'd been able to buy the place for a good price.

The last time he'd been in Beaumont Spur it had simply been Beaumont. As pretty a place as anyone could imagine. When he'd run away from it, with ash embedded in his skin and his clothes, coughing smoke out of his lungs, he'd been accused of a heartless crime.

The looks folks had cast him hurt worse than the burn on his hand. Even if he'd tried to explain that it had been an accident—one he could have done nothing to prevent—they would not have believed him.

That wicked night, everyone thought he was the spawn of the devil. Thinking of his father made him wonder if it might be true.

He hadn't seen Ephraim Culverson since then, but he'd heard that his father had been forced to shutter his freight-hauling business when the spur came to town.

The word was, he'd opened a couple of saloons in its place. In Trea's opinion that suited him better than the rough work that went into running teamsters. Not that Pa had done much but sit behind his desk, drink and curse at his employees.

From nearby he heard the snap of a leather strap, the swish of a razor being stropped.

Heavy footsteps rounded the curtain.

"Reckoned you didn't want a woman, Culverson, so I'm all you've got at this hour."

"Blamed if I don't want a woman, but I've got a reputation to repair, Goudy."

"I'll try not to tarnish it." The heavyset man plunked a stool down beside the tub. He sat on it with a grunt and a short bark of laughter. "I'll do what I can not to cut you, either."

"I appreciate that." Trea leaned his head on the back edge of the tub and lifted his chin.

He closed his eyes. Images of the past flashed on the backs of his eyelids. Mostly the faces of girls whose names he couldn't quite recall. He clearly remembered how he'd wronged them, though.

The clean scent of shaving lather filled his senses.

So did the image of one pretty young face. He hadn't forgotten that one.

Juliette Yvonne Moreland had been an angel in his

eyes. She had been consistently kind, sweet-natured and always smiling.

She was also probably the one girl he had never shamed or whose heart he had not broken—at least, he hoped he hadn't.

Oh, he'd dreamed of kissing her, all right. His boyish heart had been infatuated with her.

"You're thinking about a woman right now. Don't claim you aren't."

"Not a woman, Goudy—a girl."

"Don't forget I've got a razor in my hand."

"You could cut my throat for a lot of things—but not that. The girl, Juliette, is someone I grew up with. She's the one person from Beaumont Spur that I never could forget."

No doubt because she had been the one person who never judged him harshly.

For all that he had dreamed of it, he had never touched her. The thing was, she was too good and he was too bad. The thought of breaking her heart—he couldn't do that any more than he could pull a kitten's tail.

He'd always had the suspicion that sweet Juliette was the only person in Beaumont who saw the real Trea Culverson. He figured she was the only one who wasn't waiting to smack him on the hand with a gavel.

"Wonder if she's still there," Goudy said, stroking a shaving brush in pleasant-feeling circles on Trea's face.

"If she is, she'll be married, I imagine, with half a dozen children."

"The good ones always are."

In memory, he saw Juliette wink at him and smile, the event still clear in his mind. In that moment, at twelve years old, his heart had tumbled.

He'd been in the general store, wandering about, looking at this and that—mostly at the peppermint sticks. The store owner had been scowling at him the whole time, sure he was about to steal something.

Maybe he would have. But Juliette shot him that wink, fished a coin out of her pocket and purchased two candies. She gave him one, then blushed and ran out of the store.

No doubt she was married now to some lucky fellow. He hoped so. She deserved that kind of happiness and more.

He also hoped she was still in Beaumont Spur. There was something in him that wanted her to know the wild boy was gone, grown into a man wanting to make his reputation right.

Juliette's opinion mattered to him very much.

Juliette ought to have bid the moon good-night before her feet started aching with cold, but she'd lingered too long over its beauty.

Coming inside, she feared that, as tired as she was, she might not be able to sleep because of it. Without a man to warm her toes against, she was doomed to lie awake until they finally warmed on their own.

Passing through the parlor, she spotted the hatbox with the bright yellow bow, where she'd set it down on the table next to the fireplace.

With all the hustle getting everyone down for the night, she'd all but forgotten about the curious item.

She stirred the coals with the poker then watched the embers flare to new life. Perhaps if she sat down to read the letter attached to the delicate-looking box, her feet would have time to warm before she went upstairs.

"What on earth could this be?" she murmured to the dozing household. She could guess all night long and not come up with a logical answer.

She opened the envelope, slowly withdrew the note, then leaned close to the glow of the fireplace to better read the script written in a fine feminine hand.

Dear Mrs. Lindor,
First of all, I cannot say how grateful I am for the time the time I spent in your establishment. It was a refreshing change from the dreariness of the hotel.

"Well, yes..." Juliette muttered. "Anything would be."

And your children are sweet angels.

Hungrier-than-average angels, though. She ought to get some sleep before they woke for their middle-of-the-night feeding.

As far as her restaurant went? She was dedicated to keeping it scrupulously clean. While she might live in a ragtag town, she would not be a part of the sorry state of affairs.

She read on.

I have recently come into a large sum of money. Not through any hard work on my part, though. No, I simply collected the reward for those miserable Underwoods, a man I used to trust being among them.

I find that I do not want the money, but I suspect that you will find a way to put it to good use.

Please accept this Christmas gift to you and your beautiful babies.
With all good wishes,
Laura Lee Quinn, very soon to be Laura Lee Creed

The flower-scented paper fluttered to Juliette's feet, covering the stocking-clad toes of one foot. She stared at the letter for a long moment then reached for the hatbox.

What on earth? A gift? Of money? Juliette could scarcely believe it. No doubt she had been more tired than she knew—had climbed the stairs huddled under her covers and fallen asleep in spite of her cold feet. Clearly this had to be a lovely dream that she was about to wake from. Before she did, though, she ought to open the lid of the hatbox and see how much money was in it. No doubt she would jerk back to reality before she discovered that, but—

She lifted the lid, blinked hard at what was inside then closed it again. She didn't dare to touch the cash because dream money always vanished before one's eyes. It tended to turn into carrots or a ball of yarn or one of the many things dream objects transformed into. And here she would sit, wondering how to pay the mortgage, same as she did every month.

Tucking the hatbox under her arm, she went upstairs, got into bed and curled herself around the pretty yellow gift.

If it was still there when she awoke in the morning, she would believe it. But not until then. Not until sunlight shone on the treasure inside and it did not vanish like dreams mostly did.

* * *

Dawn came and the money in the hatbox proved to be as real as the slush Juliette swept off the porch in front of her restaurant.

Everything about the day was as normal as peas, except that she had more money than she could have ever imagined.

True to form, her father-in-law complained that the babies were fussing and that he was hungry. Levi Silver sat at his customary table, eating his breakfast of eggs and bacon cooked to a crisp.

Cold seeped through her boots while she swept, same as it always did, but this morning she barely felt it. Her mind was so full of possibilities for the future of her family that she didn't give the ordinary tasks of the morning a thought. She went through them by rote, her mind flitting among the clouds.

With her newly come tidy little fortune, she could leave Beaumont Spur along with so many others.

Or she could stay in the place she loved. Even in the state it had fallen to, this was home, the place the roots of her heart grew deep. She could build a beautiful home at the edge of town where life would be more peaceful. She could stay home all day long just watching her babies grow.

Gazing at the mountain range that circled Beaumont Spur like a snowy crown, she knew it would be a difficult thing to leave the place where her dreams and her family members were buried. Perhaps she would not be able to, even if it might be for the best.

The way things seemed now, she wondered if Beaumont Spur even had a future.

She would not want to invest her heart and her money in a place that was doomed to fail.

Her money? The idea was still fresh enough to not seem real.

Who would have imagined that a gang of scruffy outlaws would be worth so much?

Until this morning, Juliette Lindor would not have believed it.

The sound of a hammer on wood cut the quiet morning. Juliette looked up suddenly to see Mrs. Elvira Pugley pounding the tool on the front door of The Fickle Dog Saloon.

"Ephraim Culverson, your saloon is ruining my hotel!" she shouted.

After a few moments of incessant hammering, the door was flung open and the owner of the saloon burst onto the boardwalk wearing a knee-length nightshirt and a pair of argyle socks. Even with one big toe poking out of the tip of the sock, the man looked formidable.

"Stop your bleating, woman!" Ephraim's bellow had always been loud enough to shake windows. This morning, having no doubt been awoken after a night of debauchery, it was even louder.

"I demand that you keep your fleas on your own side of the wall. Folks are complaining all day and night!" Elvira Pugley was as hot-tempered as her neighbor.

"My fleas be damned!" Ephraim Culverson snatched the hammer from her hand and pitched it halfway across the road. "It's your fat, hairy rats carrying them to my place."

"Of all the insulting—I'm not the one who named my business The Fickle Dog. Dogs have fleas."

"No more than rodents do!"

Juliette was pretty sure her windows rattled, but she shrugged and continued to sweep. This was not the first time the saloon owner and the hotel owner had erupted in a battle of words.

No doubt both places had fleas borne by rats. She didn't care much who'd had them first, so long as the vermin kept to their own side of the road.

"I've a mind to sell the hotel rather than spend another day next door to you."

She had? For how much?

"Sure would suit me not to hear you hammering on my door in the wee hours."

To Mr. Culverson the wee hours were what others would call eleven in the morning.

Did she dare make an offer for the hotel?

If the saloon owner considered Mrs. Pugley a bothersome neighbor, well, Juliette would be worse. Not as loud, perhaps, but more persistent in the quest for cleanliness.

But to restore the hotel and hopefully attract a more family-oriented sort of person to Beaumont Spur, to make the ones who were leaving reconsider? The possibility niggled around in her mind until it turned into downright temptation.

"I just might take the train out of this town before that no-good, thieving, arsonist, taker-of-innocence son of yours comes back to town, and I hear he is."

At the mention of Trea, Juliette stopped sweeping, leaned for a moment against the broom handle.

The last thing she expected was for her heart to kick at the mention of that long-absent boy.

Maybe he was going to come back to town and be

his father's pride and joy—but he had never been that, not really.

He would have needed a blacker soul in order for his father to be proud of him.

For all that Trea acted like the town's black sheep, Juliette saw someone different.

She saw a boy with a decent heart looking for acceptance from people who would never respect him. And mostly because of his bully of a father.

That boy had sought affection in whatever way he could.

Just now her heart reacted to the mention of him the same way it had so many years ago, with a thump, then a yearning. She could not deny that she had been in childish adoration of him.

Over the years she'd often wondered about him, remembered the mischievous glint in his warm brown eyes, the hurt and rejection caused by those whose approval he so desperately wanted.

Of course, he would never have gotten it. *The acorn didn't fall far from the tree* she'd heard time and again in reference to Trea.

How many times had she wanted to shout that trees and their nuts were a far different thing than human beings and their children?

It was her long-held opinion that a child should not have to bear the sins of the father. It had been shocking to her to discover that, in the opinion of most folks, they did.

Most especially when the acorn, the product of a sinful man, was named Trea Culverson.

"You better take that train, Elvira. I aim to promote my son to head man around here, right under me. Don't reckon you'll like having my young hellion to answer to."

The argument over Trea and fleas continued for another five minutes before the combatants went back inside their own places of business.

It wouldn't be long before they were back at it, though, unless Mrs. Pugley was serious about selling.

If she was? Well, the idea was likely to leave Juliette distracted all day and sleepless all night.

Chapter Three

Juliette fashioned the ribbons of her bonnet into a tidy bow under her chin while she watched out the front window for Rose McAllister.

The babies were fed. Her father-in-law napped near the stove in the kitchen. Given that it was two in the afternoon and a quiet time for the restaurant, seventeen-year-old Rose should have no trouble tending things while Juliette went out to take care of business matters.

For the first time, she didn't need to fret over the money she paid young Rosc. In fact, with Christmas coming, she would give the girl extra. Rose, who was raising her younger sister, needed additional funds as much as Juliette did—or had until she found a hatbox with her name on it.

While she watched the boardwalk, her attention wandered to the hotel on the other side of the street, seeing it not as it was, but as she envisioned it.

Sometime during the wee hours of the night Juliette had made her decision. It was hard to know the moment it happened. At some point in her mind the hotel went from being the run-down eyesore she saw from her restaurant window to being hers.

Suddenly there was a coat of fresh paint to brighten its appearance. The front porch had half a dozen rocking chairs for her guests to sit in and window boxes full of blooming flowers for them to smell. Blamed if one of her guests would ever suffer a fleabite once she was in charge of things.

She was in the middle of a quick prayer that Elvira Pugley really did intend to sell when she spotted Rose hurrying along the walk, her ten-year-old sister in tow.

The door opened with a rush of frigid air. With the clouds building as quickly as they were, it couldn't be long before snow began to fall.

"I'm sorry to be late, Juliette." Rose yanked off her coat and then her sister's and hung them on the coatrack. "Cora couldn't decide which book to bring."

"Thank you for coming, Rose. I can't tell you how I appreciate the time to get a few things done." Juliette would not tell her exactly what things just yet. "I hope to be back within an hour."

"No need to thank me. Cora needs a bit of diversion. Without school, she gets restless."

"From what I hear, the new teacher will be here any day," Juliette said.

"Hope the new one's better than the last one." Cora sighed. "He didn't teach us anything. Just let the boys run wild and the girls talk about everybody."

"I hope so, too. We're lucky to get one at all, though. Most teachers choose a position that pays better than we can offer."

"I only wish we knew more about him or her." Rose rubbed her arms briskly, wiping away the lingering chill from her blouse. "Since the school board is in Smith's Ridge, and they're doing the hiring, our new teacher could come from the moon and we wouldn't know any better."

"Well—schoolmaster or schoolmistress, from earth or the moon, it will have to be better than no teacher at all," Juliette pointed out.

"Maybe," Cora muttered with a good deal of doubt evident on her young face as she sat at a table and opened her book. "I'd rather be home with my reading than hear those girls gossip when they ought to be paying attention to the lesson. And if that nasty Charlie Gumm pulls my braid one more time—I'll have to punch him, I reckon."

"And get sent home for a week?" Rose shot her sister a severe frown.

"I might learn more on my own if we get a teacher like Mr. Smythe was. I don't think he was from the moon. Maybe Mars, though."

"I suppose we shouldn't judge the new teacher, not even knowing a thing about them," Juliette said, going out the front door with a backward glance.

"I reckon so," answered Cora, but she sounded far from convinced.

Outside, wind seemed to come at her from every direction. Snow was on its way. For the first time in a long while, she didn't worry overmuch that it would keep customers home. If the widow Pugley accepted the offer that Juliette presented, there would be money to purchase the hotel and plenty for renovations, too.

She felt a lightness in her step that she hadn't felt in quite a while. At the same time, her stomach was a nervous mess.

Thanks to the generosity of Laura Lee Quinn—no

doubt Creed by now—the opportunity of a lifetime was within her reach.

But only so long as Mrs. Pugley had been sincere in her desire to leave Beaumont Spur.

Coming home to Beaumont Spur was even more taxing to Trea's nerves than he expected it to be.

Huddled into his coat against the cold, he leaned against the wall of the train station at Smith's Ridge, wondering if he was making the right decision in going home.

Not that wondering made a bit of difference, since he'd already made the decision. He was good and committed to the course he'd set.

A lot of years had passed since he last walked the streets of Beaumont. It hadn't even been called Beaumont Spur back then, just plain Beaumont.

Would folks still look at him with disapproval after all this time? His pa would. The old cuss would be ashamed to his bones.

And the girls whose affections he'd dallied with? They would be grown women—mothers, even. Would they judge him harshly?

He was a changed man now—reformed. He only hoped they would see past who he had been to who he had become. Because if they didn't…

The train whistle blew, letting the waiting passengers know they could board the train and get out of the frigid weather.

He picked up the bag of a young lady who seemed to be on her own and carried it up the steps of the train car. She smiled appreciatively at him. He let the smile warm him through, since he couldn't be sure he would get another anytime soon.

There was no telling what awaited him at home. He had a lot to atone for, and it was important that he do it. He could not be the upright fellow he'd set his course to be unless he did.

The lady nodded her thanks, then sat down on the bench across from him.

Something about her reminded him of Juliette Moreland. The sweetness of her expression—the way she tipped her head to one side when she spoke? That might be it. That, or the spark of goodwill that brightened her blue eyes and reflected a kind soul.

One of the reasons he was so nervous about going home was Juliette, even though she was probably the one person in town he had not wronged in some way.

As wild a boy as he'd been, when Juliette looked at him, he'd felt worth something.

That was it, then. He was on edge because he feared seeing her look at him like everyone else had. Over the years, growing in maturity and wisdom, she might see him differently than she had back then. As a woman grown she might judge him more harshly.

That fifteen-year-old girl who had followed him one hot summer night to the shed where he'd hidden from an angry storekeeper, the sweet girl who'd sat with him, sharing her dinner, might see him differently now.

Looking back, it seemed odd—but sitting in that secluded space with darkness coming on—blame it, he wouldn't have talked and laughed the evening away with anyone but Juliette.

He'd entertained a lot of girls in that shed. The memories were heated but vague. Visions of pretty faces melded one into one another—their sighs all the same.

The only one he remembered with clarity was Juliette.

She was—just better than anyone else he'd ever met.

Beautiful—it was the name he'd always called her. Partly to see her blush, but also because it was true. He'd called a few others that, too, but he'd only meant it with Juliette.

Just now, listening to the rumble of the great engine and feeling the vibration of the wheels on the track picking up speed, he didn't know which he feared most. Seeing her again—or not seeing her.

What had she done?

Juliette opened the door to her snug little café and came inside, shutting the door on glowering clouds that promised snow. She glanced about the well-kept space and breathed in the familiar scents.

The café was empty of customers at the moment, but clearly there had been a few. Coffee had recently been served and sweet rolls. The lingering scent of steak told her someone had just enjoyed a meal.

Every inch of this place was as familiar to her as her face in the mirror.

What on God's good earth had she done?

"You're back quicker than I expected." Rose bustled out from the kitchen, dusting flour-smeared hands on her apron. "I figured I'd bake a pan of biscuits. I imagine the folks arriving on the train will be hungry."

"I appreciate that. Thank you, Rose."

"It was no problem. The babies are asleep and your father-in-law is reading a dime novel. I needed to keep busy with—Juliette, you're pale. Are you feeling all right?"

"Am I pale?" Juliette took off her gloves and pinched her cheeks. "Well—it's just that I bought the hotel."

Cora looked up from her book and pointed out the window. "That hotel?"

"I imagine so, Cora. It's the only one in town," Rose pointed out, looking as appalled as her sister.

"But it's in worse shape than the schoolhouse is."

Juliette hadn't seen the inside of the small red building in some time but figured she must accept Cora's word on it. "Yes—that very one. The fleas and the bedbugs all belong to me now."

What in glory blazes had she done?

Turned her safe, predictable life upside down, is what.

"If I were you I'd tear it down," Cora advised.

"That will be enough of your sassy mouth, young lady," Rose scolded. "If you can't say something supportive just go back to your studies."

"I've been trying to all afternoon. But those women from the Ladies Service Society spent their whole meeting time gossiping about that no-account fellow coming to town. If they want to be of service, they should have been over at the schoolhouse cleaning it. It made my brain scatter. I reckon the new teacher will take the first train out of here once she sees where she's supposed to work."

Juliette assumed that the man the members of the Society had been discussing could be no other than Trea Culverson. Juliette was grateful that she had not been here for that conversation. Her recollections of the boy were vastly different than theirs.

And the very last thing she had time for was filling her mind with a long-ago romance, especially one that had only happened in her imagination.

"Yes, well," Juliette said. "That's what the Ladies Service Society does. They make plans over coffee, but usually don't act upon them."

"Same with our 'brave' sheriff. He took his lunch plate to the ladies' table. Sure did make some big talk about keeping a sharp eye on the man they were talking about." Cora picked up her pencil and appeared to be absorbed in study, but Juliette figured it was more focused on town trouble.

"He would, wouldn't he? After his cousins nearly robbed the bank right under his nose, he needs to do something to look like he's protecting us." Rose shrugged. "I was too young to remember Mr. Culverson much, but he sounds charming and wicked all at once."

"Yes, well, some will remember him that way, but I remember a boy with a kind heart."

When she had time she might give her memories of Trea further thought, but at the moment she had to focus on what might be the biggest mistake she had ever made.

So much was a jumble in her mind, such as how to deal with various forms of vermin while trying to keep Warren Lindor out of The Fickle Dog Saloon when it was right next door to the hotel.

But a few other things were perfectly clear.

For one thing, she would move into the hotel, once it was livable.

For another, she would open a fancy restaurant within the hotel—a steakhouse. It would be a respectable place where folks could bring their families.

Still yet another, and this was very important to her, she would keep her dear café open. It had been her lifeline, something to focus her future on after burying her family.

What she had just done was too overwhelming to consider all at once. If she tried, it made her short of breath and gave her a bit of a headache.

Tiny steps would get her to where she needed to be. In time, she hoped to lead Beaumont Spur back to the decent place it used to be. A place where a child could run free, hear birdsong instead of garish music…where one did not need to worry about being bowled over by staggering saloon patrons. That was something she hoped to change. Unfortunately, good folks were already packing.

She took a breath and let it out slowly. There was really nothing she could do about her giant undertaking right that moment.

Except—

"Rose, do you like working here?"

"I couldn't get by without the work you give me. There aren't a lot of respectable jobs for someone my age, and I'm not nearly ready to marry."

"Would you consider running the café for me?" Juliette glanced between Rose and her little sister. Whatever Rose chose to do would be with Cora's best interests in mind.

"You could live in my house. That way you would be here in town, closer to work and to school for Cora."

Rose stared at her in silence. Warren's soft chuckle drifted out of the kitchen while he read his novel.

"I know it's sudden, but—"

"I can start right now. Mercy, but I guess I already

have." Rose lifted her hands and waggled her flour-crusted fingertips. "It won't be long until the afternoon train. I'll get back to the kitchen right now."

"I can pay you, too, Cora, if you'd like to help with sweeping and keeping things tidy or watching the babies."

"I reckon I won't be going to school anytime soon, once the new teacher gets a look at the place, so, yes, I'd like that."

"The classroom is that awful?"

"As far as I can tell, and that's quite a bit, the old teacher never, ever, even wiped fingerprints off the desks."

Beaumont needed a respectable teacher. Given that Juliette would have her children attending in only five more years, and also given the fact that keeping things neat and tidy was something of a crusade for her—

"Don't you worry about what your new schoolteacher will think. If you'll help your sister with the café and with Mr. Lindor for a few hours, I'll make sure your new teacher will be happy with the classroom."

A couple hours of scrubbing ought to give her time to think and plan. There were more thoughts in her mind right now than she could keep track of.

Along with an orderly attack on dirt, she might put together a plan to make her hotel a symbol of new life for Beaumont Spur.

Wind tugged Juliette's skirt every which way while she pushed the buggy over the rutted road toward the schoolhouse. As cold as it was, she hadn't wanted to bring the babies out, but they would be getting hungry soon. Even if they would accept a bottle, which they would not, Rose would have a lot to do if the train was full of passengers.

A portion of the blanket blew loose, exposing Lena's dark, curly head. Bending over the buggy, Juliette tucked it back into place.

"I know it's cold, sweetlings," she murmured when the blanket heaved and fussing noises emerged from under it. "Almost there."

Just as she lifted Joe from the buggy, a dozen or more fat snowflakes drifted down. She hurried up the steps with him hugged close to her breast. Once inside, she laid a blanket on the floor and put him on it. Within seconds he began to cry.

"I'm sorry, little love," she called over her shoulder while she hurried back out to bring in Lena.

Lena cried louder than Joe did when Juliette laid her down beside her cousin.

There was nothing to do but let them cry for a moment, since she could not leave the buggy to fill with snow.

Making quick work of it, she dragged the buggy inside then lit a fire in the stove. She put on a pot of water to heat, since it was far too cold to scrub with anything that was not warm and sudsy.

With a child in each arm, she sat cross-legged on the floor and fed them. The peaceful moment gave her time to look about at the task she had volunteered to do.

Cora was right. Any teacher worth the pay would not consider working in this filth. How long did she have to get it cleaned?

No one knew for sure when the instructor would arrive. *Before Christmas* was all she'd heard.

"What do you think, Lena?" She gazed down at her

daughter and received a milky smile. "If I finish in time, I ought to hang a fir bough over the blackboard."

Casting a frown at the walls and the smears of grime on them, she was not sure when that would be. There was plenty of firewood stacked outside, so she could stay here until she had to get Warren home and into bed.

The twilight hours were often difficult for him, and Rose should not have to deal with his increasingly odd moods.

"What do you think about some red berries tucked into the garland, Joe?" He kicked his tiny feet.

Within half an hour the room had warmed comfortably and the babies fallen asleep.

She turned her attention to the task at hand. Walls first, then desks and the floor.

The Ladies Service Society ought to have been here to help, but no doubt some of them were intent on leaving Beaumont Spur and no longer cared about the condition of education here.

Well, this was Juliette's town—her school, in a sense—and she would see to its cleanliness. She could not understand why other folks didn't care more about the condition of their school or their town. Perhaps it was because the people who had negative things to say spoke the loudest and set the mood for everyone else, giving off an attitude of despair instead of hope.

By the looks of things, she would be here for hours, listening to the snap of the fire, the babies breathing and the swish of the cleaning rag in soapy water.

Plenty of time to make a plan to renovate her hotel.

The trouble was, being in this room—which had not changed since she'd been a student—made her look more at the past than the future.

All of her memories, good and bad, led to one thought.

What had become of Trea Culverson? He was coming home. She knew that, but not a single thing more.

Wherever she glanced in this room she saw him—a boy discounted by the teacher, flirted with by infatuated girls and resented by the other boys—even as they envied him.

And Juliette…she remembered a day…

Looking up from her work, she gazed out the window. Snow drifted softly past, very much like it had that day.

The teacher had sent her students outside to get fresh air even though the weather was bad.

Juliette stood with a circle of girls and boys who considered themselves to be wooing. Juliette believed them to be silly, since no one was of an age for courting.

The room around her faded, giving way to a vivid vision of things past.

Trea stood next to Juliette, all the while holding the hand of his current sweetheart, Nannie Breene. The name Nannie Preen would have suited her better—Juliette remembered thinking that very clearly. She was awfully proud to be holding the hand of the handsome bad boy.

Nannie had looked at Juliette with a sneer so genuine that one would not know they were friends. At least she had always thought they were, but the scorn in her expression took her aback.

"You need a beau," Nannie had suddenly declared in front of everyone.

Indeed, Juliette was the only girl in the circle without one. And no wonder. She was not like the other girls. She was too tall, quite gangly and she dressed in homemade clothes rather than the fashionable outfits her classmates enjoyed.

"Juliette Moreland, why don't you just go away?"

Nannie's words had slashed her to the heart. They were so hurtful and embarrassing, she'd wished the ground would open and she could slip away—never to be seen again.

Her cheeks had burned hotter than any fever.

She'd been certain she could never face anyone again. But then—she could scarce believe it—Trea dropped Nannie's hand and slipped his arm around Juliette's shoulder.

"She can stay," he'd said with a slight squeeze. "I want her to stay."

A day and a half later, Trea's attention had shifted from Nannie to another girl.

After all this time, she could not even recall who it was.

In the end, she was glad he'd never chosen to flirt with her. If he had, her life might have turned out very differently because there had been something, a sense of belonging, between them, a feeling that they were meant to be together. At least, that is what her romantic young heart had believed.

A silly fancy, she had come to see as time went on.

In the end, she had married Steven and never regretted it. How could she, with those two precious babies asleep on the blanket? And there was the café that had taught her how to stand on her own. And now? Well—she certainly did not regret the new venture she was taking on. It frightened her, but she would not go back from the choice she made.

Things worked out the way they were supposed to in the end.

Mostly.

When he got off the train, Trea was hungry. Seemed like half a dozen other folks were, as well.

He'd wait a bit to eat. Maybe head on over to the café he'd just spotted for dinner. The place hadn't been here when he was a kid but it looked respectable.

Picking up his valises, he tucked one under each arm then scooped up two more, one in each fist. All he had in the world fit in the four small cases. A circumstance that suited him just fine.

Anything he needed he could purchase when he received his first pay. Since his house on the outskirts of town came with furniture, he would not need much.

Glancing about, he was sorry to see the town so ragged. Seemed like no one cared about it anymore. The Beaumont he remembered had been a pretty place.

Blame it if his own father wasn't responsible for much of the blight. He imagined his pa was even less scrupulous as a saloon owner than he'd been as a teamster.

He had the sad feeling that Pa'd had Trea's mother in mind when he named one of his saloons The Fickle Dog—probably The Saucy Goose, as well.

Growing up he'd never heard a complimentary thing about his mother. Absence—death, as it was—had not made his father's heart grow fonder.

In the distance he spotted the small red schoolhouse with a bell tower on top. He'd go there before he went to his new house. It was closer, and smoke was curling out of the chimney.

With the weather turning ever colder, the wind and snow swirling, close was better.

He balanced his valises, tucked them tighter under his arms and picked up his pace. Through one of the windows he saw the stove's orange glow. It cast a welcome through the dim afternoon light.

He'd say a heartfelt prayer of thanks for whoever had had the foresight to warm the place up.

It was curious that anyone had, though, given he'd been vague about the time of his arrival.

After bounding up the steps, he set his valises on the porch then opened the door.

A woman was on her knees, facing away from him. Her slim back moved in time with her vigorous scrubbing. The skirt draped across her hips swayed with the effort she exerted.

A black braid with a pink ribbon entwined in the strands bounced between her shoulder blades.

She hadn't heard him come in because she was singing to herself.

He wasn't aware of breathing or his heartbeat because when she turned and saw him, what would her expression be? How would she look at him?

Why, after all this time, did it matter so much?

"Hello, Beautiful," he said, surprised his voice croaked past the lump in his throat.

Chapter Four

Juliette clenched the rag in her fingers then let it drop on the floor near her knees. Slowly straightening, she dug her damp, sudsy hands into her skirt.

Trea's voice was familiar and different at the same time. For some reason, it came as shock to hear it even though she knew he was coming back to Beaumont Spur.

Slowly she pivoted her head. Her gaze collided with a pair of pants, gray wool damp at the cuffs. She raised her eyes. Her line of vision slid up, over thighs that had grown muscular over the years—she noted it even under the cover of wool.

He gazed down at her, arms folded across his ribs. The coat he wore was bulky so she could not tell if his chest had filled out like his long legs had.

But of course it would have. No one stayed seventeen forever. The boy she had been smitten with had quite clearly become a man, and she scarce knew what to think or how to feel about it.

From her position on the floor it seemed that his hat touched the ceiling.

Then, for a heartbeat only, she did see the boy. The expression of vulnerability that she remembered all too well flashed across his face before he smiled.

The way his mouth curved up at one corner was instantly familiar, except, of course, for the dark mustache that had been trimmed within half an inch of a subtle dimple.

She well remembered that flirtatious dimple, having dreamed of it night after night for a good three years when she was a girl.

He grinned and the impression of vulnerability vanished.

"Trea Culverson. I imagine you still say that to all the girls." Slowly she rose, grateful that her skirt hid the way her knees quaked.

She flipped her braid over her shoulder by habit, striving to look casual and unshaken by his sudden appearance. Because why should she be shaken? He was a ghost of her past and nothing more.

"I only ever meant it for you, Juliette."

Maybe it was foolish, but she did believe him—and it made her feel…confused.

Yes, confused and lovely, which was unexpected, and silly, too. She was a widow, the mother of two, and he was—

Who was he now? Why had he shown up in the schoolhouse, of all places?

"It's good to see you after all this time, Trea."

That was so completely the truth that it scared her. How could it be that she felt as nervous as the awkward girl she had been the last time she'd seen him?

"Blame it, Juliette, you are even prettier than you

were last time I saw you. I can't see how that's possible." His smile ticked up; his brown eyes glimmered at her.

"And you are still a flirt. I was never beautiful and you know it. I was tall and gawky."

"No, that was me. You were always the sweetest person I ever met."

It was time to move on from this clumsy conversation. Or if it wasn't, of the way it made her feel.

"I heard you were coming back, but what are you doing here in the schoolhouse?" It was the very last place she would have expected to encounter him. It was in the opposite direction of The Fickle Dog, which is where she would have assumed he was headed.

He tipped his head to one side, arched a dark brow. Oh—she remembered that expression, too! It made her heart flutter, same as it always had.

Where on earth was her good sense?

Widows were levelheaded folks. Everyone knew it.

"I'm surprised to see you here, too."

"Oh, well—you wouldn't be if you saw what the classroom looked like an hour ago. The former teacher was lax in tidiness and everything else. I'm hoping a good scrubbing will keep our new teacher from turning tail and running away."

She sounded normal, her voice smooth and her thoughts casual. He would never guess how seeing him again so suddenly had shot her back in time and turned her inside out.

"That won't happen, Juliette." The jaunty smile, the teasing glint in his eye, faded and he looked at her soberly. "I'm the new teacher. And I'm here to stay."

The teacher! It couldn't be—no, not possibly.

"But—but—well." Some folks would never allow

him to teach their children. He couldn't know how they still gossiped about him. "That is—I'm glad—grateful, I mean. We need a teacher so desperately."

Trea Culverson a schoolmaster? Try as she might, she could not envision it.

Schoolteachers, both men and women, were held to strict standards. Why, they could have no social life at all. The instant there was a breath of scandal involving them, they were dismissed. It was not so long ago that a lady teacher had been fired for accepting a ride home in a buggy driven by a man who was not her father or her brother. It mattered not at all that it had been windy and getting dark.

Even if Trea had grown a halo and sprouted wings over the years, some folks would find fault.

"Surprised?" That brow lifted again, along with the crooked smile and the tick of his dimple. "You're looking at a teacher with a degree in education."

No, not surprised—stunned. Of all the things she'd considered, of all the things she'd imagined he had done with his life—she was simply astonished.

"What about you, Juliette?" he asked with a quick glance at her hand and away.

Could he be wondering if she was married? Apparently, but—

"Look over there in the corner—behind the stove."

He turned. She noticed his shoulders sag ever so slightly, but when he looked back at her his grin was as bright as summer sunrise.

"Those little babies are my life."

"Congratulations, Juliette! They are beyond precious." He reached out as though he might touch her, but instead took a step back. "Your husband must be a happy man."

No doubt. She believed everyone was, in the great beyond. More than once she'd felt Steven smiling over her shoulder.

"I'm a widow, Trea."

The regret she saw darken his expression appeared genuine. She'd bet her new hotel on it.

"I'm right sorry to hear it. Did you marry a local fellow?"

"I did. Maybe you remember Steven Lindor? But he was a few grades ahead of us in school. You'll recall his brother, I imagine. Thomas. He was in our class."

"A quiet fellow—kept to himself, as I recall."

"Yes." Thomas had been shy and kinder than many of the boys. "That was him."

And now, with her marital situation clear, she could not help but wonder—what was his?

He took off his coat, hung it on a peg on the wall.

"Hand over that cleaning rag." He extended his hand. "You must have more important things to tend to. I appreciate what you've done, but I'll finish."

It was true. She ought to get back to the café, but she was not quite ready to part company with her old friend yet. It felt nice to hear the sound of his voice, to look at him and see the man he'd grown into.

Clearly, he had changed a great deal while he'd been away.

"There's another rag beside the stove. As long as the babies are sleeping, I might as well stay and help. The students are anxious to get back to school."

"Are they?" He took the cleaning cloth, dipped it in the soapy water. "I hope so, but I can't remember ever feeling that way about it. I'll get the floor if you want to clean the desks."

"Well—one of them is, at least. Cora. She's a studious little thing."

"Like you were?"

"Not really. I was shy. Cora is—well, you'll see." She scrubbed vigorously at a dry inkwell. "Have you brought your family with you, Trea?"

The question had to be asked.

She purely hoped the answer was yes. If he'd come home a married man with children, he might be more easily accepted as the schoolmaster.

"I never married." Squatting, he scrubbed at a stubborn stain, looked up at her with that endearing crooked grin. "Came close to it once, but the lady and I both agreed we weren't meant to be."

"I'm sorry," she said, pretty sure that she truly meant it.

"Don't be. She wanted more than I could give her in the material way and I—just wanted more."

What kind of more? The meant-to-be sort of more—like she used to believe in?

Where were her emotions wandering? No place they should, and that was a fact.

She was a mother, a business woman. What she was not was a starry-eyed child.

Walking through the gently falling snowflakes and pushing the buggy with Juliette's babies inside—the pair of them sleeping like small angels under the blanket—Trea was sorry that she hadn't believed him when he'd called her Beautiful.

The doubt shadowing her eyes had been unmistakable.

Her disbelief, he felt, had nothing to do with her own self-confidence. Not at all. From all he could see, she had grown to be a strong, capable woman.

The respect he felt for her, raising these amazing babies on her own, was a mile long.

It shamed him that her doubt was because of him, of the way he'd been back then. There was no reason for her to believe that the town flirt had ever meant what he said or that he meant it now.

While they walked and chatted, even laughed a bit at old times, something became clear to him.

One day he was going to call her Beautiful and she was going to know he meant it, that it was from his heart.

It was important to him that she understood who he had become, that he no longer passed out false flattery as easily as whispers on the wind.

Of course, he'd always been genuine when it came to her. But given the mischief-maker he'd been back then, how could he blame her for having doubts about his sincerity?

Who would not?

For a long time now, he'd been preparing himself for the fact that it was going to cause a stir when people found out who would be educating their children.

"This place doesn't look much like the Beaumont I remember." It seemed dull and grungy. Not at all the respectable place he'd last seen.

"It isn't. The rail spur brings all kinds of strangers to town—thieves and gamblers, to name a few. Can you believe there are three—"

A blush bloomed in her cheeks. He saw it, even through the snowy dusk.

"Saloons, you mean? And my father owns two of them?" He smiled when he said it, to assure her that her words had not wounded him.

It had taken him years to really understand, but he did at last accept that he was not his father. He did not carry his pa's sins upon his shoulders. Only his own.

Now here he was in Beaumont Spur, hoping to make amends.

"I don't know about you, but I've worked up an appetite with all that scrubbing. What do you say we have dinner together at the café? It looks like the only decent place in town to get a bite."

She winked at him. He'd forgotten a lot of things over the years, but not how much he liked that gesture. It always made him feel warm—accepted, somehow.

"It is. And I own it." A small squeak came from under the blanket. Juliette petted one of the tiny mounds and the fussing stilled. "I needed to make a living after Steven died. The children and the restaurant gave me a reason to put my feet on the floor each morning."

"I can sincerely say I'm grateful you did. I reckon I'll be a regular customer. I can cook—I'd just rather not."

"Tonight the new schoolmaster eats compliments of the house."

"Mighty grateful." A dusting of snowflakes crusted the brim of Juliette's hat. It made her look like an ice queen from a fairy tale.

"Of all the things I ever imagined you would do with your life, I never once thought you'd become a schoolmaster."

"You imagined my life?" Judging by the way she glanced suddenly away, he probably ought to have kept that thought to himself—even if it did make him feel a bit like crowing.

Juliette had thought of him over the years! Finding that out was worth coming home for, all on its own.

"I'm sure I'm not the only one, Trea. You did have a reputation."

"Still do, I imagine." He shrugged. It was a fact. "I didn't imagine being a schoolteacher, either, not for a long time. I spent a couple of years carrying on same as I did here. Then I met a man. He taught school. Mr. Newman was his name. He told me he used to be like me, swore we were kindred spirits. He saw inside me, knew I wanted to make up for the past and showed me how."

The way she looked over at him, not a hint of condemnation in her blue eyes, made him glad he'd worked so hard to get back here. Every hour spent studying by lamplight in the livery shed had been worth it.

"So, here I am. Following in his footsteps, I reckon."

"I'm glad you came home."

So was he, even more than he'd expected.

"I bought a house not far from here, right in town, so I'll be a regular customer at your café."

Approaching the front door, he was glad for such a place to have his meals. Glancing through the windows, he saw how warm and inviting the café looked. With the wind picking up and the temperature dropping, warm was going to be a fine thing.

"Customers are always welcome. Which house did you purchase?" she asked, peeling the blanket off the babies and scooping them up, one in each arm.

"The Morrison place. A quarter mile past the schoolhouse. I recall that it was a nice home."

"Well, yes…the Morrison place was very nice, once." She muttered something under her breath that he didn't catch, then said, "We all wondered who bought it."

He opened the front door, noticed the lingering scent of soap as Juliette passed in front of him. Picking up the baby buggy, he carried it inside. He reckoned Juliette would not appreciate having muddy wheels leaving a mess on her highly polished floor.

It was odd, but he could swear she was frowning. Blamed if he knew why, what he might have said or done. Until now, she'd been nothing but friendly and smiling.

By the time he set the buggy in a corner and closed the front door, her troubled expression had passed.

The smile he remembered from years ago was back on her face as she answered the greeting of a young girl sitting at a table near the window.

No, not the same smile, quite, but more mature. Clearly, she'd lived tragedy, embraced joy and come out of it with more inner beauty than he could imagine.

Watching her glance down at her son, smile and coo—yes, he was certain he had never seen anyone more lovely in his life.

No pampered lady, this, with a maid to tend her needs. As far as he could tell, Juliette did it all on her own.

But, of course, hadn't she always? With her mother gone of influenza when Juliette was young, it had fallen upon her to care for both herself and her father.

While other twelve-year-olds were being dressed in ruffles and bows by their mothers, Juliette had been left to figure it out on her own.

As children they'd had that in common—growing up without a mother. It was a hard thing for a girl. Just as hard for a boy.

The squeak of a door hinge drew his attention from the past to the here and now.

A young woman hustled out from the kitchen, wiping her hands on a well-used apron that looked too long on her petite frame.

She stopped short, glancing between him and Juliette with a smile.

"Good evening, sir," she said. "You've come at a good time. It's quiet now. All the folks from the train have come and gone. What can I get for you?"

The girl sitting at the table drummed the end of a pencil on the cover of a book while she stared at him in open curiosity.

"Rose, Cora." Juliette tipped her head toward the girl wearing the apron, then toward the child. "Please meet my friend, Mr. Culverson."

Rose's smile fell and her brows shot up like a pair of arrows touching tips.

Cora clenched her pencil, her fingertips going white.

"I knew it!" The child's eyes grew round as a pair of full moons. "The wicked son come home to take up with his pa and wreak havoc on us all."

Funny how the prospect of his evil intentions seemed to delight her more than frighten her.

Truly, he hadn't expected to be welcomed home with open arms right off. But to be looked at so suspiciously by one of his pupils before she ever set foot in the classroom? It was disheartening.

"Cora McAllister! Mind your tongue."

"I apologize," Cora said with a deep sigh, then focused a glare on her sister. "But you know as well as I do, Rose, it's all everyone is talking about."

"Not everyone. Trea, would you mind holding my sweet boy? He's getting heavier every day."

Juliette placed the baby in his arms. He thought she intended the gesture as a demonstration that she believed him worthy of the honor. Something shifted inside of him. He wasn't sure what it was or what it meant, only that it made him feel warm inside.

"That's true." Cora tapped her pencil on her chin. "It's mostly the women Juliette's age who have been saying it. And a few men who are jealous of your handsome looks. It's what the ladies say, at any rate. Naturally, I'm far too young to take note of such a fact on my own. Sheriff Hank has a bit to say, too, but he only wants to catch you at some evil deed so that he can look reliable. Although, I doubt it will help."

"Cora! What did I just tell you not half a second ago?" Rose looked stricken. He didn't remember her, but she would have been very young when he left Beaumont.

"I apologize again. On occasion I say the first thing that pops into my mind. My sister says I lack maturity. I don't mind so much because I'm afraid I will be stifled by it. From what folks say, you were not a bit stifled. And really—truly—I do admire that."

"In that case I will do my utmost not to stifle you, Miss McAllister."

"I don't know how you could, since—" She gasped suddenly, dropped the pencil. It rolled off the table and came to rest at the toe of his boot.

Stooping, he carefully cradled the infant boy to his

chest. He snatched the pencil off the floor and handed it back to Cora.

"As I think you just guessed, Cora, Mr. Culverson is our new schoolmaster," Juliette announced, the quirk of her lips indicating that she bit back a laugh.

Juliette had always had an easy laugh. Thinking back, he remembered that she had never used it to smirk or deride, only to express humor.

"Oh." Cora accepted the pencil, set it on the table with a quiet click. "I reckon I've never made so many apologies in such a short time. I'm sorry, and welcome, Mr. Culverson."

"I accept your apologies, Miss McAllister. I hope you'll be ready for class to begin in two days. We'll be starting rehearsal for a Christmas pageant first thing."

Cora clapped her hands. "I can't remember the last time we had one of those!"

The idea of the pageant had been brewing in his mind for a while now. It seemed a good way to get to know the students and give them a chance to shine in front of their parents. Making their children sparkle was a good way to win them over. If he didn't manage to win over the parents, he might as well go back to frying chicken, since he'd be out of a job by the new year.

Watching Juliette while she smiled down at her daughter, tapping the child's button-like nose with her long, slender finger, well—he knew he did not want to leave here. And for more reasons than his need to make amends for past wrongs.

"I add my welcome, Mr. Culverson." Rose hurried across the room, her hand extended in greeting. An interesting and familiar blend of scents floated around her. Vanilla and fried food overlaid with coffee was his guess. "And you ought to know that, in spite of Cora's frankness, she is dedicated to her studies."

"Devoted to them," Cora declared. "Quite faithful, in fact. I'd rather learn than do most anything."

"That's admirable, Cora," he said.

"Practical, I'd say more than that. One day we women will have the right to vote, and I don't want to make foolish decisions."

One day women would vote, and that would be a fine thing, but for now he suspected little Miss Cora needed to learn to have some fun along the way.

"The babies are sleeping, Rose," Juliette said. "I can take over now. Why don't you and Cora go on home."

"I'll be back first thing in the morning. I reckon you'll be busy at the hotel. The gossip is that Elvira Pugley is leaving town tomorrow. She says if she spends one more day next door to that Ephraim Culver—" She shot Trea a suddenly sheepish glance. "I'm sorry—I plumb forgot that the man is your father."

"Don't trouble yourself over it. That's a fact I wouldn't mind forgetting, myself."

Rose took off her apron while Cora gathered up her book and her pencil.

At the doorway, Cora turned back and shot him a sober glance. "Mr. Culverson, I, for one, do not think you are the devil come home to roost and I'll say so to anyone."

The devil come home to roost!

Even after five minutes Cora's innocent declaration of the town's attitude toward Trea Culverson put Juliette on edge. Things had not changed in that respect over the years.

It did not matter who he had become; all some people would ever see was the reckless son of Ephraim.

Glancing through the portal window between the kitchen and the dining room, she watched Trea while she prepared his meal.

He lifted Lena in his arms, jiggled her, then smiled when she giggled.

"You letting a stranger hold my granddaughter?" Warren asked from his chair beside the stove.

"He is not a stranger, Father Lindor."

"You sure? I don't know him."

That was one good thing about her father-in-law's fading memory. Years ago, his voice had risen over the others in maligning Trea.

Still, her father-in-law's mental decline worried her. Some folks forgot everyone, in time, even themselves. She only hoped this did not happen to Steven's father.

He was not an easy man to care for, but she was his only living relative and she meant to do her best for him.

"He used to live here a long time ago. He was a friend of Thomas's. He's come back to teach school."

"All right, then, I suppose he can hold the baby if you don't have the time."

Juliette slid a steak out of the frying pan with a spatula then eased it onto a plate. She ladled a large mound of mashed potatoes beside the meat and topped it off with gravy.

Given the bad news she was about to deliver, she added more gravy. Not that it would help overmuch, but she did make delicious gravy. It was her late father's recipe and it always brought her comfort to serve it.

Coming from the kitchen to the dining room, she set the plate on the table in front of Trea, then reached for

Lena. It did not escape her notice—or her heart—that he nuzzled her baby's round pink cheek before handing her over.

Given that he was the devil come home to roost, he was quite doting.

Laying her daughter over her shoulder, Juliette sat down across from Trea. She patted Lena's small back and breathed in the intoxicating scent so unique to infants.

"I think the Christmas pageant is a grand idea, Trea. Our town needs something like that. Beaumont Spur has become such a hopeless place. Good families are threatening to leave. I hope something like gathering to hear their children sing will make them reconsider."

"It seems to me there ought to be a bit of fun along with learning arithmetic and the ABCs. I don't recall that we had that."

"You don't recall it because we didn't. It's a good idea, though."

Juliette was glad there were no late evening customers tonight. It was cozy in the dining room with the snow falling gently past the windows and the fire snapping in the hearth.

For just an instant, she thought how lovely it would be to have a home, complete with a father for her babies.

She did not let the dream linger for longer than an instant, though. The reality was that her family consisted of her babies and her father-in-law.

She was content with that. Yes, she most surely was.

Still, it was nice to look across the table and see her childhood friend—well, for honesty's sake, she would have to admit he was her *handsome* childhood friend—smiling at her.

“This has been nice, Juliette. I reckon I’ll be back in the morning for breakfast.” Trea scooped up the last bit of gravy with a spoon. “But I’d better get on my way before the snow gets any worse. I’m anxious to see the place I bought.”

“Yes—well, about that. There was a fire last week. It burned your house—half of it, anyway.”

Chapter Five

The next morning, wet ash coated the soles of Trea's boots when he walked from the burned side of the house to the standing remains. It didn't leave a mark, since the floor was already dredged in soot.

The storm having blown over, sunlight shone through holes in the ceiling, illuminating the damage.

He felt a few holes in his sense of financial security, as well. Buying this place had cost him most of his savings.

"Well, hell," he muttered, since no one was close enough to hear the dejected curse.

Had it been summer, he might have been able to live in the house while he made repairs. But in deep December the nip of the icy wind made him shiver, even though he stood in a patch of weak sunshine.

A bug bite on his rear end made him wonder if, even with the cold, he ought to live here. Juliette had warned him about the hotel, but he'd had no choice but to spend the night there.

Glancing about, he didn't wonder long. The stench of smoke in ruined furniture and black streaks coating scorched walls told him he'd be spending a lot more nights at the hotel.

Which was not such bad news as it might have been, even having insects for roommates. The woman who owned the hotel was leaving this afternoon and Juliette, he had been surprised and happy to discover, was the new owner.

When he'd left his room this morning a crew of young people was already coming in to clean the place.

"From attic to basement," Juliette, standing in the lobby early this morning, had announced with a great smile.

In fact, she had been glowing, her blue eyes sparkling when she told him of the plan she had come up with during the night to bring the town together.

Her intention was to open on Christmas Eve and host a dinner for everyone in her new restaurant. She believed this was a grand way to introduce the place.

She might have given herself an impossible task. Christmas Eve was only three weeks away. A fact that he was not about to point out to someone who, he suspected, was floating an inch off the ground when she spun away from him to follow the cleaning crew upstairs.

Then again, his impression was that Juliette had grown to be a determined woman. Not only that, she was even more industrious than she was determined.

There was every chance she would accomplish the impossible.

Glancing about the ruins of his home, he decided to take her example to heart. He would fix this place up with a cheerful attitude, a positive frame of mind. He would not allow the hole in his finances to make a hole in his intentions.

While he waited for spring and the chance to rebuild his bank account and his house, he would win over the townsfolk and educate their children.

If it was within his power, he would stand in the way of his students taking the hard, twisted path he had followed.

"Heard you were back."

Trea turned toward the voice coming from the burned side of the house. It still sounded as hard as grinding gravel.

He'd expected his father to look older, but he was surprised to see how dissipated he'd become. Hard living showed in his face and it was a disquieting thing to look at.

"Good to see you, Pa," he said, even though it was more lie than truth.

"Heard a rumor that you're the new schoolmarm." His father dabbed his nose on his sleeve then coughed, the congestion sounding thick and sickly.

"You ailing, Pa?"

"Sick at heart, thanks to you. At least tell me you faked the education that got you the sissy job."

Trea knew he shouldn't let his father's attitude cut him like it did. The man was who he was and nothing Trea did or did not do would change that.

He hadn't come back to town thinking to impress his father, only—

"Come on. Let me walk you back home, Pa. You shouldn't be out in the cold."

"What's become of you, boy? I'm talking to you like

you're spit under my boot and you act like you care that I'm sick? I raised you tougher than that."

"You did that, sure enough," Trea said while leading the way out of the half-burned house. "I reckon I take after Ma more than either of us knew."

"Tried my best to wean that out of you. I probably ought to have given you away the same time as I did that bothersome pup of yours."

And there was one mystery solved. He'd long suspected that the dog he'd brought home one Christmas hadn't just become lost. Until this moment he hadn't known for sure.

He walked beside his father, his tongue pinched between his teeth. If he said anything it would be a string of cuss words.

A schoolmaster had to be above that show of emotion. Trea was not about to let Ephraim Culverson be the ruin of his career on only his second day back in town.

Upon reaching The Fickle Dog, his father waited a moment before going inside. Rather than glaring at Trea, he glared at the hotel.

"That miserable Mrs. Pugley left town this morning. Hear tell she sold the hotel to that Lindor girl." His father scrubbed his fingers across his beard stubble, seeming to scowl at some deep thought. He still had the hands of a teamster, calloused, with a shadow of grime under his nails. "I reckon she'll be easier to control than the other widow."

"I do believe you're wrong about that, Pa." Trea opened the door to the saloon, indicating with a nod of his chin that his father should go inside. "But if you try, if you do any little thing to prevent what she's doing, I'll be standing in your way."

"Now I'm worried, schoolmarm—reckon I won't sleep a wink tonight."

"Go inside and take care of that cough, old man. And remember what I said about Mrs. Lindor. I may take after Ma, but you're the one who raised me."

Juliette took a moment to look out the window of what would become the parlor of her new living quarters at the hotel.

With the sun shining today, snow melted off the roof.

"Look at that, Joe." She pointed at the water dripping past the glass. "It looks like diamonds more than water the way the sun sparkles in it."

Beyond that there was nothing much to look at. The window faced the rear of the building. Out that way were only mud and piles of dirty, melting snow.

Come spring, though! In spring there would be a fence, a tall one to shield the hotel from the saloon, and a garden with a big patch of grass for the children to creep about on.

Turning away from the window, she gazed at the parlor, seeing it as it would be one day.

Now there was a hallway off the parlor with two rooms on each side. These would no longer be public rooms but part of her home. A bedroom for the children, another for Father Lindor, and one for herself, giving her more room than she had now in her small house.

The last room would become her private kitchen with a dining table that faced the street. If she managed to return the town to a respectable place to live, sitting in the bay window would be a lovely spot for eating and doing paperwork. She'd be able to keep an eye on her café and her hotel at the same time.

"Well, my sweet boy, there's a lot of work to do between now and then. I'll need your cooperation, yours and your sister's."

She laid Joe down on the small bed she'd set up near the fireplace. This was fine for now, but soon the babies would be rolling over and she'd have to arrange something else.

She would need to finish the renovations to the hotel quickly, not only because at this point her children were happy to eat, sleep and smile, which gave her time to work, but because she'd given herself the goal of opening by Christmas.

Accomplishing that would be a challenge, but once the dream had bloomed in her imagination, nothing would keep her from trying.

She could see it happening now, the town coming together. They would leave the school pageant, then come to the hotel for Christmas Eve dinner. After that they would walk as a group to the church, singing carols along the way.

Once upon a time Christmas in Beaumont had been celebrated that way.

Not with dinner at the hotel, but with joy and caroling.

She sighed, picked up her broom and swept up dirt embedded in the corners of the soon-to-be parlor. All that Christmas goodwill had happened a very long time ago.

Suddenly she became aware of someone standing in the doorway. From the corner of her eye she saw the silent figure of a man watching her work.

"Hello, Trea," she said, sweeping her way toward him. There were smears of ash on his sleeve and the brim of his hat. "Looks like you've been to see your house."

"Reckon I'll be lodging here for a while."

"Welcome, then, you are my first guest! And my neighbor. I'll be moving in here next week, if all goes well." She stooped to gather the dirt she had collected into the dustpan. "There's a lot to do, as you can see."

"I can help. I'm free in the evenings."

Glancing up, she realized for the tenth time—or more if one counted last night's dreams—how handsome a man he had become.

The warm expression in his chocolate-brown eyes, the way his smile tipped up slightly higher on one side—well, no wonder her heart beat faster at odd times.

Like now.

She set the dustpan aside then began to stand. He extended his hand to assist her.

Not that she needed help in rising, or that she believed that he thought she did, but she reached for his offered hand just the same.

His fingers curled around her palm, warm and strong. She'd thought her heart was thumping a moment ago, but that was nothing compared to now.

He'd touched her briefly once before, when he'd defended her pride that long-ago day when Nannie had crushed her. And again, a year later, when he'd brushed a lock of her hair away from her face and tucked it behind her ear. She'd wondered at the time if he was going to kiss her. He hadn't—at least, not until later that night in her dreams.

"I can sure use the help. Christmas will be here quicker than a blink," she said, reluctantly drawing her hand out of his because holding it any longer would not be appropriate, even for a widow.

Certainly not for a schoolmaster.

The very last thing Trea needed was a suggestion of scandal. Not that anyone could possibly know how long he'd held her hand, but still…

"I just came from my room," he said. "Doesn't look like the same place it did this morning. The kids you hired did a good job."

Juliette was taller than most women, but she still had to look up to engage his eyes. She'd had to look down a bit to make contact with Steven's blue-eyed gaze.

"I can't say how I appreciate the hard work they are putting in. I'll need to give them a bonus for it." Even if most of her money was now tied up in her purchase. "I'll lose a few of them once school starts, though I don't mind a bit."

"I'll make up for the loss."

"Once again, I'll accept your help gratefully." She returned his smile, feeling warm and content—looking forward to things in a way she hadn't in a while.

Oh, she'd pushed forward after the deaths and worked hard, but it had been for the sake of the children. What she felt in this moment, caught up by Trea's smile, well—that was for her.

"I'll cut your room rate in half for your help. And give you the same bonus as the rest."

"I'll pay the full rate, Juliette, but accept the bonus. Only it's a different sort of bonus I have in mind."

Oh? She felt her skin pulse with a rising blush. A different sort of bonus had flashed through her mind, too. Being a widow, she clearly envisioned the possibilities.

She envisioned them for a complete half second before she tucked them away.

"What did you have in mind?" she asked, as if it had been the paint color for her new parlor that she imagined.

"It's a lot to ask. If you turn me down I'll understand."

Whatever it was he wanted, he looked nervous asking for it.

"What I'd like is to be able to keep a dog."

Only hours into the day, Juliette knew it was a lucky thing that Cora was watching the babies.

There was more to do than there were moments to get it done. Hopefully everything she had ordered from Smith's Ridge would arrive as scheduled.

That was one benefit of the rail spur, she had to admit. If she'd had to depend upon delivery by supply wagon, she would not have been able to open by Christmas, perhaps not even by Easter.

And she did dearly have her heart set on a Christmas debut. In her opinion, the future of Beaumont Spur depended upon it.

Walking through the lobby on the way to the restaurant dining room, she paused to smell the fresh paint on the walls.

This evening Trea had promised to put a coat of varnish on the reception counter.

That alone was worth the price of having a dog in the hotel for a period of time. He'd promised that it would be a small, clean pup, and that he would be dedicated to keeping it free of fleas.

With any luck the dog would be a ratter. She had

cleaned and scoured the places they had been nesting, but a sharp-toothed canine reminder to not return would be helpful.

Recollecting why she had been passing through the lobby, Juliette hurried through, into the dining room and then the kitchen.

Stacks of cookware sat upon countertops. She'd been able to purchase all these things from Leif Ericman's general store, but more was coming on the train, along with beds, desks, wardrobes and rugs. She could hardly wait to see them.

Those furnishings would be for the second-floor guest rooms. For the lobby, she anxiously awaited the arrival of couches to put in front of the grand fireplace and plush chairs to scatter about the room for the comfort of her guests.

How many times had she paused to silently thank Laura Lee Quinn for her generosity and add a prayer that she would be rewarded for it. Even with the proof of the small miracle falling into place, she could scarce believe what had happened.

Juliette could see her guests in her mind's eye: chatting and smiling, perhaps waiting for dinner reservations, laughing children dashing here and there…

"Juliette!" Nannie Breene's voice echoed from the empty lobby and through the dining room. "Juliette!"

Quick footsteps padded across the bare floor, advancing in an unerring path toward the kitchen.

"Oh, there you are!" Nannie looked even more stylish than she normally did, with her lips lightly rouged and her cheeks flushing pink.

It could well be that the flush was because of excitement. Nannie looked positively bursting with some sort of news.

"It stinks in here." Nannie stood still, lifting her nose and inhaling deeply.

"That's paint you smell. I don't know if you heard that I purchased—"

Nannie snapped her fingers. "Yes, I know all that, but you won't believe what I've heard!"

"I don't have time to chat right now, Nannie. Not if I want to get anything done before the babies get hungry."

"I just saw them sleeping over at the café and, mark my words, you'll want to hear this."

Luckily, as of yet there was no place to sit down on the whole bottom floor so she would be forced to spread her gossip quickly. Juliette had little doubt what it concerned.

"What is your news?" Juliette asked quickly, to avoid a big buildup to its importance.

"Trea Culverson is here! I came straightaway to tell you, because being shut up in this dreary place you wouldn't have heard. This is heaven's own truth—and you know that's all I'd ever tell—he is the new schoolmaster! Of all the things! And here we all expected him to run the saloon. A lot of folks are uneasy about sending their children to be educated by such a rebel."

"We've all changed over the years. I'm certain he has, as well."

Nannie's grin stretched wider than her delicate, narrow mouth ought to allow for. "Not so much as you might think, except that he's more handsome as a man than he was a boy. But he's the same daring rascal inside, I'd wager."

"Why would you?" For all that needed doing, Juliette wanted to know why Nannie thought so. Her own impression had been far different. But then, it always had been.

"I saw him—face-to-face. I'm certain I'm the first person he sought out."

"Really? Where did he seek you out?"

"In the alley behind The Suzie Gal."

"What? Why were you behind the saloon, Nannie?"

"I heard his voice, so I followed it."

"You just said he sought you out."

Nannie shook her head. Blond curls shivered at her temples.

"That's how much you know about men, Juliette! He did seek me out after I put myself in the position to be sought out."

"What was Trea doing in the alley?"

"For being so busy, you sure do have a lot of questions." A fact she could not honestly deny, so did not try. "He was trying to coax a puppy to come out from under the back stairs of the saloon."

"What kind of puppy?"

"Brown, maybe. But really, Juliette, who cares? The important thing is that he's still a bit in love with me."

"Why would you think so?"

Nannie hadn't matured so much over the years that vanity was not still her guiding star.

"I could see it in his eyes, in the way he smiled at me. And he apologized for the past, the way he treated me." Nannie wrapped her arms around her middle and swayed back and forth. "I doubt you'd understand, but some of us women can feel it when a man is interested. I was tingling way down in—oh, never mind—you could not possibly know."

In spite of the fact that she had been a married woman? Really, Juliette knew quite a lot about tingles and what they led to.

Honestly, there were times when she wanted to shake common sense into her—well, her friend, when all was said and done.

Now was one of those times.

So she could not help but say, "How do you know about tingles, Nannie?"

"I've read about them in books. Frankly, it wouldn't hurt for you to spend an hour to two a day with *The Romantic Adventures of a Milkmaid.* Thomas Hardy knows of what he writes. I'll bring you my copy tomorrow."

"Milkmaid?" she murmured, then stared in silence. This was absurd, even for Nannie.

Nannie waved her hand in front of her face. "No need for thanks. I doubt if I'll have need of Mr. Hardy now that Trea is back in town."

This conversation was not going anyplace Juliette intended to travel.

"Oh, look at the time." She glanced pointedly at the mantel clock that was among the few things that she'd kept of Mrs. Pugley's. "I'd best dash over to the café. The babies will be getting hungry."

Nannie trailed behind Juliette as she walked toward the lobby door.

"Apparently I've wasted my breath giving you the news. You never did give Trea the time of day, anyway."

"As much as I'd love to chat about it," Juliette said, closing the front door behind them, "I've got to get back to my children."

"Watch out, Juliette. Infants have been known to dash a woman's hope of any sort of social life."

Trea had to take a breath, hold it, then discreetly let it out. He'd anticipated this, standing in front of his students for the first time, and it was as unnerving as he'd thought it would be.

"Good morning, children. Welcome back to the classroom."

Fifteen students heard his greeting, one returned it.

"Good morning, Mr. Culverson," Cora said from her desk in the front row.

The boy sitting behind Cora stared at the bow tied neatly at the end of her braid. He made phantom threats by clenching his fist and making a yanking gesture. The kid meant mischief. This one would bear constant watching. Having been that boy at one time, he knew he was not mistaken about this student.

The children, a nearly equal mix of girls and boys, spanned the ages of about six through fourteen.

The older students stared at him in silence. The younger ones looked out the windows where their mothers peered through the glass.

It was hard to blame the ladies for their curiosity. A teacher new to the profession was something to wonder about. But one who had been a former student and hell-raiser?

It was no wonder they braved the chill to peer through the glass at their children.

He crossed the room, opened the door and went out onto the porch.

"Feel free to come inside where it's warmer," he announced. "I'll explain what we will be doing this year and what the students will be learning."

Seven mothers came inside.

One did not. She glared heatedly at him, turned with a sharp snap of her skirt and marched away through a mist that hung heavy on the ground.

She looked familiar but he did not recall her name. Clearly, she remembered him, and not fondly.

There was nothing to do about that now but move on. To instruct her child and hope that one day she would look at him without resentment.

His mentor, Mr. Newman, had warned him that his walk toward redemption would be all uphill. On its own, teaching young minds would be a challenge, but given what his reputation in this town had been—he was half out of breath before he even began the climb.

He spent an hour telling the parents and the students what he would teach and what he would expect of them throughout the year, at school and at home.

Finished with the ABCs and American history, he talked about the Christmas pageant, how they would learn songs and poetry, and perform them in front of the parents. The children seemed interested, but it was the mothers who appeared to be the most pleased.

All around the room he saw them smile in anticipation of something fun to look forward to.

The one exception was the boy who sat behind Cora. He'd learned the boy's name was Charlie Gumm. Charlie sat at his desk, arms folded over his chest, snickering.

And why not? There was no parent standing in the back of the room beaming in pride at him.

This boy, this young and troubled prankster, was the reason Trea had become an educator. Of course, salvaging his reputation had been part of it, too—but keeping troubled children from doing what he had done was more of it.

"Today, being the first day and the weather so threatening, I'm dismissing class early."

A cheer of young voices rang out. Even young Gumm's sneer slipped to a grin.

"I'll see you all first thing in the morning. Tonight I want each of you to think of your favorite Christmas songs and stories. Bring your ideas and we'll begin rehearsing."

The children rose, making a lot of noise as they did. Many of them joined their mothers in the back of the room, getting hugs and pats on the head.

"Mr. Gumm," he said, interrupting the boy's dash toward the door. "A word with you, please."

"I didn't do nothin'." Slowly Charlie shuffled toward the front of the classroom, cutting a path through the children moving toward the door. "I swear I didn't. You won't tell my ma that I did, will you?"

"If you didn't do anything, there's nothing to tell, is there?"

"No! But sometimes—"

Sometimes he was blamed for things—yes, Trea knew a good bit about that.

Staring hard at the floor, Charlie scuffed the toe of his boot on wood that seemed to defy Trea's best efforts to polish it to a shine. The boy had made that movement often, if the hole in the leather was anything to go by.

"I was not suggesting you had done anything wrong, Mr. Gumm." Trea reached forward to touch the boy's shoulder in reassurance, but the child jerked backward.

Trea did not need to be told that Charlie's mother was rough with him. His expression all but shouted it.

How many times had Trea worn that wary look on his own young face?

"I only want to ask for your help with something. After that I'll walk you home."

"I don't want to be walked home like some baby."

"All right, then. But I do need your help and I'll pay you a dollar for it."

"What is it you want? That's a heap of money."

"There's a pup I've been trying to coax out from under the porch over at The Suzie Gal, but it won't come to me. I figure it might come to you, though. It might trust a boy your age."

"Reckon it might come to me. Animals like me more than people do."

"I do thank you, Charlie."

"Wouldn't want the poor critter to be left out in the cold, so I don't mind. Just…don't give me money. Mam will only think I stole it and give me a stropping."

Chapter Six

At the back door of the café, Juliette kissed Joe's cheek and then Lena's.

She did the same to Father Lindor, even though his reaction was to grunt unhappily.

"Don't know why you are sending me home with these strangers."

"They aren't strangers. You know Rose and Cora McAllister. They live with us now." She didn't explain that it was only for another day or two, and then he, she and the children would be moving into their quarters at the hotel. "I'll be home in just a bit."

Rose led Warren by the elbow while Cora pushed the carriage the short distance to the house.

Fog swallowed them up when they were only yards from the back door.

Still, she heard her father-in-law's voice carrying through the mist.

"I'll just make a short stop at The Fickle Dog, young woman."

"Oh, they've closed for the night, Mr. Lindor," Juliette heard Rose answer.

Shivering, she hurried back inside the café.

Welcome warmth wrapped around her as she approached the big iron stove.

Stirring the large pot of stew, she listened to the hum of conversation coming from the dining room.

She loved her small café. Truly, it was her safe place in the world. Half a dozen times a day she thanked the McAllister girls for taking over the day-to-day running of it.

One day, she imagined, she would feel the same way about her hotel.

As it was now, the task she had undertaken nearly stole her breath. Did she honestly believe she could rescue her town by reviving the place—by making it a wholesome gathering spot for families?

She had to, whether she believed it or not. She had invested nearly all her money—and her family's future—in it.

Perhaps she ought to have given more thought to the fact that her hotel, no matter how fine she made it, was knee to knee with saloons and they were not going away.

"I've packed a few things." A woman's voice carried to the café kitchen from the dining room. "I'd hoped to be gone by Christmas, but now my Anna is all in a rapture about singing in the Christmas pageant at school. I couldn't bear to break her heart, so I imagine I'll be here until the New Year."

"Adelaide Jones!" Sarah Wilcox's voice declared. "I saw the way you were looking at the new schoolmaster yesterday afternoon—I think you are half sweet on him."

Sarah and her family had only lived here for three

years, but that had been enough. They were moving along with the others.

Adelaide had a great, wonderful laugh and it rang through the dining room. "Oh, I'm completely loyal to my Ned. But one cannot avoid the obvious, and the schoolmaster is a very handsome fellow. Besides, Nannie Breene has quite set her cap for him."

"She's always been mad for him, Adelaide." Juliette glanced through the window-like opening between the kitchen and the dining room to see Flora Brown speaking between sips of tea. "Back in school she was infatuated with him."

"Oh, what a bunch of foolishness it was," Levi Silver added. "As I recall, all the girls were. The only one of you who showed any sense around him was Juliette. Now, back to the point we were discussing. I'm in favor of making our move before Christmas."

"I hate to see you go, at all, any of you," Flora said.

"And I hate to go," answered Levi. "But this town—it's dying."

"It will if everyone moves away," Flora insisted. "But now that Juliette's bought the hotel it might make a difference. Maybe if she makes it as homey and clean as the café—if we had a pleasant place to gather as a—"

The front door opened and Sheriff Hank strode inside. The scent of cold fog clung to him.

Juliette came out of the kitchen to greet her customer. "What can I get for you, sheriff?"

"Whatever you have that smells so good back there in the kitchen, I'll have that. It's colder than all get-out outside."

"Are those cousins of yours still in our jail?" Levi asked.

"US Marshal took them away yesterday."

Luckily, she only detected a bit of regret in his voice.

Beaumont Spur was not protected by the most noble of men. Perhaps if he were more reliable, people would not be so quick to move somewhere else.

"Just so you know, we are not cut off the same bolt of cloth, me and my cousins. No, sirree, they seek out crime—I hunt it down."

Juliette set a bowl of stew before him and he patted his belly.

"In fact, I'm out this late because I'm investigating a crime."

Sheriff Hank glanced about, apparently waiting for someone to commend him on his effort.

"The bank robbery?" she asked, because it seemed that someone ought to make a comment. And what a shame he hadn't felt the need to chase down the criminal when the crime was taking place.

He shook his head, licked the spoon. "Leif over at the general store is missing a can of kerosene."

"Perhaps he misplaced it," she noted.

"Naturally, that was the first thing I asked. He vowed it wasn't so. And the worrisome thing is that new fellow, the schoolteacher—didn't he burn down the livery a while back?"

"Sheriff." Juliette wondered if her face was as red-hot as her temper. "It was not a while back. It was years ago, and it came to light later that the fire was caused by accident."

"He did run..." Levi pointed out.

"Away with Nannie's heart," Flora said with a giggle. "And maybe mine."

"Really, sheriff." Adelaide set her teacup on the table

with a decided click. "Chances are the kerosene was misplaced, maybe at the worst borrowed."

"No one borrows from the general store, ma'am. It's called theft and I mean to get to the bottom of it, and I say Mr. Culverson bears watching. If he's anything like his father—well, I'd be negligent in my duty if I did not suspect him. Besides, we had a fire only a couple of weeks ago."

"It's time to close up." That announcement sounded more curt than Juliette had intended. Her customers looked in question at one another but rose slowly and shuffled toward the door.

"The thing to keep in mind about that fire," Juliette said, staring at the back of the sheriff's coat, "is that the house that burned belonged to Mr. Culverson, and he wasn't even back in town when it happened."

"I didn't realize he was the one to have bought it," Flora said, glancing back at the sheriff as she went out the door.

"An investigation is an investigation," Hank Underwood declared, thumping his boots on the floor going out the doorway.

He pulled the door shut so she hurried across the dining room and yanked it back open. She could only half see him in the shrouding fog.

"An investigation is not a witch hunt!" she called because she could not let the injustice of his attitude stand without rebuttal.

It was late when Trea looked up and realized he'd missed dinner. He must have been more involved in reviewing tomorrow's lesson plan than he'd realized. From where he sat at his school desk, he had a clear, if distant, view of the café out the window. Well, it would have been clear had fog as dense as spilled milk not been pressing on the glass.

But he was fairly certain that the café lamps had been doused only moments ago.

"Sorry about that, sweet girl. I got so caught up in reviewing the Declaration of Independence that I lost track of time."

The puppy, half hidden in the blanket in front of the stove, opened her eyes. Her tall, pointed ears twitched and so did her nose. He couldn't see her tail but he didn't think it was wagging.

She didn't trust him yet. Luckily, she had trusted Charlie and gone to him without hesitation. Trea wondered if the pup would have made it through one more night in the elements given that she had a short, smooth coat that would not have kept her warm. Even if she did survive the cold, how long would it have been before she starved to death?

Pushing away from the desk, he got up and stretched, then slowly approached the stove.

He stooped and petted the dog. She could only be a few months old, poor thing. She'd eaten all of his lunch and her belly was round, but her ribs still bumped under his fingertips.

"There ought to be a law against abandoning innocent animals."

Slowly, gently, he scooped her up and tucked her under his chin. He walked to the window, peered into the fog. Everything looked vague, wavering, but he thought he spotted the shape of a bush, or the boulder at the curve of the path leading to the little red schoolhouse.

"How would you like to be a schoolhouse dog? I think the children would enjoy having you here."

She didn't tremble when he touched her. That was something. He breathed in her puppy smell then chuckled.

He'd seen Juliette breathe in the scent of her babies the same way.

A shadow appeared in the fog about ten yards out, passing by the tree swing.

Not a bush or a boulder, but a woman. Perhaps he ought to lock the door and pretend he was not here. The last thing he wanted was an after-hours visit from the mother of a student—or worse, a girl from his past.

And the last thing he could afford was the suggestion of impropriety. A schoolmaster must appear beyond reproach in every way.

That was especially true for him, given that he had a bad reputation to live down.

Since the lamp on his desk and the fire in the stove were both burning brightly, it was impossible to pretend he was not here.

Whoever it was, he'd send them away with some polite excuse that he was scouring his brain for.

Three soft knocks sounded on the door. He drew it open before his excuse had fully formed.

"Juliette? What are you doing out so late? Come in out of the cold."

"I noticed you didn't come for dinner and that the schoolhouse lamp was lit, so I figured—"

Juliette blinked, shot him her wide, lovely smile.

"You got a puppy!" She handed him a basket with a red-checkered tablecloth folded over it. She reached for the dog.

He took the one and handed over the other. The pup smelled good, but whatever was in the basket smelled better.

"I found her under the stairs at The Suzie Gal. She wouldn't come to me but she came to Charlie Gumm right away."

"What a sweet little girl you are." Juliette cooed and nuzzled the pup's neck with her nose. "I'm glad it's Charlie you came to."

Funny how he'd felt the same way. "I haven't known him long, but the boy seems troubled to me."

"Oh, I imagine he is. His father left the family a few years ago. Just went away without a word of goodbye. The next they heard of him was in a letter saying he'd cheated in a card game and was killed over it."

"Ah…" Poor kid. No wonder he was acting up. "I had the impression his mother is hard on him."

"The whole thing left her scarred. I get the feeling she thinks Charlie is the spitting image of his father, so she resents him as much as she fears he will leave her, same as his father did."

"Bearing a father's sins is a tough thing for a kid."

"It is, but you managed, Trea. And I do have hope for Charlie. I remember what a sweet little boy he was, before." The puppy poked up her nose, licked Juliette's chin.

It made Trea…hungry.

Yes, it did, but only because he'd missed dinner and a delicious scent was coming from the basket.

Food. He was hungry for sustenance and nothing more.

As things stood now, Juliette had no reason to resent him and he intended to keep it that way.

"What's her name?"

"She doesn't have one yet."

"We can discuss it over dinner. Spread the tablecloth out on the floor in front of the stove, won't you?"

"There are plenty of desks we could sit at."

"We should eat down here with the dog. She's just so small and sweet. I can't bear to put her down."

He hesitated. A picnic in front of a warm fire was far too intimate for his peace of mind.

Juliette pointed to the floor, then the cloth, so he slid it from the basket, shook it and spread it on the oak planks with a flourish.

"Yes, ma'am." He swept his arm in a gallant gesture, as if he were a fancy nobleman. "Your wish is my command."

"Why, thank you, sir."

When she sat down her skirt billowed about her like a blue cloud. Tall and graceful, she resembled a willow swaying in a gentle breeze.

Settling the dog on her lap, she caught his gaze and smiled.

The woman plain took his breath away.

Until this moment he'd thought that to be just an expression, but for an instant he forgot to inhale.

Thinking back over time, though, hadn't she always taken his breath away? The very smile he was looking at now was the same one that had invariably made him feel accepted, worthy, even.

The same smile, yes—but it made him feel something else now. Something that he did not dare to dwell on.

"Thank you for bringing dinner. It was thoughtful of you."

"Cora would have my head if she thought I was letting the new schoolmaster go hungry. The poor girl is worried that you will decide to leave like the last instructor did."

Juliette set out bowls then ladled the most delicious-smelling stew into them. In the space between them she placed a basket of biscuits.

Before she ate, she plucked a cube of beef from her bowl and fed it to the puppy.

"I'm glad you found her."

"Me, too. Seems like a schoolhouse needs a pet. Have you ever had a dog?"

"Once, a long time ago."

"So did I. I just found out—well, let's just leave it that I'm mighty glad to have this one to watch over. Thank you for allowing it."

"It's important having someone to watch over," she said, feeding another bite of beef to the dog. "It gives one a purpose for the day—a reason to get up in the morning."

"Something you know well." He wished he could touch her cheek where it was growing pink from the heat of the stove. Of course, he didn't dare—shouldn't even be thinking of how soft and smooth it would feel. "It must have been difficult having twins on your own."

"They saved me, really. I could hardly close myself off from living, not with them to care for. But Lena and Joe are not twins. I gave birth to Lena shortly after Joe was born. His mother, my sister-in-law, died soon after Steven and Thomas did. I took Joe as my own."

"I think I respect you more than anyone I've ever met, Juliette Lindor."

"I'm sure that can't be true—besides, Joe has been a great blessing to me. And it's good for my father-in-law to have his grandbabies close by. I reckon he'd forget everything if he didn't have them to fuss and fret about."

Trea grew silent, thoughtful. She had grown to be an even more beautiful woman than he had imagined over the years, and he dearly wanted to kiss her.

She smiled softly at him, her lips looking moist in the glow of the stove. It was late and no one would ever know.

"Did you enjoy cooking, before you started teaching?" Luckily, the question snapped him back to reality.

He could not—would never be able to—kiss her.

Just as when they were kids, she was far too good for him. However—and he had to face the fact—things were not the same as when they were kids.

She was a woman grown. And he was a man who—well, hell and damn!

Cursing in his mind wasn't as bad as saying it out loud, but for a man traveling Redemption Road, he ought to be more careful.

"No, I can't say that I did. Working in the restaurant at the saloon gave me the means to get an education, but no, feeding folks was not something I cared for overmuch. How about you? Do you enjoy it?"

"I don't mind it so much—it's more, though, that I like doing things well, and cooking is something that I take pride in."

Without warning, the pup bounded off Juliette's lap, slid onto the floor and bumped its muzzle with a thud and a whimper.

Juliette lunged to the rescue at the same time he did. The result was that his nose ended up in her hair.

Hair that had fallen across her cheek only an inch from her lips.

Lifting his hand, he cupped her cheek in the palm of his hand. It was warm with the heat from the stove. He breathed in the scent of her skin—felt a bit intoxicated by it.

In another second he would lose any sense of good judgment. Become again the boy who didn't care for anything but his own desires.

He forced his hand down, curled it around the dog and scooted backward.

Juliette's eyes were closed. She bit her bottom lip.

All at once she breathed in deeply and her dark lashed eyes slowly opened. His heart slammed hard against his ribs because he imagined he saw his future in her dreamy blue gaze.

Then she blinked.

"Well, my goodness." She reached about, gathering up bowls and spoons and a crumb or two, stuffing them into the basket. "Look at how the time has gotten away! The babies will be needing me."

Rising gracefully from the floor, she hurried to the doorway.

He followed, petting the pup casually, trying to appear as if his world had not just shifted.

He opened the door and she stepped out into the cold.

"We didn't name the dog," he said because—well—they hadn't. Instead, he'd gotten lost and was not sure he could find his way back to even ground.

"Oh, yes. I think Charlie ought to name her."

And then she walked away into mist. Out of his sight, but into a thousand flights of imagination that would keep him restless all night long.

* * *

Trea had been wrong about spending a sleepless night. Dead wrong. He spent three sleepless nights.

No doubt tonight was going to be worse.

Given that Juliette was moving into the hotel today, he'd be lucky if his head ever landed on his pillow.

No matter how he tried, he could not forget about that near kiss, how she smelled and the softness of her skin. It was becoming a fantasy that lurked in his mind—or an obsession.

It didn't matter which, he guessed. In either case, it was not going away.

"Nothing for it but to take hold of the day. Focus on something else, right, Dixie?"

The dog wagged her tail. Maybe she liked the name Charlie had given her. Or, Trea hoped, she was warming up to him.

"I reckon we better check on Pa. Take him some breakfast and make sure he's feeling better."

Not that the old man would care that Trea went to the trouble or think kindly of him for it. His father resented him, and nothing Trea ever did would change that.

"Unless I become a criminal instead of a teacher," he muttered, stroking soft puppy fur. "Don't worry, though. I won't. His approval would be a twisted thing, anyway."

There were a few reasons for visiting his father. Delivering breakfast was only one.

Coming down the stairs and crossing the lobby, he knew at least one of the reasons was futile.

He tucked Dixie under his coat and went outside. The fog that had lingered for so long had finally lifted but bitter cold took its place.

He spent a short time at the café having breakfast, then asked Rose to put something together for his father.

Going outside, he stood for a moment, just staring at the saloon. Conflicting duties tugged at him.

As the schoolteacher he needed to be beyond reproach. That meant staying well away from The Fickle Dog. But as a son, it was where he had to go.

The idea of slipping over after dark in the hopes that no one would see him seemed like a good one. But that would look like he was sneaking about and trying to hide something.

Better to just march over and go inside. Folks were bound to notice but everyone knew that the tawdry business his father conducted would not begin until much later.

Crossing the street, he prayed all would go well.

It was no surprise to find the interior of the saloon dark, stifling.

The saloon Trea had worked for had been notorious, but clean.

Glancing around, he spotted thick dust on every surface but the bar. Unknown substances smeared the floor. Whatever they were must be what was making the place smell.

The pup stuck her head out from the shelter of his coat. Her small black nose twitched this way and that. He was pretty sure he didn't want to know what had captured her attention.

A scuttling sound came from a dark corner, followed by a curse.

"Miserable varmint!" A man he hadn't noticed, and who had apparently slept through Trea coming in, lurched up out of a chair, slapping his shirt.

"Hello, mister," he said, sparing a glance at Trea while he stomped the floor with one foot. "Come back at two o'clock. That's when we open."

"I'm looking for Mr. Culverson."

"At nine in the morning?" The fellow scratched his head. "He's in that room behind the bar, but he won't be up to visitors at this hour."

The slightly built fellow shuffled over to the piano and sat down. Bracing his chin in one hand, he plunked on the keys with the other.

"Long as I'm up, I might as well rehearse," he mumbled.

Not that it would help overmuch. The piano was out of tune, so even if the musician had been gifted, that would not help.

Four days ago, at three in the morning, Trea had decided this piano player was far from gifted.

The hinges screeched when he opened the door to the room the man had indicated. A figure on the bed twitched and grumbled, only halfway waking.

"How you feeling, Pa?"

"Eh?" His father sat up, but slowly, as if everything ached with the effort. "That you, Trea?"

"It's me."

"What're you doing here, boy?" He coughed, then rubbed his face with the palm of his hand. "Not scared you'll dirty your shiny new reputation?"

"I am scared of that. But here." He set the tray he had carried over from the café on the table. "I brought you some breakfast."

"What for?"

"You're sick and you need to eat."

"That don't mean it's for you to feed me like I'm a feeble old man ready to jump in the hole."

For all his surly attitude, his father lifted the cover off the tray, sniffed, then spooned up a bite of oatmeal.

"Lucky thing I've lost my sense of taste." He shoved in another spoonful, then three more. "Otherwise I wouldn't be able to eat this. Your coat's heaving, boy. Must be one of those rats snuck over from the hotel."

Driven out by a great deal of hard work, more likely.

"This is Dixie." He drew her out of hiding. "My dog."

"Sure does look like a rat to me."

"Just want you to have a good look at her." He held Dixie out toward his father. "Pet her and say something nice."

"Hell if I will."

"The thing is, you robbed me of my dog once before—he was the one thing the Christmas after Ma passed away that meant something to me. Maybe by being friendly to this one you can atone, in some small way, for that."

"Atone! Mighty fancy word from someone like you. The fact is, you weren't the only one missing your mother, boy." The admission must have cost him because he began to cough violently. "Course, she cared more about critters than she did me—always loving them up and saying sweet words."

That was probably the kindest thing he'd ever heard his father say about his mother. Growing up, he'd been convinced the old man was glad to be rid of her.

"You and her, just the same. Caring about a mongrel more than your own pa. You shouldn't be surprised I sent the mongrel away."

"The funny thing was, I knew the dog loved me. I never did know it with you."

"Let me see that thing," his father said, wiping crumbs of the toast he had gobbled off his chin.

His father stretched his hand a few inches toward Dixie then curled his fingers into a fist and lowered it to the bed.

"Sure ain't got no use for dogs. That's why you pranced over here and woke me so early? To pester me with a mangy critter and half-spoiled food?"

"Partly why."

"There's more! I'm going back to sleep." He lay back on the bed, closed his eyes.

"I also want to tell you that Mrs. Lindor is moving into the hotel today with her babies. They don't need to be kept up all hours by that awful piano. If you can't shut it down sooner, move it to another part of the building where it won't keep decent folks awake."

"Decent folks like you? Aw, you even nag same as your mother did." His father yanked a faded brown blanket over his head.

A moment passed with no further comment from under the cover so Trea picked up the tray and left.

He could not recall a time when he was more grateful to be out in the fresh, icy air.

Well, he would have been, had not two women on their way into the café stopped to gawk at him.

Chapter Seven

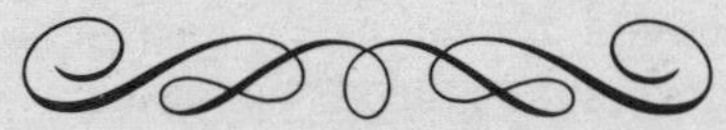

It would have been a good day to stay inside.

Juliette hugged her billowing cloak tight to herself, leaned into the cold wind while she pushed on toward the *Spur Gazette*. If she allowed a dash of blustery weather to get in her way, she would never get anything done.

Along the way she noticed a bough of holly and red berries draped over the window of Flora's Feathered Bonnet Shop. A few doors down Leif Ericman had decorated his storefront window with glass ornaments that caught the cold-morning sunshine. It made for a pretty, twinkling scene. Even The Suzie Gal sported a wreath in the front window. What had become of the black drape that normally hung there? The sight was so odd that Juliette stopped and stared.

The saloon sported a festively decorated door while Juliette—who adored everything about Christmas, every pretty bow and fresh-smelling fir bough—had yet to decorate a single thing.

Yes, life was exceptionally busy at the moment, but one should never be too involved in the day-today rush that one forgot to rejoice in the beauty of the season.

Just as soon as she had her new furniture arranged, the babies and Father Lindor settled in for the night, she would do something about that.

Yanking the hood of her cloak back over her hair, she hustled toward the *Spur Gazette*.

Across the street, footsteps bounded up the boardwalk. Sheriff Hank rushed past.

Spotting a wreath on the saloon door had been odd, but seeing the lawman in a hurry was unheard-of.

As curious as those things were, she didn't have time to puzzle over them.

A pretty wreath hung on display, tacked to the door of the newspaper office. Even Frank Breene had beat her to holiday decorating. Or perhaps it had been Nannie who'd put it there, given all the frills and fuss that adorned the circle of fir boughs.

Tonight would be the night, she decided while opening the door and stepping inside, she would correct her holiday neglect.

"Just because you saw him coming out the front door doesn't mean—oh, hello, Juliette." Nannie looked up from her conversation with the Winston sisters. "Papa's not here, if you came on *Gazette* business, but I can help you. He's been training me all week because he thinks it's time I learned something useful. Don't go just yet," she said to her companions, then she took a position behind the counter. "This won't take but a shake."

"I want to run an advertisement," Juliette said.

"Oh, good. That's something I know how to do." Nannie glanced about, looking for something to write with. "Did you know that Trea was seen coming out of the saloon? I'm trying to convince Abby and Stella it was all perfectly innocent, but you know how those two love to spread tales." Nannie lowered her voice for the last since the girls were standing nearby.

"You can tell them that Trea's father is ill and he was taking breakfast to him."

"I already have," she said in a louder voice. "He confided in me when we met behind the saloon."

"What else did he 'confide,' Nannie?" Stella asked.

"If I go behind the saloon, maybe he'll confide in me, too," Abby added with a giggle.

And this is how Trea would be ruined. Folks were too ready to believe wagging tongues.

"Nannie?" she said. "My advertisement?"

"What would you like to sell? I've found that I am good at describing goods for sale—I would never have imagined it."

"It's the grand opening of the hotel and restaurant. It will be on Christmas Eve and the whole town is invited for dinner. The time will be after the school pageant is finished."

"Oh, how lovely." Nannie's gaze slid to the sisters, her attention focused on what they were saying about Trea more than on business. "I'll write up something wonderful about it. Christmas Day, did you say?"

"Christmas Eve, after the school pageant."

"Of course. And mark my words," Nannie whispered. "Trea will never dally with them in the alley. He's much too taken with me to even give them a thought."

"You did write down Christmas Eve?"

"Yes. Right here." Nannie tapped the pencil on a word that was so scribbled that it might have said Easter—or Halloween.

"This is crucial, Nannie. So much depends upon getting the word out to everyone. Families might not move away if they have a nice place to spend an evening."

"Possibly, but you are next door to the saloon." She snapped her fingers, grinned. "But I do promise, you can count upon me and Trea to be your first customers."

Perhaps. He was certainly free to choose who he wanted to spend time with.

But while the other women fantasized a romantic encounter with Trea, she had an actual memory.

No matter how she tried, and she did—on occasion—she could not quit feeling the slide of his fingers on her cheek, the huff of his warm breath on her skin.

In that moment when he'd nearly kissed her, she'd felt her world shift and not quite right itself again.

Trea had been avoiding making this visit since the moment he came back to town. Now, walking the uphill path that led to the cemetery gate, he could no longer delay the pain visiting his mother's grave would cause.

Grief, he had found, could not be outrun. Even after so many years he would hear a sound—sometimes close at hand, other times distant—or catch a half-remembered scent, and his heart would squeeze.

The way it did now, as he opened the gate and gazed across a hundred feet of snow-dappled gravestones.

Partly because his mother's marker was half toppled and grimly adorned with last spring's dried-out weeds, but also because Juliette was there, kneeling in the far corner of the cemetery.

With her back to him, she plucked dried vegetation from the base of a gravestone. By the gray light of a cloudy afternoon, he could tell that the headstone had not been worn down by passing years.

She must be vising her husband's grave.

The crunch of his boots as he walked across snow and gravel caught her attention. She looked up with a smile that must have been on her face before he opened the gate.

"Good memories?" How many people weeded a grave and smiled over it?

"Good afternoon, Trea." Wind caught her cloak, fluttering it about her. "Most of them are, once you get past the tears."

He set his mother's small, plain marker to rights then crouched in front of it and yanked out a weed.

Luckily, Juliette was not so far away that they could not carry on an easy conversation.

"What is the one that's got you smiling now?"

Truly, he wanted to know because he could not imagine anything that might rise from his mother's grave to make him smile.

"Actually, I was thinking of my sister-in-law. How on our shared wedding day, we did up each other's hair. Mine refused to take a curl for all of Lillian's best efforts to tame it. She accidentally cussed. We laughed ourselves silly. So when I think back, it makes me happy."

"You must miss her terribly, miss all of them. To have had to bury them so young, and so close together." He felt a lump constricting his throat just thinking of what she must have gone through. "And yet you visit the cemetery without letting grief overwhelm you. I envy that."

"I was overwhelmed, Trea. But I was also busy with

the babies and Warren. I gave myself a time to cry, but even more important, I gave myself a time to laugh. Truly, how could I look at those sweet baby grins and do anything but smile back?"

"You always have been quick to smile. It's something I always admired about you." He glanced down at the small pile of weeds he had extracted. Perhaps he should not admit this, but— "Did you know that when I was a boy, I took something from the general store without paying for it? Course, I felt wicked and returned it the next day. I got caught putting it back. No one would believe I meant to, so I went along with being a thief. Figured I'd get a whipping from my pa, but he said he was proud of me. I couldn't sleep that night, thinking about how I could only make him proud by shaming myself."

He traced one finger over the letters engraved on the tombstone. "Or worse, shaming Ma. She'd only been dead two years by then."

"It took me forever to smile again after my mama died."

"The point I'm getting at is—you did smile. I want you to know that it's your smile I saw in my bed some nights. Seeing it in my mind was the only way I was able to sleep. I don't know why I want you to know that, but I do."

"We were friends, are friends. It's not so surprising."

No, she had been more. But he would keep that to himself.

"Tell me how you do it. Come here and smile."

"It's not such a mystery, Trea." Standing, she rubbed the dirt off her hands then came to crouch beside him. "Tell me something you loved about your mother."

"How she smelled."

"But you don't think about it because it makes you sad?"

He nodded. Even now the loss made him feel hollow.

"Try doing this. Close your eyes and imagine how it was." He didn't want to, not after her eyes fluttered closed in illustration. All he wanted to do was look at the sweep of her dark lashes against her fair skin, gaze freely upon the way her lips puckered slightly while she thought. "Now, unless I'm wrong, this makes you sad."

He closed his eyes. "It does."

"That's because you are looking backward, through the grief. Try and take yourself to a place before that. Your mother isn't dead—she's holding you, tickling you, and she smells good."

The warmth of Juliette's hand covered his where it rested on the cold stone. He opened his eyes to see her looking at him and, yes, smiling.

"Do you see? Looking at a memory through loss hurts, but putting it back in its time and place—it's a joy."

"You are a joy."

"And you are still a flirt." She stood up, brushed snow and bits of dried grass from her skirt. "That's enough looking back for one afternoon. I've got a thousand things to tend to at the hotel."

She looked as graceful as a willow walking away. At the gate, she turned, winked and waved goodbye.

He looked again at the headstone, searching for another memory to look at for what it had been.

Somehow, all he could see was that blue-eyed wink.

The next morning, Trea strode over to the schoolhouse stove and pitched in another log. Even though it was sunny outside, the wind was blowing and cold air seeped in through cracks he hadn't been aware of.

"That sounds lovely, Cora," he said when her *fa-la-la-la-la* rose above the other voices.

All the voices sounded lovely, in fact, whether on key or off.

"All of you do. I appreciate the effort you are giving. Your parents will be proud of you."

Six-year-old Maxwell Finch raised his hand in the air, waggled it.

"What is it, Maxwell?"

"Mama says if we don't move away, we can deck our halls. She'll be glad I can sing fa-la-la-la-la-la-la-la. Was that enough la's, sir?"

"The more the better. How would you all like to decorate the classroom?"

Judging by the cheers and smiles, the answer was yes.

"Bundle up, then. We're going to the woods behind the school to gather boughs."

It was a shame that Charlie was absent today. The boy would have enjoyed this outing more than he did most things they did in class.

Trea didn't think he was wrong to worry about the child's absence.

Not only was he falling behind in his studies, but with his part in the Christmas pageant, as well. The boy had a clear, fine voice and was supposed to sing "O Come, O Come, Emmanuel" solo.

Trea followed the children outside, carrying his ax. They selected the branches and he hacked them off.

The idea was for each child to decorate one for the classroom, then, after the Christmas program, take it to adorn his or her own home.

It was good to hear the students' laughter, see them leaping and running around.

Education ought to be fun. There was no reason that learning had to be a somber affair.

A movement caught his eye, a flash of brown plaid on the hillside dashing between a tree and a boulder.

Ten to one odds it was Charlie. What he could not figure was why he would be hiding instead of coming inside. For all that the boy claimed to hate school, Trea did not believe him.

He was smart—clever, too. At times, Trea believed he pretended to be ignorant of things he actually knew.

Unless he figured wrong, it was not that the boy hated school so much as he felt an outsider among the group.

Lord knew, that's how Trea had felt. It's why he'd raised the devil as a child. Somehow he thought his misbehavior would earn the respect of the boys—his flirtations the affections of the girls.

It's why, after he had been accused of the theft he'd told Juliette about, he committed a couple more, just to see if he felt good enough about his father's approval to be a thief.

He didn't, and even though he never took anything else, the image of being a bad seed had stuck to him like an ugly smell.

Trea was dedicated to all his students, but Charlie—that boy needed him in a way the others did not.

"Good work, boys and girls." He called loudly enough for Charlie to hear from his hiding place. "Drag your branches back to the porch. When we get inside, I've got a surprise for each of you."

Moments later the children sat at their desks, wriggling and grinning in anticipation.

He drew a blanket off the books he had hidden under his desk. Picking up the stack, he passed out new copies of Clement Moore's *'Twas the Night Before Christmas*.

He supposed he ought to have spent the money repairing his house, but there was not much he could do until spring, anyway.

The children cheered at the gift. A moment later, as he had hoped would happen, he spotted Charlie's face peeking briefly through the back window.

"I'm dismissing class a little early, but I want you to take the books and spend some time reading. Tomorrow we'll discuss the poem."

Within a minute, the classroom emptied of students and he sat at his desk pointedly thumbing the pages of the book he intended for Charlie.

It took ten minutes, but the door finally opened.

Trea looked up and smiled as if he were surprised to see him.

"Good afternoon, Charlie." He stood up and crossed the room because the boy seemed hesitant to come past the desk closest to the door. "We've missed you. Have you been ill?"

"No, sir, Mam's needed me at home, is all."

It was evident that Mrs. Gumm put no value on education. He would have to fight for Charlie, do his best to make sure the boy got what he needed to be successful in life.

"This is for you." He put the book in Charlie's hand. It was good to see his frown give way to a smile, even if it was half smirk. "Read it tonight. We'll be discussing it tomorrow in class."

Charlie stared at him in silence, but he tucked the book inside his coat.

"You'll be here?" Trea clapped the boy on the shoulder. "We miss you."

"You're the schoolmaster—you have to say so."

With that, he spun out from under Trea's hand and raced out the door.

A smear of ash dusted Trea's hand. The scent of kerosene lingered in the air.

"Here's one for you, Lena." Juliette held up the stocking she had spent the afternoon sewing. "Yes, I should have been organizing the kitchen, but Santa will be coming soon and he'll need someplace to put your new rattle."

Bending down she kissed Lena's cheek then turned to attach the stocking to the lobby mantel.

There was a mantel over the fireplace in her living quarters, but this room was the one that needed decorating.

Some of the furniture had been delivered and arranged in groupings about the room. It looked as elegant as she'd imagined it would.

The only thing lacking was heart. The room needed something that stated, *Come. Enjoy a peaceful moment at the fireside. Rest your feet and feel at home.*

Stockings hung by the chimney with care was a good start.

"And here's one for you, my sweet Joe." He was waving one round little fist in the air, so she put the stocking close to him. He latched onto it and stuffed the toe into his mouth. "You're just a little man already, hungry all the time."

She tacked Joe's stocking beside Lena's, stood back and nodded.

"The room is still sparse looking as far as decorations go. But…" She turned around and clapped her hands, gazing down at the twins. They both smiled and kicked their feet. "By the time Santa comes, it will look as festive as anything you ever saw. Not that you have seen a decoration before."

She bent over, tickled a round belly and was rewarded with a giggle.

"But you will." She tickled the other belly and got a coo for her efforts. "I promise Santa will not be disappointed and neither will you."

Nor would the guests who would fill this room on Christmas Eve.

She could barely wait to see the display in the newspaper. Hopefully Nannie was as good at advertising design as she believed she was.

Mentally going over everything that still needed to be done, she sighed, straightened up and placed her hands at her waist. She arched her back, easing away some tension. With a groan, she closed her eyes and reveled in the stretch.

Many tasks flitted through her mind. She tried to pluck the most urgent one.

Seeing to Father Lindor's dinner. She hated to wake him from his nap. During the two hours he'd been dozing in his new room, she had been able to finish the babies' stockings, feed them and even do a bit of organizing in the kitchen.

Half reluctantly, she opened her eyes.

Her gaze collided with Trea's. He stood on the stair landing, holding his small dog while staring raptly down.

There was no telling how long he had been there. Long enough, she supposed, for her blush to be deserved.

Judging by the half grin pushing his mustache up on one side, he'd witnessed her indulgent performance—heard her groan out loud.

From now on she would keep in mind that the lobby might feel like home, but it was not the same thing as being in the privacy of her own quarters.

"You are just in time," she said, deciding to pretend he had not seen what he had seen. It would be easier not to speak of it.

"I was just thinking the same thing."

In spite of his effort to reform, Trea Culverson was still a tease. The thing was, she was not sure she minded.

Well, she would if his teasing was directed at another woman. Nannie, for instance. She would mind that.

It was astonishing to discover how much. Yes, astonishing and not exactly welcome.

She had quit envying other girls long ago and was not about to begin again.

The handsome man on her stairs was her friend, her boarder and nothing more.

Not only her boarder but the schoolmaster. Any hint of impropriety between them would be the end of his career.

If this town was to survive, it needed its children to be educated.

For that they needed Trea Culverson. Finding a new teacher would not be a quick or easy thing to do. Besides, from what Cora had told her, the students liked him, looked forward to going to school, even.

That was bound to have an influence on their parents. Perhaps enough to convince them that moving to another town was not the best thing, after all.

Juliette would not do anything to jeopardize the future of her town.

Not only had she invested her heart in Beaumont Spur, but her newly come fortune. Nearly all of it, in fact. The success of the town was now critical to her financial future—to the security of her family.

"The dog is more who I was speaking to." She plucked a red sock off the chair cushion. "She's just in time to see her stocking being hung."

"You made a stocking for my dog?"

His dark eyebrows arched, causing small furrows to crease his forehead while he came down the stairs.

"Poor sweet girl, I just thought she ought to have one."

"You are an exceptional woman, Juliette Lindor." He set the pup on the floor then stepped closer to her than he ought to. "In every way."

His gaze on her seemed appreciative—and…and was he going to thank her with a kiss?

It seemed so. He lowered his head, inch by slow inch. The appreciation in his brown-sugar gaze flared, turned hotter. To pure desire—a quickening in the blood.

She knew because she recognized the answering heat thrumming under the surface of her skin.

Nothing would be as sweet as leaning into that kiss, forgetting every caution that she had just ticked off in her head.

Would it be so horrible to indulge in what she had long dreamed of?

A tinkle of water softly tapped the floor near her feet.

Trea grunted then, stepped back.

Apparently she was saved from taking an ill-advised step by a puppy's full bladder.

"We were on our way outside." He frowned and shook his head, causing a wave of rich, dark brown hair to dip rakishly across one eye. "I'm sorry. I will not let that happen again."

"I wouldn't take it to heart if it does," she answered with a wink. "Don't forget I've got two babies who spring leaks all day long."

"Juliette, I meant—"

"She's squatting again," she said quickly, because she knew what it was he meant. She just did not know how to feel about it.

To be honest, it was not an apology she wanted.

It was a kiss.

A kiss that would not happen. For the sake of so many, it could not.

Trea carried Dixie to a leafless bush a short distance beyond the hotel kitchen and set her on the dirt.

"Good girl. You wouldn't know it but you rescued me from behaving like my old self. Juliette will never believe I'm changed if I pounce upon her like an undisciplined heathen. Be quick about this, won't you? It's freezing out here." He stared up at the stars while he waited. If it was this cold down here, what must it be like way up there? "Shouldn't have been staring at her like that, either. But you saw her, she was just so damn pretty. I may be a changed man, dog, but still, I'm a man."

And she was temptation in a buttoned-to-the-chin blue-checkered dress.

Dixie scratched the dirt, apparently finished. He scooped her up and tucked her under his jacket.

"I forgot how good it is to have a dog to talk to. Let's go back in and admire your stocking."

Opening the front door, he saw Juliette with her arms raised over her head, tapping a nail into the rustic mantel. The stocking was not the only thing he admired.

Right there was the proof that it was going to take more than five minutes in the frigid air to cool off his yearning for her.

"Ouch!" She dropped the hammer and sucked on her thumb.

"Let me do it." He set Dixie down, hurried over and snatched her hand.

She blinked and her blue eyes shot wide, startled. He shouldn't do it but he laughed. "I'll pound the nail, is all I meant. Although—?"

He turned her hand this way and that, checking for injury—all the while admiring the long, slender fingers, the delicate knuckles and the smooth texture of her fair skin, slightly reddened by hard work.

"You can't not do that, can you?"

"Hammer nails? I've done it all my life."

"Flirt. It's something you can't help—like some folks tell jokes and others—" Her voice trailed off. "I'd better check on my father-in-law. He's been quiet for longer than he usually is."

The thing was, even though she said that, she made no attempt to pull her fingers from his touch.

"I came here to teach school because I owe this town a debt. But flirting with you—"

The front door opened with a crash.

"Hate to interrupt this tender scene, but I reckon this belongs to you, Mrs. Lindor."

Trea's father spotted a chair, a new one that no one had used yet. He dumped Warren Lindor upon it. Given the scent of alcohol on him, he'd no doubt been dragged from The Fickle Dog.

"Father Lindor!" Julia rushed to him, knelt down beside the chair. "What have you done?"

"He's peed himself."

In Trea's opinion, his father didn't look much cleaner.

"You don't look well, yourself, Pa." Trea crossed the room, touched the old man's forehead with the backs of his fingers. His skin felt feverish.

His father slapped his hand away. The only thing surprising about the rebuff was the way it made Trea feel. As a kid, he'd always felt crushed by his father's rejection.

Tonight, he didn't. The man was who he was. Trea was under no illusion that his father would ever welcome him with open arms.

Which did not lessen Trea's responsibility to take care of him.

"Father Lindor, you mustn't leave the house by yourself." Juliette skimmed her fingers over the line of his jaw, then his shoulder, as though searching for hidden injury. "It isn't safe."

"I know how to walk next door on my own, girl."

While Warren Lindor did know how to walk, he had lost the ability to care for himself.

"Can you stand? I'll clean you up and get you in bed."

"Don't forget my dinner."

"Oh, I wouldn't forget that."

Juliette turned to Trea with a smile and a wink—he

adored that wink. When she might have been angry or resentful, she was cheerful.

"Trea, if you'll watch the babies, I'll run over to the café and bring back dinner for us all. Can you stay, Mr. Culverson?"

If he'd ever seen his father so stunned, he could not recall the occasion.

It took a few seconds but the old man gathered himself. "Why would I want to do that?"

He spun, cussing as he marched toward the still-open door.

The odd thing was, his father cursed under his breath instead of at the top of his lungs, and he didn't slam the door but closed it with a quiet click.

Yes, Christmas was coming closer each day and bringing with it the spirit of love and goodwill. The thing was, Trea had never known his father to be touched by yuletide goodwill before.

This had been an interesting evening, so far. Watching Juliette lead her father-in-law to their living quarters, he wondered what else the night might bring.

Chapter Eight

Trea watched Warren Lindor take a bite of his meal then grunt over it, shake his head. "See what happens when a woman stays home like she ought to? Meals get served on time."

"And," Juliette said, patting the man's blue-veined hand, "bedtimes are predictable."

"I'm not sleepy. Don't think you can tell me what to do and when to do it."

"The thing is, Father Lindor, you are still a bit drunk and someone needs to look out for you. I don't imagine you feel very well."

"That might be true, Juliette. Food isn't setting right in my belly."

"As long as you insist on sneaking over to The Fickle Dog, it won't."

"Who's that stranger eating with us?"

"Trea Culverson," Trea explained. "I'm the schoolteacher. I live here in the hotel."

"My boys went to school." Warren Lindor set his fork on his plate. "Put me to bed. I've got a headache."

Juliette helped him up from his chair, which he did

seem to resent, but he did not fight her when she led him away to his room.

While she was gone, Trea cleared up the dinner dishes, washing them and setting them on the counter to dry. While he worked, he glanced about at what her hard work had accomplished.

He'd seen this room before she moved in. It must have been an exhausting task to transform the bleak place it had been into the cozy kitchen it was now. The table at the window might have been one of the most welcoming places he'd ever eaten a meal.

The thing was, Juliette did not look exhausted. She never looked anything but fresh and engaging.

"I hope he didn't say anything to ruin your meal. I don't think he understands things the way he used to," Juliette said, coming back into the kitchen.

"You are good to him." She set a whole pie on the table along with a couple of plates, so he plunked himself down with a grin. "He's a lucky man."

With a return smile, she cut a large slice of pie and set it in front of him.

"I don't know. He lost his sons and a daughter-in-law. With his mind as it is, he doesn't always understand."

"Still, I say he's a lucky man in spite of what he's lost, which is unbearable. But you did bear it, Juliette, and so he has you and his grandchildren." The sweet-tart flavor of cherry exploded on his tongue. "Heaven on a fork! This is dang good pie!"

"Well, I've made hundreds of them." She shrugged away his praise. "As I see it, it's your father who is the lucky one. Truly, Trea, I remember how he was with you. He doesn't deserve your forgiveness—and from all I can see, it's what he has."

"Never thought about it as forgiveness so much as me doing my duty. Can I have another slice of that pie?" She cut one. He shook his head. "Bigger."

She laughed, scattering issues of forgiveness and duty, and leaving behind a glow. It beat in his heart as warm as anything he could remember.

And he did remember.

"Juliette, do you recall the time you brought me dinner in the shed?"

"The time you were hiding from the store clerk?"

"One of the times." He felt his smile tic up on one side, saw hers widen in response. "I just want you to know how I appreciated it."

"We laughed for hours that night, just talking about silly things. It was raining, wasn't it?"

"Pouring down so hard I thought the roof would leak. It was late when you finally went home. I always felt bad that you might have gotten in trouble."

"I imagine I would have if Papa hadn't been caught up in a grieving spell." She must have noticed his empty plate because she filled it once again. "The truth is, Trea, it was the anniversary of Mama's death. If I hadn't been laughing with you, I'd have been home crying with Papa. I dearly needed the company of a friend."

For a moment they simply looked at each other. Affection—no, that was a lie—love, pure and simple, was blooming in his heart so fast that for the moment he could not speak.

This was not the fanciful, she-is-so-beautiful, makes-my-heart-skip-and-my-palms-sweat kind of ardor.

No, he'd always felt that for Juliette. This was more *your soul has touched mine, danced, melded, and life will never be the same again* kind of love.

"What is it you want, Juliette?"

She closed her eyes, took a deep breath, bit down on her bottom lip. He saw a shiver run through her when she let it out, then she slowly opened her eyes.

"A piece of pie, but you've eaten it all."

He glanced at the tin. Hell, he had done that!

"From life. What do you want from life?"

"I want this town to flourish. I've invested all my money in it so it has to." She dabbed the pie tin with her finger, caught up a crumb and licked it. "And a dozen Christmas trees for the lobby."

"That's a lot of trees." It was clear that she did not want to discuss the feelings he thought were ripe and aching between them. Not now, at least.

Not that he could blame her for it. She carried a lot of responsibility. And, damn it, he had run away once.

He doubted that she thought he would do it again, but it wasn't only herself she had to consider in the decisions she made.

"As long as I'm dreaming, why not a dozen?"

"Why not?"

And as long as they were dreaming, why not stare at her lips and wonder…

Walking through the woods the next afternoon, huddling into his coast against the wind, Trea thought about the previous night.

He hadn't touched Juliette, hadn't so much as held her hand. They had simply shared a meal while sitting at the kitchen table, eaten pie and fallen in love. At least, he had.

And they had talked, the same as on that rainy night in the shed—laughed the same way, too.

They had spoken of Steven, of Thomas and his wife. But mostly they had discussed the babies. He enjoyed watching her when she talked about them. The love she felt for those children shone out of her eyes. And when she touched them? It was with utter devotion.

Speaking with Juliette was as easy as breathing.

Yet there was one thing he did not admit to her.

He did not confide that while she fed her babies by the fire's glow, cuddled and cooed to them, he'd imagined she would one day love his babies that way.

That was a notion too intense to consider for a man who had never pictured himself as a father.

The trouble was, once he did consider it, the idea would not go away.

A rock on the path caught the toe of his boot, brought him neatly back to the here and now, the issues of the day.

Charlie had not attended school—again.

A visit to Mrs. Gumm was in order. Signs of the boy being in trouble were all there, and Trea was not about to let him slip away.

As it turned out, the Gumm residence was well outside of town. The road to get there wound through woods grown thick with brush. He didn't see the rundown dwelling at first. Not until a dog burst out of the growth, barking an alarm.

"Who's there?" A thin woman stood on the porch, craning her neck to see what had distressed the animal. "Show yourself!"

"It's Mr. Culverson," he called in answer as he stepped into the open. "Charlie's teacher."

"Well, he ain't here." Mrs. Gumm fidgeted with the collar of her faded dress while she fixed a stern glare on him.

His first impression of her was that she had a cold soul and an icy temper. For all that her son was a mischief-maker, Trea would bet a month's pay that Charlie did not take after her.

"I'm here to see you, actually."

"Wha'd that boy do now to set the teacher on me? I'll take him to task, don't you worry."

"He hasn't been in school for a few days. I want to make sure he's not ill."

"Not so far as I know, he ain't." Mrs. Gumm scratched her head, then her neck.

"He's a bright boy, ma'am. I'd like to see him in class on a daily basis."

"A daily basis! Imagine a Culverson using such fine language. Reckon you don't take after your pa overmuch. Old Culverson, he's a purveyor of sin, is what he is, with his saloons full of alcohol and gambling. Dens of iniquity is all I have to say about those places."

"As I said, I'm here because I'm concerned about your son."

"Oh, that boy does take after his pa. Curse his dirty soul. Made sure I lost everything I had and left me with a hellion to raise."

"Raising a child on your own can't be an easy thing to do."

Unless you were Juliette Lindor. She faced the challenges of raising two babies alone, along with caring for her declining father-in-law, and she made it look pleasurable.

No doubt it had been a long time since Charlie received so much as a smile from his mother.

"I get it done. Me and my switch." She inclined her

head toward what appeared to be a branch more than a switch.

"Mrs. Gumm. I'll agree that Charlie can be a handful, but I believe he is a good boy at heart. Without help, I'm afraid he'll go wrong."

"Don't know what kind of help you're talking about. But don't fret. He always lands on his feet."

One thing was clear. When Mrs. Gumm looked at her child she didn't see him. She saw his father.

An old ache threatened to rise from the grave Trea had buried it in.

"Did you know that your son has a beautiful singing voice?"

"For all the good that'll ever do him. Rather see him be good at cleaning the chicken coop."

"We're having a Christmas pageant. Won't you come? I know you'll be proud of him. He's singing 'O Come, O Come, Emmanuel,' solo."

"Rather see him cleaning up after the chickens."

Apparently that was all she had to say. She spun and went back into the house.

The door slammed closed. A snowflake drifted out of the sky. He watched a half-hearted wisp of smoke twirl out of the chimney.

Judging by the short stack of wood on the porch, it was going to be a cold night inside that house.

A hundred or so feet from the porch under low-hung tree branches, he spotted a stack of logs with an ax leaning against it.

He strode over, snatched it up and began to split wood.

A curtain stirred then fell back into place.

Still, he felt eyes watching him, but not coming from

the house. Unless he missed his guess, a boy in a brown plaid coat was hidden in the trees, observing him work.

Trea prayed that Charlie would understand that someone cared that he was worthy of a warm place to sleep.

"I want to go home," Father Lindor announced.

Juliette set the garland that she had been about to hang on the mantel across the back of a chair. She turned to see him standing in the middle of the lobby, his gaze shifting from object to object.

"We are home, Father Lindor," she assured him.

"You sure, girl?" The poor man looked confused and a bit afraid.

The alcohol he'd had far too much of last night must still be having an effect on him. In the past he had been forgetful, but never of where he was.

"Are you hungry?" He'd had breakfast early this morning, but perhaps some time in the kitchen of the café would help him regain his mental balance.

Decorating the lobby would have to wait.

Within moments she had bundled everyone up for the short walk across the street.

"Isn't the snow lovely?" It fluttered down, softly whispering in the still air. "What a fine Saturday morning."

"Must be snowing at home, too."

What? He had lately considered home to be the café and it was only steps away.

"Oh, I imagine so. See it just ahead?"

He stopped dead still in the middle of the road, staring hard at her.

"You think I'm an old man whose mind has wandered? Either that or I've gone blind? I know where I belong."

Maybe, she thought, following him. But she could not help wondering what he saw when he was in the café. The home where he raised his boys, perhaps?

They came inside. As always, warmth wrapped around her.

Whatever her father-in-law's mental condition, there was nothing she could do about it. Life did take its course. She would do the one thing she was able to, and care for him as dutifully as a natural-born daughter would.

"Feed me something," he grumbled.

And she would do it with a smile.

Juliette followed him into the kitchen.

She greeted Rose while she settled the babies into their cradles a safe distance from the stove. Warren sat down in his familiar chair and picked up the book he had left on the side table.

Hopefully, he would never lose the ability to read. It was the one thing that kept his mind occupied.

When she set a plate of food in front of him, he nodded, even gave her a half smile.

Juliette went back into the dining room. Cora looked up from the book she was reading at the same time three members of the Ladies Service Society hurried in from the cold.

They plucked off their gloves and rubbed their hands as they stood in front of the fireplace. After a moment of absorbing the warmth, they sat at a table in front of the window.

She felt like she ought to take their orders, but Rose

bustled into the room, a writing tablet in one hand, a pencil in the other.

A busy schedule demanded that Juliette return to the hotel and keep working. Christmas Eve was in ten days and she still had a lot to do. On the other hand, duty demanded that she stay for a while and make sure Warren was content.

Cora sat at a table, reading a book while silently mouthing the words.

"Hello, Cora." Juliette sat down in the chair across from her. "How is school?"

"It's clean as a whistle, although I do wonder how clean a whistle really is. Being blown into all the time, it might not be."

"What are you reading?" In the brief glance she got of the book before Cora closed it up, it looked festive.

"It's *'Twas the Night Before Christmas*. Mr. Culverson gave each of us copies."

"That must be easy reading for you."

"It is, but do I like looking at the artwork. Besides, I'm memorizing it for the pageant."

"That's wonderful, Cora. I'm really looking forward to the program, even if I don't have a child in school yet."

"I only hope that Charlie Gumm doesn't ruin things. He's supposed to sing all by himself and he's hardly been to school."

Rose set a teapot on the table where the members of the Ladies Service Society gathered for their meeting.

"The rules clearly state that any teacher who frequents a public hall will be suspect." Sarah Wilcox whispered, but since she was sitting only feet away, Juliette clearly heard.

"He was seen doing it." Adelaide Jones shook her head. "And as much as I hate to repeat that news, it does not make it any less true."

"And Nannie says he invited her to meet him behind The Suzie Gal," Stella Green added with a wink.

Rumors of impropriety seemed to be in full bloom. Untrue comments would doom the career Trea had worked so hard for.

There was nothing to do but speak up.

Juliette pivoted on her chair. "The only reason Trea went to the saloon was to bring his ailing father breakfast."

All three of the women set down their teacups with a unified clink and stared at her.

"It's true," she said in the face of their speculative gazes.

"How would you know that, Juliette?" Stella asked. "I realize he's staying at your hotel and that it is a perfectly reasonable accommodation in and of itself, but… I wonder…does Nannie need to be worried?"

"I'm absolutely certain that courting two women at the same time is against any sort of moral conduct for teachers," Sarah pointed out with a sly half smile. "And he does have that reputation."

"Mr. Culverson is not courting me. I doubt that he is courting Nannie, either."

"Nannie does tend to fantasize, Sarah…you know she does." Adelaide nodded while taking a sip of her tea.

"I think we need to call a meeting of the school committee. If he's not behaving to the moral code required, it ought to be noted and reported to the board in Smith's Ridge."

The scrape of a chair interrupted conversation. Cora lifted off her seat like a tight spring suddenly released.

"You oughtn't gossip. That's against the Good Lord's moral code." Cora pressed her book close to her heart. "Mr. Culverson is the best teacher we've ever had… just ask any of us."

Cheeks flaming, Cora whisked around then dashed into the kitchen.

"If that's the kind of behavior he's inspiring, I say we call a committee meeting this afternoon."

"My child quite likes him. And I know some others do, as well," Adelaide said.

"Newcomers, who didn't know him way back when." Stella accented her comment by arching her finely shaped brows.

Out of the window, Juliette spotted a woman dashing through the snowflakes. She came inside, hung her coat on a peg and settled at a table near the back of the dining room.

How odd. Suzie Folsom, the owner of The Suzie Gal, rarely came to eat at the café.

With Rose busy in the kitchen, Juliette took her order.

And not a second too soon. If she had to hear another mean-spirited comment about Trea, she might lose her composure. The steam she felt building inside her chest might whistle out her ears.

"Coffee, please…and a word with you, Mrs. Lindor."

Juliette poured two cups and sat at the table with Mrs. Fulsom.

If the ladies of the Service Society thought it was unseemly for Juliette to be speaking to the saloon owner, and judging by the narrowed gazes of two of them, they did…she did not care.

Mrs. Fulsom was a customer the same as they were and would be treated with the same courtesy.

“I just want to tell you I like what you are doing with the hotel.”

“I appreciate you saying so, Mrs. Folsom.” Truly… more than she could say.

“The thing is, I’m not getting any younger and there’s a lot of headache goes with owning a saloon…and not much profit with having to compete with that underhanded Culverson…father not son. I reckon the son is decent enough.”

She sipped her coffee, nodding her head. “With the puppy and all he took from under my porch. Didn’t know the poor wee critter was there until I saw Mr. Culverson and the boy take it away. Anyway, all that aside, I’ve been thinking. With the way you are fixing up the hotel, might be that other places ought to shape up, as well.”

“Are you speaking of your place, Mrs. Fulsom? I appreciated the wreath in your window.”

“Pretty thing, isn’t it? And I’d be pleased if you’d call me Suzie. We’ve been neighbors for a while, now.”

“Suzie, then…and you’ll call me Juliette?”

“In private, maybe. But judging by the looks those women are shooting your way, I’m not doing your reputation a bit of good.”

“The thing is, Suzie, I don’t reckon I care. It seems to me that if one picks one’s companions by appearance… or reputation alone, it could lead to taking up with the wrong friends and missing the true ones.”

“I hope once I make my change, folks will be as understanding as you are…Juliette." Suzie's smile crinkled the corners of her mouth and creased the lines at the corners of her green eyes.

"What change is that? I'll help if I can."

"You already have. If it weren't for you making town nicer by giving us a decent hotel, I never would have considered calling my son home."

"I didn't know you had a son. He'll join you in the business?"

"Oh, my, no!" She waved her hand in front of her face as if trying to brush the idea away. "My boy is a doctor. He's new to the profession and I'm just so proud I could burst."

A doctor setting up practice in Beaumont Spur! It was Juliette's daily prayer.

"If it weren't for you, I wouldn't have thought to close the saloon and give the building to my son for his clinic. I just came over to say thank you."

"I'm so pleased for you, Suzie." And for the future of Beaumont Springs. She could scarce believe that folks would no longer have to take the train to Smith's Ridge to get medical attention. "When will he be here?"

"By Christmas, he says. He's anxious to help me clean out the saloon and get his practice going."

"I know some young people who—"

The front door burst open. A rush of cold air blew inside along with Sheriff Hank.

Trea entered the café then closed the door behind him. He'd noticed it standing open when he'd come out of the hotel. He'd wager that half the warm air had rushed outside already.

Probably shouldn't even think about betting, though.

He spotted Juliette going nose to nose with the sheriff over something. He could not recall ever seeing her so het up.

The heat in the room would be replenished in about a minute.

"You will not post that nonsense on my wall!" She snatched what appeared to be a handwritten notice from the sheriff's fist when he lifted a hammer to try and nail it to the wall.

"It's a crime to interfere with the duties of a sheriff, missy," he mumbled past the nail he bit between his teeth.

"I'm certain you meant to say *Mrs. Lindor.*" Trea had to bite his tongue to keep from shouting something that would get him fired.

With a neat swipe, he took the hammer from Sheriff Hank's fist then set it on a table where three members of the Ladies Service Society sat, their eyes grown wide…their teacups stalled halfway to their mouths.

Making a room full of folks gasp was not what the schoolteacher ought to be doing, but he could not let the insult to Juliette stand.

"Mrs. Lindor," the red-faced lawman amended with clear resentment. Was that a quiet laugh coming from the back of the dining room? "A crime has been committed and you are required to post this notice."

"A trash fire in back of The Saucy Goose is hardly a crime," Juliette said.

"When a can of kerosene goes missing and then there's a mysterious blaze…I say that's a crime."

"It could be coincidence," Adelaide Jones, the mother of one of his students, pointed out. "I do not believe there was ever any proof that the kerosene was stolen."

Trea's face turned hot, the pit of his stomach cold. Recently, he'd noticed that Charlie Gumm had ash on his coat and the scent of kerosene lingered about him.

"Well, ma'am—" the sheriff glanced at his hammer but did not pick it up "—I've been informed that this town has a history of fires."

"I don't think that's true," Stella declared. "Other than the house, we haven't had an unexplained blaze since—"

Her gaze shot straight to Trea.

"And even that one was eventually determined to be an accident," Juliette said. "Isn't that right, Stella?"

"A broken lantern that someone left burning fell into a pile of straw," Sarah added, her gaze settling on him, same as Stella's had.

Obviously, even after all these years his honor was in question.

"Oh, indeed," Juliette added. Her gaze never leaving the sheriff's. "The livery owner felt wretched over his carelessness."

No wonder he was in love with Juliette Lindor. She was as bold as she was beautiful.

A man could not ask for a better friend. He would have kissed her in front of everyone if it wouldn't have doomed his fledgling career and her reputation.

Everything he did with regard to her must be above reproach, given that he was living under the same roof as she was. The slightest show of personal interest on his part would start tongues wagging.

He was under no illusion that he was not a bull's-eye for gossip.

Silence clung to every corner of the café dining

room. He reckoned it made everyone as uncomfortable as it did him.

The kitchen door swung open and Cora came out.

She dragged a chair to the center of the room and, of all things, stood upon it.

"'"Twas the night before Christmas and all through the house, not a creature was stirring, not even a mouse.'" Her voice sounded lyrical, as sweet as an angel's.

While she stood reciting the poem with her hands folded before her, smiles flashed, flicking on, one after another, like candles being lit in a dark room.

She stepped off the chair, leaving the last few paragraphs unsaid.

"If you want to hear the rest, you'll need to come to the Christmas pageant at school. You'll be there, won't you, sheriff? Mr. Culverson is working ever so hard with us to make you all proud."

"I'd be happy to attend, little miss. Just so long as I'm not protecting the town from a wanton criminal."

"I expect to see you then, sir. Everyone knows even desperados take a day off for Christmas."

Chapter Nine

It was late when Trea decided that he would not be able to sleep.

He left his room and walked through the lobby, being careful not to wake anyone.

A clank of metal drifted from the kitchen, but softly muted by distance. Juliette must be busy putting away the stacks of cookware that had been piled on the countertops.

He wanted to go in and lend a hand with the chore, but wasn't sure he ought to. Not given the way his feelings for her had intensified.

The last thing he wanted was to give anyone reason to gossip. And, truthfully, being alone with her late at night…he was not sure he wouldn't give them something to talk about.

For that reason and because he carried a burden of another sort on his heart, he huddled into his coat, closed the front door behind him and went for a walk in the snow.

Music from The Fickle Dog disturbed the tranquil, otherworldly peace of walking in the falling snow.

Seemed like he'd have to go a bit farther in order to find peace of mind.

Hell, maybe he wouldn't find it anywhere tonight.

Trea was pretty sure that Charlie had started the fire behind The Saucy Goose. He was also pretty sure that, as a mere teacher, there was not much he could do about it.

Confronting Mrs. Gumm would do no good. In his opinion, it might even do harm.

After walking long enough that he could no longer feel his toes, he came to one conclusion. It fell to him as the boy's teacher to make him feel worthy.

That was something he could do. Something that would have helped Trea when he was young.

Only one person had ever done that for him. A sweet, tall and gangly friend whose smile had lit up his world. For all he'd tried to find acceptance by sweet-talking other girls, it was only Juliette who'd made him feel worth half a cent.

Charlie was worth a half a cent and more.

A block from The Fickle Dog, he heard shouting over the harsh thrum of music. Some gambler, drunk and unhappy with the turn of a card game, he guessed. Across the street, at The Saucy Goose, he heard a woman laughing, her bawdy guffaw lifting across the road.

Curiously, The Suzie Gal was closed, every window dark.

As much as Juliette wanted this town to thrive, be a decent place to live and raise a family, so did he.

His students called this place home. For their sakes he wanted it to be a good one.

When he was ten feet from the front door of The Fickle Dog, the door opened and a beam of light spilled onto the boardwalk. A second later a man tumbled out and down the steps.

He lay facedown in the snow, a twitching foot the only sign of life in the fellow.

Trotting down the stairs, Trea knelt beside him, helped him sit up. He patted the flaccid cheeks to try and bring the young man's eyes into focus.

A shadow in the doorway blocked some of the light falling on the road.

"What'd you do, son? Become a damn do-gooder?"

"How are you feeling, Pa? Must have gotten some strength back in order to toss him out like you did."

"Green kid, can't hold his liquor or play his cards right. Would have got himself shot if I hadn't."

"It was good of you to take a care for him."

His father was silent for the time it took Trea to get the boy on his feet. For half a second he thought he saw the old man's expression soften…but not more than half.

"You ever tried to scrub blood out of the floor, son? It's nasty business."

"Are you still coughing? Eating right?"

"You a nursemaid or the schoolmarm? Can't tell from here."

"Better get back inside. It's cold as blazes out here. I'll see to the kid."

With a nod and a grunt, his father backed through the doorway then closed the door.

Trea's first thought was to take the kid to the hotel, but he glanced up the street and noticed that the lamp was still on in the sheriff's office.

"Won't hurt you to get a feel for the place. Just so you know to avoid it in the future." Whether the young man heard him or not, he couldn't tell.

Even though the door to the sheriff's office might not be locked, since it was late, Trea thought it best to knock. It was after hours and the lawman's private time.

The door swung open.

"Brought you a customer, Sheriff Underwood." The sheriff greeted him with a scowl. "Got himself kicked out of the saloon."

"This ain't the hotel."

"I'm told he was drunk and disorderly."

"Now, that's a legitimate crime. Reckon I'll accept him."

Trea leaned the boy toward the sheriff, who caught the half-limp weight with a quiet curse. He probably didn't care for having his solitude interrupted by business.

Since Trea didn't have much to say to the man he'd recently exchanged words with over his insult to Juliette, he turned without further comment.

"I don't believe you didn't start that fire. Once an arsonist, always one."

Trea pivoted on the bottom step, looked up at the lawman and the half-conscious burden sagging in his arms.

"Whatever I was in the past, I no longer am."

"That right? Well I've got my eye on you, Culverson."

"Good. I hope to see you at the pageant, just like you promised Miss McAllister."

"I'll be there. Unless I've got fire-starter in my jail by then."

Trea nodded then went on his way, leaning into increasingly heavy snowfall. He wished he was already at the hotel and in his room with a fire lit.

His conversation with Sheriff Hank left him uneasy. Ordinarily, he would have denied the charge of arson. But if he convinced the sheriff he was innocent, he would look elsewhere for the culprit.

Elsewhere might lead straight to Charlie Gumm.

By the time Trea stepped back onto the front porch of the hotel, snow was mounded on the shoulders of his coat. He hoped the storm moved on before morning so the children could attend school.

He took off his coat, shook it before he went inside. The doorknob felt cold, even through the thick padding of his gloves.

Lamplight from the kitchen carried through the dining room and dimly illuminated the lobby.

Glancing about, he admired Juliette's hard work. The room looked nothing like it had before she purchased it. Didn't feel like it, either. Ever since she had set her hand to renovating, he hadn't suffered a single fleabite.

Come Christmas Eve, folks were going to feel right at home.

He didn't hear any noise coming from the kitchen or the dining room but he didn't believe that Juliette would inadvertently leave a lamp burning.

He hung his coat, hat and gloves on the hall tree then put a towel beneath to catch the melting snow. Taking off his shoes, he set them on the towel then followed the light through the dining room and into the kitchen.

Juliette sat asleep on the floor, her back against a row of low shelves, her long legs stretched out and a stewpot on her lap.

Sleeping Beauty would not look more enchanting.

Her festive green-plaid skirt was hitched about her calves and revealed a froth of lacy petticoats.

Red ones. She wore red petticoats?

With her braid half undone, the green ribbon she had twined through it lay across her throat like a glossy vine.

If she'd had a pair of wings, he'd have sworn she was a Christmas Angel…colorful undergarments notwithstanding.

But there were no wings and that was where his problem lay.

Juliette was not ethereal. She was a flesh and bone woman. And, at this moment, the very lovely flesh was positioned on the floor in an enticing way.

Her head rested on her arm, which was draped across the top of the shelf, which in turn shifted her posture a few degrees to the left. This accented the curve of one breast. It rose and fell in time with her dreamy breathing.

Hell…damn.

Gathering a great dose of moral fortitude, he shifted his gaze to her hand, where her slender fingers dangled, relaxed in slumber.

He did not recall ever seeing such beautiful fingers. Certainly other hands were as lovely in structure; they might not even have the redness, the work-worn nails that Juliette's did.

But would pink and pampered hands set to a task and work until it was completed…even fall asleep in the act? Would they, no matter how weary, touch a baby with tenderness…tend to a cantankerous old man with patience?

In his opinion, no woman had more beautiful hands than she did.

He noticed that she did not wear her wedding ring. Some women did so long after the death of their spouse. Could this mean that she was open to finding new love?

That he might hope she would stroke him with those exquisite fingers?

Hell…damn…again. It did not!

Not unless he was willing to cause a scandal. He had the rules of conduct for a teacher in the top drawer of his desk. He had them burned into his brain.

A woman teacher would lose her position for courting. Not a man, though. He could court once or twice a week, depending on how often he attended church and read the Good Book.

What Trea had to keep in mind is that he was not just any man. He was being watched, judged. No doubt he would be held to the same strict regulations that a woman would.

Even if he gave up the career he had devoted himself to, he could not give up Charlie. Without being the boy's teacher, there was no way he could reach him.

Life was a complicated thing.

That is why, in fantasy, he knelt down beside Juliette, touched her hair, let his fingers glide across her cheek and turn her face toward him. As clearly as if it were real, he breathed in the warm, womanly scent of her skin, felt her slowly come awake while he kissed her…touched—

Hell and damn…for the third time now. No matter how he wanted to wake Sleeping Beauty in this manner, he could not.

Deliberately, he kicked a pot lying among half a dozen others scattered over the floor.

The clatter woke Juliette with a start. Her eyes flew open, wide and blurry, but quickly coming into focus on his.

She slapped her skirt down over her ankles and upset the pan on her lap. It hit the floor with a sharp report.

"Glory blazes! I didn't mean to fall asleep!"

She tried to stand, but rose too quickly and half stumbled.

There was a bit of good fortune. He was able to touch her, after all…just his hand under her elbow, but it was a touch nonetheless.

"The babies!" She placed her hand on his shoulder. The funny thing was, he was pretty sure she was already in control of her balance. "Father Lindor!"

"Asleep, at least, I think so. I didn't hear anyone stirring when I came in."

"In that case, the babies will be soon." She withdrew her hand. Did he imagine…hesitantly? "I'd better get this done before they do."

"Go to bed. This can wait."

"Not really. My list for tomorrow is a mile long." She stooped and snatched a skillet, slid it inside in the cupboard. "I'm making a Christmas dress for Lena and the sweetest little suit for Joe."

"A suit for a boy?"

He bent over and picked up a saucepan, his recent fantasy still red-hot enough to sear his heart.

Locating the lid, he placed it on top with a clang, then stood up again.

"Oh, well, I know boys wear dresses as babies," she

pointed out. "But think how cute it will be to have him looking like a little man."

Maybe, but what he would call cute was her expression in revealing her project.

No…not cute so much as enchanting, even if she was dead tired on her feet and her night not yet ended.

While they worked on putting the kitchen in order, he was more aware of her bare wedding finger than he ought to be.

Part of owning a hotel was to clean the guests' rooms.

Given the heavy snowfall last night, the woman Juliette had hired for the task was housebound.

And with no school today, Trea took advantage of the chance to take lunch to his father.

"I'm sure we can finish this quickly, before he gets back," she said to her babies as she wheeled them in their buggy into Trea's room.

It seemed awkward entering his private space without him present.

And wouldn't it be more awkward if he were here? She simply would not have been able to do it.

It was still warm inside the room because he had only recently banked the fire. She stirred the embers to add a bit more heat for the children.

She glanced about, deciding where to begin.

There was a stack of McGuffy Readers on the desk in front of the window. Cold sunshine illuminated a pen and writing tablet beside them.

She took a dust cloth out of the pail she had attached to the stroller handle. Dabbing on a bit of wax from a jar, she set to her task of polishing the desk.

It was easy, quickly finished with only a bit of twinge to her conscience.

Of course, there would be no twinge at all if this room belonged to anyone but Trea.

But everything about his space felt intimate. Cleaning, touching his things, it all felt intrusive.

Perhaps because she paused to smell his hairbrush when she dusted the washstand.

She needed to gain a bit more control. If she went this weak inside over the scent of a grooming tool, what would happen when she put fresh sheets on the bed?

She glanced over her shoulder at the intimate piece of furniture.

Oh, dear. She should not have done that. In her mind the bed was not empty. Oh, dear…dear…dear. Her imagination saw Trea lying in it, sound asleep, the sheet drawn only to his hips… What a surprise to discover that he did not wear a sleeping garment.

A delightful surprise. One that she was free to stare at, given it was only in the confines of her thoughts. But to be honest with herself, she had to admit that her thoughts were not all that confined.

With a shake, a good mental one that shot her back to the here and now, she finished every chore but making the bed.

Now, though, it needed doing. She would simply have to remove those rumpled, no doubt sweaty, male-scented sheets from the bed.

Skimming her hand over the top sheet, she sighed out loud. Only the babies would hear and they would not know why she made such a yearning noise.

She gripped the sheet in both fists then raised it to

her cheek and drew it across her nose. It felt soft and the scent was even more erotic than she'd expected it to be.

There was no denying she missed that part of marriage.

"I better think of something else," she said to the room at large, or perhaps to the bed…or maybe even to the babies who blinked up at her from the carriage. It didn't matter. The point was to turn her attention in another direction.

"Do you know what I'd like more than anything?" Well, clearly not *anything*, since she still stroked the sheet across her cheek. "Those dozen Christmas trees in the lobby. Maybe Santa will bring them since I can't think of another way to get them here."

"Santa has been known to grant all sorts of wishes."

She opened her fists, dropped the sheet and grabbed the fresh one out of the buggy before she turned.

"Back so soon?" Hopefully her face did not appear as blazing as it felt, because it felt perfectly singed. "I was just changing the sheets on your bed. Mrs. Cromby could not get in today, so here I am."

"Yes, here you are."

He glanced at the bed. Judging by the mischief lurking behind his smile, he had been standing behind her long enough to see past her show of industriousness.

"Discussing Christmas decorations with the babies?"

"Oh, yes, a dozen of them," she said while she bent over the bed, tucking the sheets this way and that. "I'll need all of Santa's special magic to get those trees."

With the bed fresh, the sheets smoothed, she straightened then turned…in time to catch the most interesting expression on Trea's face.

The last thing she was going to dwell on was what it could mean.

"How is your father doing?"

"He seems a bit better. Still pale, but he ate the food in a hurry. It's why I'm back so soon."

Did the corner of his mouth twitch when he said that? Yes, she was certain it did.

"I'm glad to hear he's eating." If only he'd done it more leisurely. "Well…I have a lot to do."

She caught the buggy handle and pushed past him. There was not much clearance in the doorway. He did not move aside to allow more.

"I should be on my way."

"Juliette…" He was close enough that she felt the beat of his warm breath on her face. He touched her hair, tugged lightly at the green ribbon entwined in her braid. "Yes, I reckon you ought to."

"I am…on my way, that is."

Pushing the buggy swiftly down the hall, she made the decision that she would not clean his room again. If Mrs. Cromby was not here, the task would wait.

It would not hurt the man to spend an extra night in rumpled sheets that smelled so…so virile.

Oh! Her balance shifted without warning.

It was a lucky thing she had her hands clamped to the buggy handle because she tripped over the curling end of a rug.

She'd come so close to falling…and not just into the carpet.

"Thank you, Charlie. Your strong, clear voice is just what we need," Trea announced.

The students stood in two rows, flanking Cora and

Charlie, who were shoulder to shoulder in the center of the group.

"Let's show him our gratitude."

Cora clapped her hands with enthusiasm. The girl was always appreciative of anyone putting forth the effort to make the show a success and did not hesitate to show it.

The rest of the class applauded, but with much less animation.

A movement at the window caught his attention. A flash only moving across the bottom pane of glass.

Curious parents had been known to peer inside, wondering how their children were progressing. A few times he'd seen members of the Ladies Service Society with their noses to the glass.

He was under no misconception that they were there to admire his students' progress. His former classmates would not be here for any reason but to catch him doing wrong.

Strolling to the window while Cora recited *'Twas the Night Before Christmas*, he peered out.

Wind shivered through the tree branches, knocking off snow and dropping it in globs on the ground. It fluttered the coat of a familiar-looking woman running uphill into the woods.

It surprised him that Mrs. Gumm had come to hear her son sing, after all.

Trea only hoped she would attend the pageant, when her presence would truly matter.

He knew it would mean everything to Charlie if she did.

An hour later the wind had picked up enough that he felt he ought to send the children home early.

He passed out copies of the McGuffy Reader that he had ordered for them and gave the older children a reading assignment from it.

"Do any of you need me to walk you home? It's blowing hard outside."

No one did, which left him free to bank the fire and catch up with Charlie.

"Where are you off to, son?" Charlie glanced over his shoulder but kept walking. "Home's the other direction."

"I know where it is, sir. But I ain't going there."

"Where are you going?"

"Just someplace that ain't there."

"Isn't there, Charlie. The correct word is *isn't*."

"Why do you care how I talk? I'm not your boy."

"I care about how you speak because I'm your teacher. I want the best for your future."

The boy was quiet while they walked to wherever it was he had in mind…assuming he did have someplace in mind.

"Why?" he asked at last.

"You've heard the rumors about me?"

Charlie glanced up, the beginnings of a smirk on his face. "A few."

"I was you, Charlie. Like you, anyway. So I know the truth and I'm going to tell it to you."

The kid shot him a scowl. Trea would have been surprised at any other response.

"If you keep on the way you are, you won't like where you are headed. It's a hard place to come back from." Trea shrugged out of his coat and set it across the child's thin shoulders.

Trea did not miss the sigh of relief when Charlie settled into the warmth.

Still, he said, "Only place I'm going is to get some privacy."

"I wonder if old man Cleary still has that shed behind his property. It's where I used to go."

"A hundred years ago?"

"Naw…hundred and fifty." Charlie almost smiled at him, but caught it back just in time. "I need to ask you something, and I know you might not want to tell me all of it…maybe not any. But sometime, if you want to, you can and I will help you."

"What? I ain't… I'm not…going to sing but the one song all by myself, if that's what you want."

"I smelled smoke on you the other day…and kerosene. Was it you who set the trash on fire behind the saloon?"

"Weren't me! And I don't know who did!" He took off the coat, slammed it on the snow. "Folks are saying it's you who did it."

Then he was gone, sprinting away through the woods in the direction of home.

It was true, what he'd told Charlie. He had been him, and so he knew the boy was lying. Either he had lit the fire or he knew who had.

Chapter Ten

Juliette dragged Joe's cradle out of his bedroom and into the lobby.

She built up a fire in the large hearth. From out here she could not hear him fussing and fretting on her bed, but she knew he was.

He'd fallen asleep feeling fine but woken near ten o'clock, unable to find comfort unless she walked and swayed with him.

It was eleven thirty now, and she still had not completed the last thing on her list of chores.

Hurrying back into her bedroom, she scooped up Joe, then her sewing kit. Sitting in her private quarters put her too close to Lena and Warren. The last thing she wanted was for them to wake up, too.

There was still the chance that the wind racing about the building would wake them. Or that the loud banging on the piano, carried from next door on the gusts and sounding worse than normal, would.

"All right now, my sweet boy." Settling into the chair, she held him close and nuzzled his hair with her nose.

Did he feel feverish? It was hard to tell. He might.

She had never dealt with this before. With all that might cause a fever, this was something every mother dreaded.

If he fell ill it would be her fault. She should have devoted more attention to him instead of trying to save the town. And, yes, he did need a good place to grow up in, but what if her focus on the hotel and not her family caused…no—no she would not think of that.

But if he did get sick, perhaps her father-in-law had the right of things when he said she ought to have stayed at home.

Stayed home…which would mean doing nothing to help her town survive. Sit by and watch while it became a place unfit to raise her children.

No matter what she did, it was wrong.

She took a breath, pushed back at the as-yet unfounded worry.

It was very likely that all he had was gas…or colic. Both of those were normal for babies and nothing to fear.

A fever, on the other hand? She did fear that.

He was so young and vulnerable. It broke her heart to see him in such distress and not know why or what to do about it.

The wind howled. The clank of the piano shivered faintly in the air. The grandfather clock ticked away the seconds.

Suddenly it was an hour closer to Christmas… Joe's suit an hour further from being finished.

"Hush, now, love, morning's coming. Things will be better then."

Did he feel hotter all of a sudden? Sometimes a sudden elevation of temperature would bring on a seizure. Hadn't she heard that before?

If only Suzie Fulsom's son was here. Juliette would feel much better with a doctor across the street. Without a husband to turn to, Joe's health was in her hands alone.

Her hands, along with everything else in her body, were bone weary.

"Hush, hush, baby Joe," she half sang, half said. "Sweet little baby."

Standing, she wondered if more walking might help. Of course, it wasn't walking so much as pacing.

Over to the window, glance out…walk and rock all around the rug…over and over again.

One time, when she looked out, she saw a customer from the saloon sitting on her front porch, a bottle raised to his lips. For a second she thought he might be frozen in place, but the next time she paced to the window he was gone.

Joe's cheeks looked flushed. Perhaps that high color was the beginning of a fever. His hands were cool to the touch, but his forehead felt overly warm under her lips.

What was going on inside his little body? Whatever it was made him squirm, then stiffen in her arms. In between doing that, he fussed.

If only Steven were here… She shut the thought away before it fully formed. He was not here, would never be here.

Whatever happened tonight, if Joe became raging ill or became suddenly soothed, she would be dealing with it on her own.

All of a sudden she felt very small in a world that had grown frightening.

"Hey there, Beautiful, what are you doing up so late…again?"

Pivoting from the window, she saw Trea standing

at the foot of the stairway. Firelight reflected off his mussed hair and glowed warmly on his face.

"I think Joe might be sick." Something inside her cracked, allowed tears to smart in the corners of her eyes. "I don't know what to do."

"Sit down."

"I can't, I—"

Evidently she could, because Trea lifted Joe from her arms then led her to the chair and gently pressed her shoulder until she sat down.

"Dry your tears, now."

"I don't even know why I'm crying. There's nothing really wrong with him. I'm nearly certain." Her nose began to run, so there was nothing for it but to give an unrefined sniff. "It's more of what my imagination says is wrong. Just because a baby fusses does not mean… it doesn't indicate that—"

He had some fatal malady. Those words would not come out of her mouth but her imagination tucked around the horrid thought and ran with it.

Although not on such a wild course as it had before Trea came downstairs. But still, she felt half sick to her stomach.

"What's wrong, little man?" Trea rocked the baby, same as she had, but with no better results. In fact, the fretting increased. "Let's just see."

He put his finger in Joe's mouth. It looked like he was rubbing the baby's gums.

Joe relaxed. She heard him coo.

"Ah…that's your trouble, is it?" He glanced down at her with a smile. "I feel a tooth trying to come in."

Truly? "He's young for that. How did you know to check?"

"A woman who helped out in the saloon in the kitchen where I worked had a baby. She used to bring him to work sometimes. I learned more than you'd guess."

"I suppose all I need to do is rub his gums for the rest of the night and he'll be happy."

"Reckon he would, but, honey, you look dead on your feet. I'll tend him and you go to bed."

The mention of bed made her remember how she was dressed…or rather, not. Her sleeping gown was flannel and not a bit revealing, except that she was naked underneath and things would jiggle when she moved that ought not to be seen jiggling.

"I still have things to do."

Things that could be accomplished while modestly sitting. She glanced at the clock again.

Two hours closer to Christmas now.

Trea settled into the chair across from her, massaging Joe's sore gums.

Since her son was content for the moment, she snatched up her sewing and began to stitch.

"I wish you would go to bed."

"As an unmarried woman, I'm free to make my own decisions," she stated. That should put the discussion to bed even though he was correct. She did need to rest.

A fact that did nothing to change how much still needed to be done.

The advertisement she'd placed in the *Gazette* would be out tomorrow. It would be too late to back out of what she had set her hand to do, even if she wanted to.

Which she absolutely did not. Especially now that her fear for Joe had subsided.

While she stitched, she watched Trea hold her son. Her heart melted like butter left out in summer sunshine, which made her sigh and add another chore to her list.

A pretty new Christmas dress for herself would be in order. She was not so foolish as to think she could whip one up with her shiny little needle, but she might be able to manage a trip to the dress shop and buy something ready-made.

The plain bald fact was that she wanted to look pretty for Trea.

"I just want to say, I'm glad you're here," she admitted. This night would have been far different had he not come downstairs. Funny how the world was not so frightening with him close by.

"So am I. Even though those new sheets you put on the bed are the stuff of sweet dreams…so to speak."

Clearly he meant to bedevil her over her earlier behavior cleaning his room. It was a lucky thing she had not actually been rolling in his sheets like she had imagined doing.

"I suppose you wish you were upstairs dreaming instead of keeping company with me and my fretful child," she said, refusing to rise to his bait…as delicious as that bait might be.

"I think—" slowly he withdrew his finger from between Joe's lips "—that he's gone to sleep."

He glanced over at her, his smile soft and his eyes appearing whisky brown by firelight.

"And, Juliette, as far as me wishing I was upstairs dreaming? I'm not sure I'm not doing it right here where I sit."

"Here, then…" She reached her arms out for Joe. "Best get on up to bed where you can do it in comfort."

"Naw, this a waking dream. If I get up…if either of

us moves an inch…it might go away. So let's just sit here awhile and keep on talking."

"All right. Tell me about the pageant. Will the children be ready?"

"Cora was born ready…the rest will be. Charlie is the one I don't know about. The boy has a voice, but… blame it… I'm worried he might have started the trash fire behind The Saucy Goose. He wouldn't admit to it, but he looked defensive when I brought the subject up."

"Maybe he didn't. It could be that he was just scared. Think how frightened you were when you were accused."

He thought about that for a bit. What she said made sense. Sense that he desperately wanted to believe.

"I only hope he doesn't run. He's a good boy who got some lousy breaks… Juliette? Hey…Beautiful."

What? She blinked. "What?"

"Your eyes are closing. You're going to poke yourself with that needle."

She glanced down at her hand. "I think I already may have. I suppose I will go to bed, after all."

She put aside her sewing and reached for her sweetly dozing baby.

"How the blazes is a man to sleep with all the racket?" Father Lindor shuffled barefoot into the lobby wearing his nightshirt and sleeping cap. "Durned piano is about to shake the walls down."

Joe squealed then began to cry. She was not a woman to curse, but if she was, she would have shouted the word that just exploded in her brain.

Trea didn't put on a coat for the short walk from the front door of the hotel to the front door of The Fickle Dog.

Temper over the noise coming from the saloon already had his blood boiling. Sure didn't need to add any heat to that.

Going inside, Trea wished he didn't have to breathe. The saloon was crowded with men, and nearly all of them had cigarettes dangling from their mouths or were blowing smoke out.

He spotted a large man sitting at the end of the bar who didn't appear completely drunk.

Trea pushed past a couple of fellows arguing politics. Wouldn't be long before those two came to blows.

With any luck he would complete his task before tempers exploded.

"Good evening," he greeted the fellow and got a nod in return.

"I'd like to hire you for a quick task." He got right to the point since he doubted the man cared to socialize any more than he did.

"Is it legal?"

"I'm not sure."

"How much do you pay?"

"Two dollars to help me slide the piano from this wall to that one." Trea pointed to the wall farthest from the one that abutted the hotel.

"Mr. Culverson know about it?"

"No, sir, he does not."

"Four, then."

They shook hands on the agreement then approached the piano where the musician bent over the keys, pounding them hard and producing no tune known to mankind.

"Here's a dollar." Trea said to the piano player… Felix, if he recalled right from his visits to bring his father food. "Have a drink on me."

"I do appreciate that, young Culverson."

Trea nodded at the burly fellow he'd hired.

The piano screeched against the floor as the two of them pushed and pulled it toward the far wall.

"Doesn't sound any worse than it did when it was being played," he muttered, certain that no one heard him over the surprised exclamations folks were making.

With the piano deposited in its new spot, Trea gave his accomplice another dollar.

Nodding, he tucked the money into his shirt pocket then returned to his place at the end of the bar.

"What gives you the say-so to come in and act like you own the place, boy?"

Trea glanced over his shoulder at the sound of his father's voice and spotted him, hands braced on the bar and fingers clenched in tight fists.

"I asked you to have it moved and you didn't do it." Resigned to being here longer than he wanted to, he walked to the bar, taking note of the red flush on his father's face. He was angry and that might account for the high color. Then again, his fever might have returned. "You feeling all right?"

"That's none of your concern. Put the piano back where it was."

"I wish it didn't concern me. The thing is, I was born your son, so it does. And as for putting the piano back… it stays where it is."

With a narrowed gaze and a string of curses erupting from his mouth, his father pounded his fist on the bar. Once. Which was enough to make folks set down their drinks.

"Let's go talk about this in your office." Trea inclined his head toward the half-open door.

"You insolent pup." His pa started cursing again but ended up coughing violently.

"Water," Trea ordered. "Clean water."

Within seconds a glass was plunked down on the bar. Liquid sloshed over the sides.

"Drink it all."

Trea expected to have it tossed in his face. To his surprise, his father gulped it down. He didn't ease up on the glare, but he did set the glass down without slamming it.

"The thing is, Pa, the piano is bothering everyone at the hotel. One of the babies is teething and the noise keeps him awake. It keeps Warren Lindor restless, too."

"Hell's blistering beans! Sure don't want that crazy old coot wandering over here, so I suppose the instrument can stay where it is, don't you, Felix?"

The piano player shrugged. "Don't make no nevermind to me which wall I perform next to."

With the drama apparently over, customers turned to their pursuits.

"Ain't you worried about soiling your pretty new reputation, son? Better get along."

When was the last time the man had called him *son*? He couldn't recall.

"I'll go, just as soon as I know you don't have a fever." There had been enough fever scare for one night. "And, yes. I am worried about my reputation. Seems like I have to fight to keep it every day."

"That's what comes from being a Culverson. Like father, like son."

"When was the last time you ate?"

"None of your concern."

The bartender gave a long swipe of his cleaning

rag over the bar, which brought him within speaking range. "He ate enough at dinner for three men, if you ask me."

"Hell, Clarence…no one did. Go serve that man waving the coin in his fist before he goes home and hides it under his mattress."

Clarence served the man, then leaned one elbow on the bar, looking about.

"Better rest up now, Clarence. Just as soon as my new advertisement in the *Smith's Ridge Herald* comes out, you're going to need three hands to serve the drinks."

His gaze swung back to Trea.

"Don't look at me like I'm dirt for promoting my business. Just because you turned over a shiny new leaf, don't give you call to judge me. You were every bit the hellion I was as a boy…a real love-'em-and-leave-'em-crying bad boy."

"I can't deny that." Trea leaned across the bar. What he had to say was for his father's ears only. "The thing is, all I wanted was the attention I never got from you. After Ma died, I would have been better off raising myself."

Trea hadn't expected his father to be stung by the truth and apparently he wasn't. He laughed in his gravel-grinding way then went into his office and slammed the door.

Making the short trip from the saloon door to the door of the hotel lobby, Trea yawned. With any luck he would not fall asleep later in the day while teaching multiplication tables.

At least everything here had grown quiet. If Felix had resumed playing, Trea could not hear it.

* * *

"Something cheerful…red, maybe? Or green?" Juliette said to young woman working in the dress shop. "Perhaps something green and red in one gown?"

The salesgirl did not answer, her gaze having slid to the buggy where the babies slept.

"I'd like one of my own someday. I doubt I'd raise it in this town, though."

"Things could change."

The girl's attitude disturbed her. She and others like her would determine the future of Beaumont Spur. Perhaps once she saw the advertisement for the Christmas celebration in today's *Gazette*, she would feel differently… or, at least, begin to.

"I will say, there are more Christmas decorations going up in windows than last year," the girl admitted, then she smiled again at Lena and Joe.

"I, for one, want to look festive this Christmas… I'm looking for a gown that will suit."

"Let me think." The girl tapped her finger on her lip. "There's a green one up front."

Juliette followed her to the rack of gowns near the front window but had to glance down because of the glare of bright sunshine on the snow.

"Here!" The girl removed a dress the color of a holly bough from the rack. She spread out the skirt to show off the subtle sheen of the fabric. "You'll need to let out the hem, but it should do. Just sew some red silk berries here and there, and voilà, it's festive!"

A movement on the boardwalk caught Juliette's eye. She lifted her hand against the glare, glanced out the window to see Nannie hurrying past with several copies of the *Gazette* tucked under both arms.

"Oh, my, yes. This will be lovely."

Juliette paid for the gown and asked to have it delivered to the hotel.

She was far too anxious to see the advertisement in the *Gazette* to wait for the gown to be folded and boxed.

Pushing the buggy toward the café, her heart thudded against her corset. In moments, everyone would know about the grand Christmas fete!

She only hoped Nannie had done as good a job as she had promised in promoting it.

By the time Juliette maneuvered the buggy over the icy boardwalk and through the front door of the café, some of the customers would already have seen her invitation. No doubt they would greet her with smiles of anticipation.

"I don't know what things are coming to." Levi Silver shook his head, a severe frown dipping his gray brows. "I remember when this used to be a safe place to live."

Three other customers sat at tables, each of them with their attention riveted on the *Gazette* that Nannie held up.

"With an entire shed burned this time, I think we have good reason to be afraid," Nannie declared…the tic of her narrow smile indicating that she was more intrigued than frightened. "Poor old Mr. Cleary was distraught when he reported the news to me."

"First the theft of the kerosene, then the trash on fire behind The Saucy Goose and now the shed!" Sarah Wilcox glanced from person to person, holding each gaze. "There's villainy afoot, I tell you. I'm quit of this town."

Lena blinked, suddenly awake. Juliette lifted her from the buggy so that she would not bother Joe, who was still sleeping in spite of teething pain.

She picked up a copy of the *Gazette* and sat at a table.

No doubt, when everyone's nerves settled, they would turn past the first page of the paper, give their attention to something far more pleasant than the imminent ruin of the town due to a burned shed.

Juliette opened the paper. She had hoped her advertisement would appear here, since the paper only had four pages.

A last-page announcement is not what she had paid for. Hopefully folks would see it—

It was not on the second or third, or fourth page. Juliette checked again.

It wasn't there. She flushed hot and cold all at once… felt irate and distressed in equal measure.

"Nannie?"

Her friend—of sorts—turned about, the paper gripped tight in her fists and her blue eyes glowing. "I know, it's perfectly horrid. Believe me, as soon as we discover who committed this crime it will be front-page headlines! We may even print a special edition."

"Where is my advertisement, Nannie?" She strove to keep her voice as calm as possible, so as not to alarm her small daughter, who smiled up at her, unaware of her mother's stress.

If folks were uninformed about her event, they would not attend. If they did not attend, how would they be convinced that a new day was coming for Beaumont Spur?

They would not! Folks would continue with their plans to leave town, not aware that a brighter day was coming.

"Your advertisement?" Nannie turned the pages, quickly scanning her narrow gaze over them. "It isn't here. In all the excitement of real news, I must have forgotten to give it to Father."

"But I was counting on having it in today's paper."

"I'll be sure and tell Papa first thing when I get back to the office. We'll run the ad next time."

"That will be too late."

"Everyone!" Nannie raised her voice. "Juliette is having a party at the hotel on Christmas Eve. You are all invited."

Juliette pressed her lips together to keep an uncharitable string of words inside her mouth.

"There," Nannie declared. "The news will spread in no time."

Chapter Eleven

This afternoon Juliette had expected to be sewing curtains for the lobby windows…they would match the ones she had already stitched for the guest room windows.

Anyone approaching the hotel would feel instantly welcomed by the charm of them. Pretty curtains, she had noticed, always made a person feel comfortable and at home.

But she was not sewing curtains, she was stewing. And not something delicious on the new stove in the hotel kitchen.

She felt a jumbled mess inside. Hugging her arms about her ribs, she huddled into her cloak and walked toward the schoolhouse.

She had spoken to the babies for an hour about her frustrating predicament, even tried to find a bit of solace by telling Father Lindor about the problem.

Naturally, he'd pointed out that if she stayed home and cared for her family like a proper woman ought to, she would have no reason to be stressed.

In the end, she'd taken him, along with Lena and Joe, to the café.

She'd settled him into his familiar chair and set his lunch tray on his lap before she bent down to kiss his cheek. The man probably could not help saying the things he did, given that his world was not at all what it used to be and that he did not understand why.

It occurred to her that when he wanted her to stay home, in fact, he was longing for the days when she did do that. When she and Lillian had a meal waiting for their husbands at the end of the day and laughter reigned at the dinner table.

This was a far different time.

But even though it was, she still had someone to turn to. An old friend who, over the course of a few weeks, had become a new one…a dearer one.

Trea would understand her anxiety. Especially since their events were closely linked.

Coming up the schoolhouse steps, she was glad to find the children at lunch. Because of the cold, Trea kept them inside.

She did not remember school being such a cheerful place. Peering through the window, she saw students playing games and laughing.

She had no idea why she should be proud of Trea's success. She hadn't had a thing to do with it. He'd made the best of his past all on his own.

Truly, she respected him more than anyone she had ever known.

Seeing her, he stood up from his desk, crossed the room and opened the door.

"Don't stand out in the cold, Mrs. Lindor," he said. "Please come inside where it's warm."

He picked up a chair from the back of the room and carried it to his desk.

The noise level in the room died, then picked up again once the novelty of having an unexpected visitor had passed.

Trea set the chair beside his desk and motioned for her to sit down.

"You look upset. Are the children well?"

"Well enough, considering the fact that their mother spent her God-sent fortune on a hotel that will fail and she now does not have the money to move anywhere else, so they will be forced to grow up in this sordid town."

"Sounds dire."

Was he suppressing a smile at her breathless rant? Yes…she believed he was.

"Nannie did not print my advertisement."

"Why not?"

"Mr. Cleary's shed burned down. In all the excitement of having something dramatic on the front page, she forgot to give the information to her father… Oh, I reckon she remembered to give him my money, though."

"Don't worry, Mrs. Lindor." Trea's gaze shot to Charlie, then quickly away. He lowered his voice when a student passed by close enough to hear their conversation. "We will think of something. Christmas is only around the corner, but it's going to work out."

Clearly this was not the time or place to throw herself into his arms and weep away her frustration. Truly, that was not what she intended by coming here, only what she felt like doing in the moment.

Somehow, seeing the reassurance in his warm brown eyes, knowing that she was not as alone in the world as she sometimes felt…well, she did want to weep.

"I'll be on my way," she said, instead. "You have a class to teach and I have curtains to sew."

"Try not to worry." He walked with her toward the door. "We'll talk tonight."

On the way back to the café she did feel more optimistic. She was even deciding where to sew the red silk berries to her new dress when she passed by Sheriff Hank in deep conversation with Herbert Cleary.

Perhaps Herbert had seen the person who burned his shed.

Trea feared it was Charlie. The concern she saw shadowing his eyes when he looked at the boy was evident.

She hoped…prayed…that Charlie was not the culprit.

Trea rose earlier than he normally did. He gathered the artwork that his students had created yesterday afternoon then tucked the pages under his arm. Swiping up a handful of small nails along with a hammer, he stuffed them into his coat pocket.

Down in the lobby, everything was still quiet. He hoped that Juliette was sleeping.

He'd promised to sit up with her last night, to help figure a way past the failed advertisement, but by the time he had come back to the hotel she'd already closed the door to her private quarters.

It was for the best. In his opinion, which did not influence anything since he was not her husband, she was working too late and too hard.

As she had pointed out the other night, she was unmarried and therefore free to do what she pleased.

By that logic, so was he.

It was why he had gotten home late last night. It was also what brought him out early this morning.

Something needed to be done to make up for the missing advertisement.

While he figured he could count on the parents of his students to attend the pageant and the opening of the hotel, everyone in town needed to turn out.

If his idea played out the way he envisioned it, folks would come from beyond Beaumont Spur for the opening.

This town needed the revival that Juliette was striving for. The odd thing was, his unwitting father had played a part in what, Trea hoped, would turn out to be a successful event.

If The Fickle Dog could draw folks from out of town by running an ad in *Smith's Ridge Herald*, so could the hotel.

Folks did like to say *Like father, like son.*

Closing the door with a quiet click, he stepped into the brisk morning. The sun was coming up and he couldn't recall ever seeing a prettier dawn.

Sunshine pierced a bank of clouds on the horizon, shooting rays of light onto the snow and making it glitter like a scene in a snow globe.

This was a perfect morning for success.

Things did not always work out just how one planned, but if this did, it would be a very good day.

Better than yesterday.

A day ago, it had cut him deeply to see Juliette so worried. It's not what he was used to. Juliette was the most confident person he'd ever met, facing whatever life dumped on her with a smile and a wink.

Had it been appropriate, he would have taken her in his arms when she'd come to him, soothed her by folding her to him, stroking her hair, kissing her forehead… or lower.

But given that she had come to him at the schoolhouse, he could not.

Mrs. Lindor had come on school business, having to do with the pageant.

It's what the students thought, and to an extent that was true. The pageant and the grand opening were all but one and the same event.

The students would not know that there was so much more to the visit than that. They would not understand that Juliette had come to him, sharing her predicament.

She couldn't know how deeply that simple act of trust in his friendship had touched him.

Trea pivoted right, took the few steps to the front door of the saloon.

He tacked the painting of a Christmas tree that young Maxwell Finch had painted to the wall.

Writing the actual invitation on each painting was what had kept him at the schoolhouse so late.

Next he went to The Saucy Goose, tacked a likeness of Santa beside the window.

When he was putting up a painting of Christmas bells on the wall of The Suzie Gal, the owner stepped out of her front door. When he told her what he was doing, she offered to take four of the advertisements and give them to other business owners.

He had only three left when he heard footsteps tapping the boardwalk with a quick rhythm.

"Trea Culverson!"

Halfway into a swing he lowered the hammer, slowly pivoted toward the voice.

"Hello."

Nannie Breene looked flushed, her nose red tipped from the cold air.

"What are you doing out and about so early?" he asked.

"Looking for you. I just came from the hotel but couldn't tell which room was yours. I opened half a dozen doors before I gave up looking."

It seemed to Trea that tapping discreetly on the doors would have been more appropriate than opening them.

"Visiting me at the hotel is not acceptable, Miss Breene."

"Don't be silly." Her eyelids closed halfway, her gaze from under them could only be called sly. His use of her formal name had not put her off in the slightest. "It's only me—you and I are—"

"In the future, if you wish to speak with me, send word and we can meet at the café."

Her brows furrowed, her blond frown severe.

"I'm sure you encounter Juliette at the hotel. Is that acceptable?"

"It is." Nannie would like nothing more than to gossip about him and Juliette, and it turned his stomach sour. "Mrs. Lindor and I have a business arrangement. There is nothing inappropriate in my encountering her from time to time."

Nannie's expression brightened as quickly as the flick of a dog's tail.

"Oh! I didn't think." She stepped too close to him. He backed up. "Yes, of course, since our relationship is more intimate than business, yes, it would not be appropriate for me to come to your hotel room during daylight hours."

"Not during any hours."

"Oh, surely once you announce your intentions to court—"

"Why was it you were looking for me?"

"Since you are too respectable now to meet me at the hotel, let's go the café. We can have a nice long chat over coffee."

"I've got to get to the telegraph office before school starts. You can walk along with me if you like."

Hell's business. Why did she have to slip her hand into the crook of his elbow, lean close in a way that implied familiarity?

"Well, you know I don't like to tell idle tales."

It was true, she didn't like it—she lived for it.

"But I overheard the sheriff and Mr. Cleary speaking. I thought you ought to know that Mr. Cleary saw you near his property shortly before his shed burned."

Trea stopped midstep, stared down at her.

"Did he see anyone else?"

"He didn't mention anyone."

Trea started walking again. His heart settled back to its normal rhythm. Relief flooded him. Rumors about him bounced around town like a rubber ball in the wind. He could handle that.

What he could not abide were wagging tongues talking about Charlie.

"Trea, surely this trip to the telegraph office can wait until later. We've barely exchanged a word since you came back to town."

Oh, how true. And that was how he intended to keep the situation. The problem was, Nannie apparently wanted them to be seen together, arm in arm.

It took some effort, but he managed to dislodge her grip on his elbow.

"This has to do with the school pageant and the grand opening of the hotel. Since the advertisement that Juliette placed was not posted as it should have been, we've got to find another way to promote the event."

"I did scold Papa for that." Nannie shrugged one shoulder, dismissing the error as trivial. "Those quaint little drawings ought to do as well."

"Good day, Miss Breene." There was nothing else he had to say to her that would be polite.

Tipping his hat, he hurried along, listening for the sound of her footsteps following. Thankfully, the only noise was the fall of his boots on the boardwalk, that and the rat-tat-tat of a woodpecker pecking the trunk of a nearby tree.

Juliette tacked a garland over the frame of the front door. Stooping down, she picked up another off the floor and draped it over a painting, her attention only halfway on her task.

There had been an unannounced visitor to the hotel early this morning.

The footsteps had not belonged to Trea. She knew the sound his boots made crossing the floor, the rhythm of his pace. She'd heard him go out earlier this morning.

Believing she was alone, it had been startling hearing doors opening and closing overhead while she dressed Lena.

She'd settled the baby in a safe spot then hurried into the lobby with a broom gripped in her fist just in time to see Nannie's ruffled skirt in a swish, going out the front door.

Why in blazes had the woman been skulking around

up there opening doors? And how long had she been up there?

It didn't take too much guessing to know the reason. Nannie was drawn to Trea like a bee to spring nectar.

Wondering—stewing over, to be honest—how long she had been up there had Juliette's stomach twisted in a knot.

Trea was a changed man, no longer the boy seeking affection wherever he could find it—wasn't he?

She would have bet her heart on it—had, in fact.

Still, jealousy—and she knew what that sickening emotion felt like from long ago—snaked about her heart and squeezed. She fought the tear that leaked out of her eye, fought it valiantly.

She was in the process of wiping it on her sleeve when the front door burst open and Trea swept in with a great grin on his face.

What had happened to make him look so joyful? No—she did not want to know that.

Trea and Nannie?

Even though Juliette and Trea had no understanding between them beyond friendship, and he was free to pursue a future with any woman he wanted to—no, not Nannie Breene.

"Come outside with me." He caught her hand and drew her onto the porch.

Schoolchildren, bundled up in coats, hats and scarves stood in two rows on her porch, tallest in back and shortest in front. Maxwell Finch held a painting of a Christmas wreath bearing a hand-painted invitation to the grand opening.

With a sweep of his hand, Trea gave his students a

signal. They raised their voices, happily singing "Jingle Bells."

What a joyful sound!

Folks on the street smiled, nodded. A few of them sang along as they passed by.

What a very sweet thing for Trea to have done. Even the fact that Nannie stood twenty feet away, grinning as if she had played some part in this performance, did not diminish Juliette's pleasure.

Looked at in a certain way, Nannie *had* played a role. Had she published the advertisement the way she was supposed to, Trea would not have called upon the children to promote the Christmas event in this way.

She could scarce believe he had done this wonderful thing, but there the children were, singing with their hearts as well as their voices.

She had half a mind to thank Nannie for her neglect. But only half.

After singing "Jingle Bells," the children stood silently smiling.

A gust of wind whooshed softly around the building, as if sighing its pleasure.

Trea nodded toward Charlie.

"'O come, O come, Emmanuel…'" Charlie's song drifted sweetly across the morning. "'And ransom captive Israel…'"

People passing by stopped.

"'Rejoice… Rejoice, Emmanuel…'" The strains of his clear, beautiful voice carried across the street.

People came out of the café, stared, silently stunned.

She saw the awe and the questions on observers' faces. Could this be Charlie Gumm, the terror of the schoolroom?

Juliette heard footsteps behind her. She turned to see Father Lindor at the door, smiling and holding his grandchildren in his arms. She could not recall the last time she had seen him smile or touch the children.

"'Emmanuel shall come to thee, O Israel…'"

Felix came out of The Fickle Dog, rapture on his thin, wrinkled face. Clarence came out after him. He did not look enraptured, but stunned.

"'Rejoice… Rejoice…'"

The blacksmith stood outside his shop, hammer forgotten in his fist. Suzie Fulsom leaned beside her front door, her hand tapping her heart. Levi Silver, Mr. Bones and Leif Ericman watched, shoulder to shoulder.

If a voice like Charlie's had ever been heard in this town before, she could not recall it.

The pride shining out of Trea's eyes very clearly shot straight from his heart.

Now she understood why he had looked so happy a moment before, and it hadn't had a single thing to do with Nannie Breene.

When Charlie's pure voice sang "Rejoice!" that was exactly what she did. Yes, it was for the redemption of mankind, like the ancient carol told, but also for the satisfaction evident in Trea's expression.

She could not ever remember him looking so joyful. She understood that he meant to showcase the boy's worth as much as to promote the pageant and the hotel opening.

Sheriff Hank came out of the saloon. He did not look at Charlie, but at Trea. He, for one, was not caught up in the magic spell, but studied Trea with sharp speculation.

A second after the sheriff cleared the doorway,

Ephraim Culverson stepped outside wearing his nightshirt, cap and baggy socks.

If Trea bore a look she had never seen before, his father did, too.

One corner of the man's mouth ticked up. Apparently father and son had something in common, after all—that intriguing half smile.

The tender expression passed in a heartbeat. Long before Trea noticed his father had even come outside.

The devotion, the affection Trea felt for Charlie and the rest of his students was evident in his gaze upon them.

Then he turned that gaze upon her—meant that devotion for her.

He had done all this for her—the singing, the posters.

The emotion reflected in Trea's eyes nearly brought her to her knees. It was a very good thing that Warren was holding the babies.

Truly, she doubted that Trea intended to reveal so much.

Did she dare trust that depth of feeling? In him or in herself?

With some effort, she looked away from the gaze pinning her heart—right into the startled eyes of Nannie.

Clearly she'd noticed the longing that shot between Juliette and Trea, because her expression looked like thunder—like a green-eyed monster ready to spit fire.

The very doubts and the jealousy that had assaulted Juliette moments ago were now reflected on Nannie's face.

With the performance ended, Juliette applauded vigorously. So did everyone standing in doorways and down on the street.

All but one.

There was Mrs. Gumm, a tattered shadow standing in the alley between the mercantile and the bank, her arms crossed over her bosom while she shook her head. It was a lucky thing that Charlie had his back to his mother and could not see her frowning before she spun about to retreat down the alleyway.

At noon the next day, life was peaceful—for an hour or two, at any rate. With the babies napping and Warren having dozed off in his chair while reading, Juliette took a few precious moments to sit at her dining room table, to look out her window with a cup of coffee warming her hands.

This was her favorite spot in her private quarters. With a view of the street, she could watch life parade past her window and yet be apart from it. This was an ideal spot to keep watch over the café. Most of the time she could look out this window and into the one across the street with only an occasional passing wagon to get in the way.

She took a sip of coffee, felt peaceful. Christmas Eve was only four days away and she was nearly ready. She hadn't been able to get a Christmas tree, let alone her fanciful dream of twelve. Life was just too busy to get it all done. But maybe next year, and she did have garlands and wreaths to make things festive.

She took another sip. Try as she might to indulge in the tranquility of the moment, she felt agitated—but in the most lovely way.

Thoughts of Trea had her turned inside out. The look he had given her yesterday when the children were singing, well, she had never felt more desired.

Her husband had been a good man, and for a time he had made her nerves sing. However, one glance from Trea and she felt like a symphony shivered under her skin. The thing she had to bear in mind was that he also made Nannie's nerves strike a tune.

With cause or without? And why was Juliette allowing suspicion to follow her about like a hovering cloud?

She drummed her fingers on the warm mug. At least there was coffee. She breathed in the aroma and tried to let everything but the peace of the moment, of napping babies and a resting father-in-law, slip away.

Across the street, the door of the café opened and Cora stepped outside. She marched across the road toward the hotel, looking something like a teakettle and carrying a stack of books under her arm.

Juliette heard the lobby door open. She set down her coffee and hurried toward the public space.

There was every chance that Dixie would rouse from her bed by the lobby fireplace and start barking.

By the time Juliette reached the lobby, Cora was kneeling and hugging the pup to her.

"Do you mind if I study here, Juliette? Those women over at the café are making me crazy."

"There's no school today?"

She shook her head and stood up, lifting Dixie with her.

"No. Mr. Culverson had something important to do so he let us off for Christmas Recess a day early."

Had he? He'd left earlier this morning than he usually did. She hadn't seen him since.

"Did he say what it was?"

"I only wish he had." Cora rolled her eyes then set the puppy down. "That's what all the gossip is about over there. How's a girl supposed to learn anything with them all so het up on other folk's business?"

"Feel free to stay as long as you like, Cora. It's nice and warm here by the fire." Juliette pointed toward the big stuffed chairs. "Everyone's asleep so you won't be disturbed, for a little while, anyway."

"Thank you! I suppose I should go back and put at least one story to rest—I might do it, too, if it weren't so cold outside."

No doubt the rumor had to do with Trea. It seemed that every unexplained thing that happened lately had to do with him.

"What story can you put to rest, Cora?"

"Oh, the one about you and Mr. Culverson carrying on a scandalous tryst right here in the hotel."

"What?" Oh, dear, she hoped her outburst hadn't woken the babies.

"Here—in the middle of the day with the babies and Mr. Lindor underfoot?" she asked more quietly. And wasn't Cora too young to know what a scandalous tryst was? Those women should be ashamed of discussing such a thing in front of a child. "That is just not logical."

"Yes, well, gossip hasn't much to do with logic." Cora sat down and shrugged. "That's what my sister says."

Unless Juliette missed her guess, there was one person who would be the leader of the wagging tongues. She should not ask but—

"Is it Nannie spreading rumors?"

"Well, no." Cora's brows lowered, as though she were puzzling something out. "Really, that is the other rumor. No one has seen Nannie all day, either."

That made Juliette feel half sick.

"They haven't? Are you sure?"

"I'm not—but they are. Some people are convinced Mr. Culverson is here with you—some think he's with Nannie. Some of the old biddies, when they thought I could not hear—but really I do have young ears and I don't miss much—they say that all three of you are secreted away together in a lewd liaison."

"Well!" That's all she could say really, just, "Well…"

"I don't know what they think you've done with the children during the wicked melee."

"Made them nap in a trunk, perhaps."

Really, the whole thing was so absurd it made her want to laugh. Or cry. Because if Trea was not with her—where was he? Where was Nannie?

And now, on top of it all, she felt ashamed for even thinking such a thing. It made her no better than the women at the café.

Trea had changed his ways, she was certain of it—nearly positive.

And yet…

No! There was no *and yet*. She would not let herself succumb to the low-down, mean-spirited thoughts others were suggesting.

It made her blood simmer, thinking how things hadn't changed around here. Even after all these years had passed, even though Trea had come back and shown what a fine person he had become, all they saw was trouble.

"What I would like to know is how, between behaving like the devil with you and Miss Breene, he had time to light the fire in the straw behind the livery."

"There was a fire at the livery?"

"Just a small one. Smoke more than flames, really,

and the livery owner stomped it out with his boot. But I imagine by now the story is that it was a massive blaze."

Now Juliette felt truly sick. A fire at the livery, of all places! And Trea nowhere to be found?

Someone was igniting fires and trying to make Trea look guilty on purpose. She almost wished he would be caught with Nannie.

She would absolutely not believe he had run in fear again. He would not do that to her.

Wouldn't!

"Should I tell them that I saw Mr. Culverson near the train this morning?"

"Did you?"

"I can't be sure. I saw someone, though. It might as well be him."

"No. Better that he is thought to be having an affair with me or Nannie—even both of us—than to have them believe he ran away from a fire at the livery."

Again.

"That's what I thought." Cora tipped her head to one side. "The babies are crying."

Chapter Twelve

It wasn't far to Leif Ericman's store, but it was bitter cold, even with the slanting rays of afternoon sunshine streaking through a gathering bank of clouds.

Luckily Cora had been willing to tend her family while Juliette went shopping.

With Christmas Eve four days away, it was time to purchase what she would need in order to feed the town.

Her list was a long one. She tried to go over it in her mind while she walked. A list was only as good as what one remembered to write on it, after all.

"Flour for the cookies," she muttered under her breath. "Butter, eggs, vanilla and—"

A shadow moved in the alley. She stared hard into the winter shadows. Trea?

No—a cat. None of the last four shadows she had spun toward had been Trea, either.

Where was he? Not warm and safe at the hotel. She knew because she had strained her ears listening for his footsteps most of the day.

She walked faster, thought harder about her list in order to purge the images of his possible fate from her mind.

Blame it! In her mind he was lost in the snow, half frozen and unconscious—wait—now he was sitting in jail because he had been arrested for the smoke in the livery.

Not likely that, though. People would be talking about it.

So that put him looking out a train window speeding toward who knew where. Was he thinking of her? Of Nannie? Of the students he'd left behind? Perhaps Nannie was with him!

No. It was unthinkable that he would have left town—not with the pageant coming up. He'd poured his heart into it and into his students.

She was sure he would not just up and leave. He did not deserve to be dragged to the places her imagination carried him.

Juliette lifted the hem of her skirt to climb the steps to the store. Perhaps he was with Nannie.

As much as it hurt, as much as her logical mind did not believe it to be true, this last nightmare was better than the one with the snowy ditch where Trea turned blue and lifeless before her eyes.

She ought to organize a search party. Sundown was coming and the weather would grow even colder.

The bell over the door jangled as she opened it and went inside.

Oh, no! The first person she spotted was Nannie, her back toward the door while she ran her fingers over bolts of fabric on display along the back wall.

If Nannie was here—where was Trea?

Juliette's first impulse was to dash over and interrogate her. She would not, though. Finding out that Trea had been with her all day would be horrible, but not as horrible as finding out he had not.

She turned toward the counter and handed Leif her list.

He confirmed that he had all she needed and agreed to have a boy deliver it to the hotel in the morning.

Nannie, looking in a mirror and holding a bolt of blue fabric beside her face, was apparently deciding whether it matched her eyes or not.

The woman knew the answer to Juliette's inner turmoil.

Either she could ask Nannie and deal with whatever heartache arose from it, or she could spend who knew how long in fear of the unknown.

"Thank you, Eric," she said while handing him the payment for her goods. "Will I see you Christmas Eve?"

"Me and my wife will be there. We don't have a child in the school, but if the Gumm boy is going to sing again, we wouldn't want to miss that."

Tucking the list back into the small beaded bag strung about her wrist, Juliette approached the fabric wall.

"Hello, Nannie."

"Juliette! You are just in time." Nannie held a bolt of yellow fabric next to her face. If she felt any lingering envy from yesterday it did not show. "Does this color make me look washed out?"

"The blue is better." Why wasn't Nannie envious? As much as Juliette had tried to banish the petty emotion, she had been a bit green all day.

"Have you seen Trea?"

"Well I—have you?"

"No."

"Oh, perhaps I have." Nannie shoved the yellow bolt back into the row and picked up the blue again. "I can't say—a lady does have her secrets. You understand?"

Juliette did not understand! The very last thing she could imagine was a man like Trea being interested in a woman like Nannie.

It made no sense.

But if it didn't make sense, if she could not accept that he had been with Nannie, she would fret the rest of the day over where he really was.

Even hours after leaving the store, that is exactly what she continued doing…fretting and worrying.

Even if Trea had been with Nannie this morning, he had not been with her several hours ago.

Juliette paced in front of her dining room window with Joe in her arms, staring out into the dark.

The clock had struck nine o'clock an hour ago.

She reminded herself that he was a grown man and could go where he pleased, but surely he should have been back from wherever it was by now.

"Are you hungry, Joe?" Given the way he plucked at the buttons of her bodice, he was. "Lena has been asleep for hours already. Are those little gums sore, sweetling?"

She carried him to her private parlor and sat with him in front of the hearth. The flames snapped and sent out wave after wave of warmth. She took off her shoes and stockings. Not her dress, though.

As soon as Trea got back, she would find out where he had been. Kiss him or smack him—she was not sure which. It didn't matter. She would be relieved to see him safe, either way.

She set Joe at her breast, stroked his hair and sang him a Christmas carol.

Halfway through "Silent Night" she began to dream of frosted cookies, mulled wine and sugar-dusted mountaintops under a starry sky. She was vaguely aware of drifting off and welcomed it. Imagining the scent of Christmas trees was ever so much better than… gumdrop frogs.

A foray into the forest to cut a dozen trees was harder and took longer than Trea had thought it would.

Even though he'd left the hotel at dawn, the adventure had taken all day and into the evening. The morning had begun when he went to the train depot and picked up the crate of candles and metal reflectors he'd ordered from Smith's Ridge. Then he'd gone into the woods to find twelve perfect trees, cut them down and load them into the wagon.

It had been a huge undertaking. One he could not have completed without Charlie's help.

He winced now and again at newly sore muscles and a collection of scratches, but he did not regret them. They were a small price to pay for what he had gained today.

Not only was he going to fill Juliette's lobby with trees, but the hours spent with Charlie had been invaluable.

While sharing the labor of cutting and hauling, a man-to-man sort of activity, he had been able to speak with Charlie about dozens of things. The kid seemed to bask in the attention like a lizard soaking up sunshine.

They'd spent the previous evening stringing popcorn garlands, and he had been able to talk to Charlie about life—how at his age it could go one way or another. That it was his choice to pick success or failure for his future.

At some point while they were tying up berries and ribbons, he'd thought Charlie understood—success was hard and had to be worked for. Failure was easy and just naturally slipped into a life of failed dreams.

It had taken Trea a long time to learn that. Hopefully the way would be easier for his student.

Deep down, he was a good boy. Truly, Trea could not have pulled off the surprise for Juliette without the boy's hard work.

When they parted ways at the schoolhouse, Trea swore the boy walked taller. A bit of pride straightened his posture.

That had been at eight o'clock. It seemed like it took an awfully long time for Juliette to quit looking out her dining room window and settle in for the night. Watching and waiting from the alley between The Suzie Gal and the dress shop had been a cold business.

He didn't even know what time it was now, but late—or early, depending upon how one looked at the wee hours.

Everything had been worth it, in the end.

Twelve trees were now scattered about the hotel lobby, decorated and glowing with the light of too many tiny candles to count. He hoped this was the enchanted forest of her dreams. He could not wait another minute to see Juliette's joy when she first saw them.

For half a second he thought he should not disturb her, but no longer than that. There was something he wanted to tell her and he needed to do it while everyone was asleep.

Barefoot, he walked to the door of Juliette's private quarters. The floor had been chilly when he removed his boots earlier in order to complete his task as silently as possible. It still was.

Dixie didn't seem to mind. She trotted from tree to tree wagging her tail and sniffing low branches.

Knocking softly on Juliette's door, he listened for movement.

Nothing, not a shuffle or a sigh.

He would have to wake her, but he doubted she would mind after seeing the bewitching shimmer of the transformed lobby.

Fortunately, the door was not locked. Neither was the one to her parlor. It stood ajar, the glow of the dying fireplace leaking out the gap.

Inch by slow inch, he pushed it open.

Softly illuminated in the flames' last glimmer, Juliette slept in her chair. Her dress was open to the waist and Joe's pink cheek lay against her breast. Even in the baby's dreams, his small pink mouth made sucking motions.

It was wrong to stand, dumbstruck and staring, but he could not recall ever seeing anything more touching, more beautiful, in his life.

Maybe having missed a mother's love growing up was what made his eyes moist, made his heart swell and his breath catch in his throat.

This woman deserved to have all of her dreams come true. He was grateful to be able to fulfill a dozen of the smaller ones.

With great care, he lifted Joe from her slack arms, resisting the very great temptation to glance where he should not.

He carried Joe to the bedroom, laid him down in his cradle then paused for a moment to watch Lena sleep. Sweet little thing, she was the image of her mother.

Tiptoeing back to the parlor, he kept his gaze steadfastly on the floor. With the baby removed the scene had changed.

Where a moment ago it had been tender beyond bearing, it was now pure titillation. Yes, his reaction to Juliette not being modestly covered was unlike what it had been with Joe to chaperone.

It was not the tender vision of a mother with her child that kept his eyes riveted on the roses woven in the rug, but ripe and forbidden fruit.

He'd be a fool to think otherwise and he'd outgrown being a fool years ago.

If he succumbed to temptation, looked at her in lust, it would only prove that he had not changed at all.

Hell and blazes, it didn't mean he didn't feel lust. A man could not control what he felt, only what he did.

Kneeling in front of her, he gently tugged on a lace ruffle to slide up her chemise. It was not his fault that smooth warm skin grazed his knuckles or that his body reacted to the velvet brush against the hairs of his fingers.

With his eyes still closed, he located a button on her shirt and tugged the chemise across her skin—didn't button it up, though. That was not a job for a man on the verge of tossing away restraint.

Since he had so far survived temptation, he figured it would be safe to open his eyes.

He'd figured wrong. His heart tumbled, free-falling at the sight of loose tendrils of hair kissing her temple and the sweep of her long dark lashes closed in deep sleep.

For as much as he wanted to kiss her awake, he didn't. He stood up, ever so quietly, then backed up three steps. Perhaps she would not realize he was the one to set her clothing to rights.

"Juliette… Beautiful, wake up."

She jolted, grabbed her empty lap and gasped.

"I put him to bed."

With the barest of glances, she took note of the fact that her clothing was not as it had been when she fell asleep.

She leaped out of the chair without seeming to care that the crescent-shaped curve of one breast had popped back into view.

He cared—greatly. Mouth dry, he pointed his finger, urging her to cover herself.

If she didn't, years of self-discipline might be for naught. Reformation had its limits.

"Where have you been?" she exclaimed, launching herself at him while she buttoned up.

For a moment he thought she would fall into his embrace. But no, she poked his chest with one finger… forcefully. "You aren't dead."

She touched his cheek, blinked her eyes against the gathering moisture. "I don't even care if you were cavorting with Nannie Breene—well, I do, but I thought you were dead!"

"Why would you think so?"

"You just disappeared! Not a word to anyone! Poof—you were gone. You couldn't have left me a note?"

"I nearly did, but I didn't want to lie about where I was."

She went from flushed to pale, quick as a gasp.

"I'm sure it's none of my business what goes on between you and Miss Breene, although if you ask me, she isn't—"

Wrapping his hand around the finger that had begun another assault on his shirt, he led her out of her parlor and toward the lobby.

"Nannie Breene?" he muttered, pulling her along. "I'd rather be alone the rest of my life."

"You would?"

"Come with me." When she resisted, he tugged her along the hallway.

"If you aren't dead and you haven't been with Nannie—then what? I will not believe you started the smolder in the livery."

"There was a fire at the livery?"

"A small one that the liveryman was able to stomp out. But no one knew where you were, so everyone assumed it was you and you'd run away."

"They'll have to assume something else."

The glow cast by hundreds of candles came into view before the trees did.

At the lobby door, he heard her gasp his name. He let go of her hand.

Silently she entered the parlor, slowly moving from tree to tree, touching one, breathing in the pine scent of another. She did not seem to be aware that Dixie jumped up and down on her skirt in greeting.

"This is—it's just so unbelievable—I might still be asleep." It had to be his imagination that her bare feet didn't quite touch the ground while she glided from one tree to another.

"How did you get the angel all the way on top of that one?" she said, looking up and up, nearly to the ceiling.

The angel she spoke of was simply a handful of straw, twisted this way and that, with white feathers stuck in it for wings.

It was something of a rustic masterpiece, he had to admit. He was particularly proud of the small wooden star attached to the back of the angel's head that Charlie had carved and Trea had painted white.

"I stood on the landing with it stuck on the end of a broom handle and then—"

She must not have cared about the *and then* of things so much, because she rushed across the room and into his arms.

"I am so relieved you aren't frozen in a ditch." Her arms went around his neck, hugging tight. "Truly, Trea—I could accept you being with Nannie, but the world without you in it? No, never that."

He felt the chill of her bare toes brush his warmer ones, smelled the feminine scent of her cheek so near his lips.

"That so?" he asked casually, but life as he'd known it was about to change.

Maybe it was too soon, but he had something to ask of her. The answer would determine the course his life would take.

On the other hand, it might always be too soon. Better too soon than too late, though, so he was going to do it.

"Yes, it is. I've never had a better friend than you."

"A better friend?" He gripped her shoulders, held her back just far enough so that he could look into her eyes, judge the sort of emotion flooding them. "So good a friend that you wouldn't mind if I courted Nannie? And one you would hate to see dead?"

* * *

"Hate it very much," she agreed, nodding vigorously.

Judging by the slow narrowing of his eyes, perhaps she had said too much—or not enough.

The thing was, she was so completely and enormously overwhelmed by this gift he had given her, she could scarce form a logical thought.

The one and only thing in her mind was kissing him and admitting how truly devastated she would be if he courted Nannie.

"Why?" he asked.

She backed up a step, but he lifted the braid that was dangling over her heart, then drew her close again.

"Because I—what are you doing?" Or rather, why was he doing it? She knew what. He was untying the ribbon that secured her braid and unraveling it from the tresses—fondling the strands with his fingertips.

"Watching the reflection of candlelight in your hair." He shot her the lopsided smile that made her insides buzz like a hive of honeybees. "You didn't tell me why you would hate to see me dead."

"Naturally, I would hate to see anyone dead," she whispered. Where was her breath all of a sudden—her logic and sound judgment? Gone to a place she could not find them and where, in that moment, she did not care to go looking for them. "But in your case—I couldn't kiss you if you were dead, Trea."

Looking at her silently, his grin evened out. He withdrew the ribbon from her hair, opened his fingers and let it drift to the floor.

Dixie snatched it up and ran off with it.

"I'm mighty glad I'm not lying lost in a ditch." He lifted her chin with his big firm thumb. Evidently one could drown in another's gaze because she was doing it. His steady brown eyes utterly took her breath away and she didn't care to get it back. "Do you know how long I've been waiting to kiss you, Juliette?"

She shook her head because she did not know, but she wanted to—desperately.

"Since I was fifteen years old." The warmth of his breath inched closer to her lips.

"That's a very long wait. I think you ought to do it—now."

In case the Christmas trees were not blessing enough, the warmth, the possessive pressure of his lips coming down upon hers were half a heartbeat from a miracle.

For as long as he claimed to have dreamed of this moment, so had she.

Dreamed of it, given up hope of it, then dreamed it again.

His grip on her waist was firm, his fingers warm, tender as they inched up her ribs in a possessive advance. Muscular arms circled her back, drew her in.

With heartbeat pressed against heartbeat, Trea Culverson changed her world.

Life might appear normal once he released her lips, but she would never be.

In time she might have recovered from a kiss given by the fifteen-year-old boy, but not one from the man. No, she would never recover from him.

And if he didn't feel the same way?

She could not let herself think it. Right now, in this moment, they were not simply meeting mouth to mouth, but soul to soul.

In her marriage she had been kissed, pecked and petted. This was different.

She was consumed—taken by this man. With one embrace, she was forever his.

Slowly, he let the kiss go, but he hugged her close, breathing hard.

She clung to him. As much as she wanted to draw back, to look into his eyes and see if the life-shaking moment had touched him as much as it had her, she was frightened to, because if it hadn't she—

"Juliette." His voice stirred the hair at her temple. His breathing began to slow but his heart still beat as madly as hers did. "There's something I've been wanting to ask you. I hoped to do it here among the trees."

"Yes?" She pushed out of his embrace, felt bereft of his warmth. But then she looked into his eyes and found them gazing down at her, as full of heat and yearning as the kiss had been.

"May I court you?"

"Yes!"

"May I begin now?" He crooked his elbow so she placed her hand upon it. "Will you honor me with a barefoot stroll among the evergreens?"

"It's a lovely night for it, don't you think?" she asked politely, then winked.

"It's enchanting by candlelight. Especially in the company of such a delightful companion," he said, equally proper and formal.

For five minutes they toured the room, chatting affably while pointing out various ribbons and berries adorning the trees.

"I enjoyed our courtship," he announced with a grin and a nod.

"Are we finished already?"

"Transitioning." He ran two fingers along her brow,

the curve of her cheek and the line of her jaw. "There's something I want to tell you, Juliette. Actually, I've been wanting to say this to you for a long time—maybe for years. The length of our courtship won't make it any more or less true."

Her hands and face grew damp, her stomach flipped and swirled. There was every indication that she was going to faint—or float.

Trea cupped her cheeks in his rough, warm hands, his touch grounding her to the here and now.

"Juliette Lindor, you are the most amazing person I have ever met. I respect you more than anyone I have ever known—"

"As I do you, Trea."

"And I'm completely in love with you."

Her face was moist, dripping, in fact, and there was not a single thing she could do to stop the tears.

"Well—I love you, too."

Going up on her toes she wrapped her arms around him, pressed her face against his throat.

"I always have." Her lips grazed his skin with the whisper. "And I don't mean to take away from what I felt for Steven, but Trea—somehow it's always been you."

He closed his eyes for a moment, his head nodding ever so slightly. "You know how I was as a kid, all those girls. But in spite of how that appeared, there was only ever you. You are the only one who was ever in my heart, Juliette."

He held her for a long time, bare toes touching while she clung to him as tightly as he did to her—rocking, holding on to the newfound joy of confessing their hearts.

"I've got something else to say before we quit this

courtship. Let's continue our walk in these magical woods."

He did not extend his arm but hugged her close to his side. This time there was no polite, courtly conversation.

A silent awareness, an awakening, pulsed between them while they strolled between the trees. He drew her to a stop behind one, kissed her and told her again that he loved her and how much.

Pausing at each tree he did the same, revealing one more reason that he loved her.

She was not completely certain this was not a dream. How could one go from complete misery to complete joy in such a short time?

He led her to the tallest tree, the one with the angel on top.

With a great grin, he hugged her then released her with a kiss on the top of her head.

Kneeling down, he took her hand, kissed her palm and then her knuckles. "Marry me, Juliette. Let me be your husband. I can honestly say I will love you for a lifetime. I know I'm not Joe's or Lena's father, but I'll be devoted to them, love them every day, as if I was. I promise you. Please, just marry me."

Candlelight cast his hair in glimmering light, and it reflected the love in his eyes as a living flame, leaving her speechless.

"Is it too soon?" His expression fell. "Don't you feel—?"

"I do—yes!"

"You do—as in, you will?" Bounding to his feet, he glanced about as if it was someone else she had just pledged her life to. "You will!"

"You knew I would before you asked," she said between the quick kisses he was raining on her mouth and cheeks.

"I prayed, but I didn't know."

"Me, too, Trea."

Upstairs, there was a bed. There was one down here, even closer at hand.

No words were needed. The knowledge of that intimate piece of furniture lay ripe between them.

Chapter Thirteen

"We could." He bent his forehead to his betrothed's, whispering an answer to the question that lay unspoken between them. "No one would know."

"No one but us. And we are the only ones who matter."

She mattered, she was everything to him and would be for the rest of his life.

"My bride-to-be…" He pulled away, but only enough to look into her eyes, judge what she was thinking. "I like the sound of it."

"So do I, husband-to-be." She winked at him. "We have a very long time to be married, God willing. I think I would enjoy anticipating the mystery of our marriage bed for a while."

"Me, too, honey. Somehow *betrothal bed* doesn't hold the same depth of commitment. I want to have you for the first time as my wife. You deserve the respect of that and I, I need to give it to you. You don't mind?"

"No woman I ever heard of minds being respected by her man—and you will not actually be my man until the preacher says so."

"But don't think that bed won't be on my mind every minute from now until then."

"Yes, mine, too. And quite apart from my desire to steal away with you right now, Lena will be waking soon to be fed. Since you are going to be a father and a husband, it's something you'll need to get used to." The look she gave him was a little too somber. She must think that was something he had not considered.

"Do you mean I'll need to get used to watching you nurse your babies instead of squeezing my eyes shut?"

"You did that?"

"Could have broken my toe tripping over something, but yes. And, honey, it was damned hard."

She laughed. The sound went straight to his heart, wrapped it up and squeezed.

Staring and smiling, neither of them spoke with words for a moment.

"I don't know about you, Trea, but I won't get any sleep tonight. Let's go to my kitchen. I've got muffins and I'll make us some tea."

On the way there, they passed by her bedroom door. It was cracked open and he saw the bed, neatly made and calling for its sheets to be tangled and the blankets tossed on the floor.

She intercepted his stare. "We are going to need a very short engagement." She caught his hand and drew him into her cozy dining room.

With a sweep of her finger, she indicated that he should sit down at the table in front of the window. With a quick dip she leaned down and kissed him, then, with a swish of red-and-green plaid, went to the stove.

A few minutes later she placed a cup on the table

in front of him. The scent of black tea swirled about the room.

"Christmas Eve, we'll be married then," he announced.

"Thank goodness. I couldn't wait a day longer than that."

She set the tea on the table then came to his chair and bumped him sideways with her hip so that they shared the seat.

Side by side they gazed out at the night. It was pretty with the light of a full moon reflecting off snow, every bit as magical as the Christmas trees were.

Adding to the peace was the fact that there was no noise from the saloon. Hadn't been since the piano was moved. He could tell The Fickle Dog was still open for business because someone had just staggered past the window. Hopefully the fellow didn't pass out in the snow. He'd freeze to death if he did.

Trea tried to pay attention to the man, but he and Juliette could not quit kissing each other.

"I love you," he said again for the—he didn't recall how many times—but it was only the beginning of a lifetime of making that declaration.

Another kiss was called for, so he gave it, deeper and less playful than the last several. He felt laughter bubble under his lips.

"Someone is going to see us," she advised with a grin that indicated she didn't care if they did.

"At this hour, I can't think of who that would be, but I'm going to talk to Preacher Gordon first thing after sunrise."

With the next kiss his hands got tangled in her thick, black hair. It slid between his fingers, gloriously lush.

From down the hallway he heard a baby cry. Lena, judging by the high-pitched squeal.

He broke the kiss, let his hands fall away and found that he was grinning like a loon.

"Welcome to nearly married life, Trea."

"Let me get her."

Standing, he gave a start. Someone stood outside the window, staring in with his nose smashed on the glass.

It was his father, his arm supporting the drunk man.

Their gazes caught and held for an instant. The old man nodded; Trea nodded back.

Walking down the hallway to get the baby, he wondered about that. An expression had crossed his father's eyes that he'd never seen before.

If he didn't know better, he'd have thought the look bordered on tenderness. But it was dark outside and hard to read anything clearly. No doubt his father was only showing the strain of holding up his customer.

In spite of the fact that her heart was living among the clouds, Juliette's feet were planted firmly in Beaumont Spur.

She stood in front of her dining room window, sipping coffee and watching the town wake up. The breakfast crowd at the café was larger than usual, so she bundled everyone up and took them across the street.

It felt good to put on her apron again, to take orders and serve her customers.

"Good morning, Levi," she said. What she really wanted to do was hug him.

She missed seeing him and the rest of her regular patrons each morning.

It was hard to think about how much she would miss the ones determined to move away.

"You've got a sparkle about you this morning, Juliette. Your smile looks all full of Christmas cheer."

"The big day is almost here. Can't you just feel it in the air?"

"I can when I look at you."

"What can I get for you?"

"The usual, and some of your holiday cheer. With the move coming—well, I could use a bit of it."

"You could stay in Beaumont Spur."

"Things around here are beginning to look up, I'll admit, but still—I just don't know. Those fires say that no good is afoot."

"Folks build bigger fires when they burn leaves in the fall, and don't forget, Mrs. Fulsom's son is due in on the train today. He's a doctor. Did you know The Suzie Gal will become his office?"

"It's all the talk, and as fine as that is, there's still two saloons in town and old Culverson keeps advertising in Smith's Ridge. Strangers keep on coming and going. One doctor isn't going to change that."

"The hotel—"

She lost track of the thought when Trea walked in the front door. This was the first time she had seen him since the wee hours of the morning when they had each gone to their own rooms.

As much as she wanted to dash madly around the tables and into his embrace, they had not yet announced their engagement.

"Good morning, Mr. Culverson," she said. "What can I get for you?"

"Just some toast and coffee to take with me to the

schoolhouse, Mrs. Lindor." His smile indicated that he wanted a bit more than mere food from her. Did anyone else notice? she wondered. "And a moment of your time?"

He indicated with a nod of his head that he wanted to speak with her outside.

"Of course. Just let me get your breakfast first."

Within moments, she stood beside him on the boardwalk, casually handing over his toast and coffee. Folks looking out the window would see her positioned a respectable distance from the schoolmaster, but in her mind she leaned into his embrace.

"Here," he said, digging in his coat pocket. "I just came from the telegraph office. These are for you."

He handed her four pieces of paper.

"Reservations," he explained in the face of her bewilderment. "For the hotel. Sure do hope you are ready, Beautiful. Your first guests will be here tomorrow."

"They will? Why? I never—"

"I put an advertisement in the *Smith's Ridge Herald.* Figured if my father could attract customers that way, so could you. I also invited them to our party." He lowered his voice even though no one was close enough to hear. "Hope you don't mind, but I reckon they'll be attending our wedding, too. I visited the preacher this morning. He says this will be his first Christmas wedding and he's looking forward to it."

"I'd give you a giant hug, but it would cause a great scandal."

"In a few days it won't. But I reckon we need to keep this to ourselves. For some teachers it wouldn't matter—but for me? I reckon it would, and honestly—

I almost don't care." He must not, because he lifted his hand toward her braid.

"Helloooo!" Nannie's voice carried from half a block away. Trea snatched back his hand, took a big step backward.

"Good morning, Trea," she said, filling the space that was, by rights, Juliette's.

For all that Nannie noticed her, Juliette might have been turning pancakes in the kitchen.

"Good morning, Miss Breene," Trea answered.

"Pish. We've discussed that. It's Nannie and you well know it."

"Good morning, Nannie," Juliette said, because it had been a good morning a moment ago.

"Oh, Juliette! I've come to see you, actually."

"Well, here I am."

Nannie withdrew a newspaper from the basket she carried over her arm. "I just feel horrible about neglecting your advertisement. I convinced Papa to run a special Christmas edition to rectify it. Your grand opening takes up half the second page."

Juliette turned past the front page, which was filled with the announcement of Dr. Fulsom's setting up business in town.

In reality, her advertisement of the hotel took up only a quarter page. Still, it was nicely done and Juliette said so.

"I am rather proud of it," Nannie answered, addressing Trea. "I've discovered that I have a talent for this sort of thing. Father is giving me more responsibility every day. I don't mind being gainfully employed one little bit." She inched a step closer to Trea, if that were possible, and blinked up at him. “At least until I’m a married woman.”

“Thank you, Nannie. This is lovely,” Juliette briskly put in. “Mr. Culverson was just on his way to the schoolhouse. Wouldn’t you like to come in for some breakfast?”

“Oh, I would. And I’ll pass this along to everyone at no charge. Papa said that, in the spirit of the holiday, I could.” She lowered her voice to a murmur. “Good day, Trea. Perhaps I’ll see you later.”

“And perhaps,” her fiancé murmured after Nannie went inside, “I should just kiss you right now. Let that woman know where I stand once and for all.”

“A part of me would like that, but it wouldn’t be right.”

“Do you reckon I ought to have a private conversation with her before the wedding?”

“No, I do not. She can find out when everyone else does.”

He reached for her hand and squeezed it.

“Maybe, but, how many more hours until Christmas Eve?”

“Too many. I’ll see you at dinner tonight.”

Spinning about to go back inside, her gaze crossed over the front window of the dining room.

Nannie’s nose for gossip must have been in fine fettle because she was staring hard through the glass—well, glaring, actually.

It was difficult to hide anything from Nannie.

Guests were booked and arriving tomorrow!

Juliette felt like a bee flitting from task to task. There was a basketful of final details to be seen to.

Scrubbing floors, cleaning windows, putting fresh linens on the beds, shaking out the rugs and, perhaps most important of all, preparing food for the party.

Juliette had planned on doing most of the work by herself. Of course, that was before she knew that Christmas Eve would also be her wedding day. Thank goodness Rose had volunteered to cook and Cora agreed to tend the babies and Warren on that day, even without knowing about her wedding.

Even given all that she needed to do, she could not help but take a moment to gaze—dream, more rightly—upon the wedding gown hanging on a hook on the wall of her bedroom.

She hadn't known when she purchased the green satin gown, when she'd sewn the festive berries on it, that it would be for her wedding day.

The first time she married she had worn an elegant white gown that she had spent months picking out.

This one was also elegant, just in a less frothy way. Smiling, she straightened a red berry she'd sewn to the waistline.

A Christmas-colored wedding gown—nothing could be more wonderful. The only white she'd wear this time would be the new petticoat and the pretty, lacy chemise she had purchased this morning.

When Trea unwrapped her, so to speak, he would untie the pink satin ribbon on the bodice. Feel soft lace under his fingertips when he drew it down over…

She would continue this lovely fantasy before she went to sleep tonight. With so much to do, she could hardly stand here indulging in intimate dreams of her future with Trea.

Hurrying into the kitchen, she snatched up a bucket of cleaning supplies then rushed back to the lobby.

From upstairs she heard Mrs. Cromby singing "Jingle Bells" while she prepared the guest rooms.

Apparently Juliette would not be cleaning the outside of the windows today. Sunshine beating on the roof melted the snow, which slid off the eaves like raindrops. There was really no point in attempting to keep the windows sparkling.

She turned her attention to polishing the reception desk. It already gleamed, but a layer of wax gave it a mirrorlike sheen. From a shelf under the desk she lifted out the guest register and placed it on top.

This was really happening. Only a short time ago she had purchased a building with a dirty reputation, overrun by bugs and vermin. Today it was a jewel. One that had enough refinement and charm to revive her town, if folks gave it the chance.

It would not hurt having Dr. Fulsom setting up business across the street, either. If he was as gifted as his mother claimed him to be, folks might move here purely for reassurance of having a healer nearby.

That did still leave two saloons to attract criminals and drunks, but—the bell over the lobby door tinkled. Juliette looked up with the smile that sang in her heart.

Oh—well, clearly Nannie Breene did not have a smile in her heart.

"We need to discuss something, Juliette," she said, charging toward the desk without greeting.

It was true that they did. More than poor Nannie knew.

"Would you like to do it over tea?"

"I would not."

"Coffee, pastries?"

For a second Nannie seemed to consider the idea. "I rather think not. My stomach is all in knots because of you."

"Maybe we ought to sit down and you can tell me why."

Was it silly to pretend she did not know? It was, but this was a conversation she did not want to have and she was stalling.

"I can't sit, either. Feels like I've got fleas jumping in my veins."

"That can't be healthy, Nannie. You should try and calm down."

"I will, once I've had my say."

Juliette heard a rustle of skirts on the stairs. Nannie did not appear to notice, being caught up in turmoil as she was.

"What is it, then? I have a lot to get done."

"Oh, you always do and that is part of your problem. You are so caught up with babies and cleaning and business, you neglect yourself."

"I like being caught up in those things."

"Well, you oughtn't. The neglect of your appearance shows." Nannie slammed her hands on her, admittedly slim, waist. She narrowed her close-set eyes in accusation. "Just look at your hair!"

"My hair? It's clean." It was hard to take the accusation to heart. Not when she remembered the feel of Trea's hands undoing her braid and caressing the strands. Something a man would not be able to do to Nannie's hair, being as looped and tightly curled as it was.

"I'll give you that, but the style is dowdy. That braid makes you look like you are just off the farm."

"That's a disrespectful thing to say about the women who work hard to provide what we eat."

Nannie blinked rapidly. "Oh, I didn't mean that about them. Living out in the middle of nowhere, no one cares what they look like. But we live in town and ought to dress the part."

"I'm not going to change my hairstyle to make you happy, Nannie Breene. Do not hold your breath for it." Although she might do her hair up in a few curls for the wedding. Yes, and place a white silk flower sporting slender satin ribbons to suggest a veil.

"Juliette! Your attention is wandering. I don't think you are listening to what I'm saying."

"I'm doing my best not to. But, honestly, why would you come here to malign my hair?"

"Oh, it's not only your hair. Just look at your dress and that dirty apron. If you want to attract a man, you will have to do better."

"I have attracted a man." Juliette stepped from behind the desk, her rising temper making her too riled to stand in one spot. "I married him, as you will recall."

While you have married no one, she wanted to shout. But aside from it being a cruel thing to say, it would wake the babies. They had never heard her shout and it might frighten them. When she thought about it, she doubted if anyone had ever heard her shout.

In the moment she thought she ought to, but refrained.

"Yes, Steven was a good man," Nannie admitted. Juliette's temper cooled a bit. "But he is not the reason I'm bringing all this up."

"May I assume Trea Culverson has something to do

with this attack on my appearance? Do you know what I think, Nannie? I think you are envious."

"Envious!" Nannie's face flushed bright red. "Why would I be? Really, Juliette. I only want to point out that you are not at all right for Trea. I would not want you to be hurt by pursuing him. Don't you remember when we were young girls? How you were the only one he had no interest in?"

A thousand replies sprang to her tongue but it was Mrs. Cromby, standing on the landing, who voiced them. Mrs. Cromby did not bother to refrain from shouting.

"You, Nannie Breene, are a contentious troublemaker! If you ever have a hope of capturing any man, it's you who need to change. Go away and quit pestering Juliette. She is far lovelier than you can ever hope to be."

"Well! That is the most insulting and untrue thing I have ever heard." Nannie backed toward the door, moisture glittering in her bright blue eyes. "I'm a successful businesswoman. I don't need to capture a man. He needs to capture me!"

With that, she spun about and dashed through a fall of cold water dripping from the roof.

"Oh, mercy me. Maybe I shouldn't have been so hard on her." Mrs. Cromby wrung her hands at her waist. "She is who she is, we all know it. It's just that she riled me with those awful things she said to you! I just could not keep hold of my tongue."

"She was nasty." And Juliette ought to be more offended by it. And might have been, if not for the fact that she was about to be married to the very man Nannie thought she was not good enough for. "But you are right about her being who she is. Ever since we were young she's been trying to feel important to someone."

"Just don't you go believing what she said. I can think of a dozen men in town who would be interested in you and those beautiful babies. Probably not in having Warren in their home, though. He's turned cantankerous of late."

"He can't help that. He's gotten confused about things."

What Juliette did not confide in the woman was that she did not need the interest of a dozen men. The one she was about to marry was a blessing she had only dreamed of. And he wanted to love her children, as well as having no qualms about helping her care for her father-in-law.

Trea remained in the classroom until after dark, making sure everything was ready for Christmas Eve. The place looked festive, with the garlands the children had made decorating the windows and walls and the risers in place for them to stand on when they sang.

The students had not been in attendance today because of the holiday but they would come by tomorrow for a brief rehearsal before the performance. It would be a fun time for them, since Juliette had promised to bring cookies and hot chocolate.

Day off or not, one child still came to school. Charlie had knocked on the door late in the afternoon.

Poor kid needed some reassurance about singing his solo. Apparently his mother had been criticizing his voice. Telling him he had no business putting on airs like he was "somebody."

"It's late," Trea said, clearing up the remains of the

dinner they had shared. "Better get on home before your mother worries."

"She never does. Can't think she'll start tonight."

"She might. You can't know for sure what someone is feeling. Wait until the pageant. She's going to be proud of you, for sure."

Trea didn't think that was true, but he did think no one could know what someone else was feeling.

His own father had him confused. He was still as surly as an old bear, but every once in a while of late a softer expression crossed his face. What, if anything, did that mean?

"She says she's not coming," Charlie called over his shoulder as he walked away, the full moon lighting a path for him through the trees.

"Lots of other folks are coming," Trea called back. "Every one of them will be proud of you."

When he could no longer see the boy, he locked the door and began the walk home.

His thoughts went where they always did—to Juliette.

She'd probably be busy with last-minute details, which he intended to lend a hand with. Partly because keeping his hands active with chores would keep them off her, maybe.

Christmas Eve suddenly seemed a very long way away, not the forty-eight hours it actually was.

Trea reached inside his vest pocket, checking to make sure the wedding band he had purchased earlier today was safe where he'd put it.

It was. He had verified its presence no less than fifteen times already.

The gold band felt warm from being next to his heart.

He ran his finger over the engraving on the outside. He thought the circle etched with fir boughs would suit his bride. He couldn't quite believe the goldsmith had been able to engrave the design so quickly. It was what was on the inside of the band, though, that meant the most. He had asked the jeweler to write Forever My Heart.

It was appropriate, because Juliette had been there ever since he could remember.

He was nearly to the hotel, going at a half run against the falling temperature and eager to be home before the sidewalk turned icy, when he heard a shout.

He looked toward the sound, saw a man waving his arms and pointing.

That's when he smelled smoke.

Pivoting suddenly, he nearly lost his balance.

The sky to the east pulsed bright orange. A twisting, leaping finger of flame scratched the black sky.

The schoolhouse was on fire!

He ran, shouting for help, heard another cry of alarm and then another.

Slipping on the gathering ice, he went down hard, scrambled up and pushed on.

At a distance of fifty yards he felt thrumming heat, smelled wood burning—knew the school was lost.

Flames ate up the back of the building. He raced for the front, yanked the rope attached to the bell tower.

Raising the alarm would not help a damn thing, but he jerked and pulled until his shoulders ached. Men would show up with buckets and shovels, but it would be too late.

A block away he saw them running, shouting, waving their tools.

He squinted through smoke that rolled in a sinister gray cloud across the road.

There was the banker, along with Levi Silver, Leif Ericman and a dozen others.

Was that his father charging ahead of a group of his patrons, some of them half weaving and going down on the ice?

Heat seared Trea's face and clothes. He had to back away.

His father's voice rang out above the others, urging them to run faster.

And then he heard another sound. He listened hard over the roar of flames and the crash of lumber.

There it was again! A scream, coming from the rear of the schoolhouse.

On the run, he followed the screech. Rounding the corner as flames jumped out, singeing the elbow of his coat.

He saw a woman, the hem of her skirt ablaze. Leaping, he caught her about the waist, went down on top of her and rolled with her in the snow.

Another shout came from the edge of the woods.

"Mam!" Charlie's voice screeched over the chaos. "Mam!"

"Mrs. Gumm!" Trea gasped, coughing. Her eyes focused on his face, looking angry more than injured, praise the Good Lord.

"Oh, Mam!" Charlie skidded on his knees, caught his mother's arm, batted at her burned skirt. "You weren't supposed to be here!"

Charlie looked away from her long enough to glance briefly at Trea.

Had he been kicked in the gut by mule, he'd not have felt half as stunned.

The boy's eyes filled with tears, his mouth turned down, trembled. The remorse he saw on that young face nearly laid him flat.

"I don't think she's hurt. Just her skirt burned and a bit of hair singed."

He heard shouts near the front of the building.

"Get out of here, son. Take your mother and get home."

"But I—"

"Now! Before anyone sees you."

Charlie's mother leaped up, shooting her child a hateful look.

When the boy bounded to his feet and reached for her she wrenched away. A sneer cut her mouth in a ugly, jagged line.

She fled for the woods, Charlie a few yards behind.

Charlie? Charlie had burned the school! Everything pointed to his guilt. He'd been there moments before the fire began, was still there in the woods while it was burning. And he'd told his mother she was not supposed to be there.

It all added up, but damned if it made any sense.

Trea wanted nothing more than to sit down in the snow, cover his face and weep away the grief squeezing his heart.

Then a hand clamped down on his shoulder. "It's a hell of a thing, son."

"Pa! What are you doing here? It's too cold for you to be out."

"Like I said." His father shook his head. "It's a hell of a thing."

"Damned shame is what," declared Felix, who had been the second man to come around the corner. "Wouldn't know it now, but I always liked school as a kid."

"Damned shame," repeated his father, a red glow glittering off the sweat that dotted his forehead.

"Take him home, won't you, Felix? There's nothing to be done here."

"There's one thing," said a voice a several feet to his left. With all that was going on, intense grief over the loss of the school and the reason for it, Trea hadn't noticed Sheriff Hank's approach.

The man had a gloating—almost triumphant—look on his face. He dangled a kerosene can from his finger. It had to be empty, judging by the way it swung so easily. Hell if it didn't keep time with the heavy thump of Trea's heart.

Charlie, no—it seemed impossible. And yet—

"Trea Culverson, you are under arrest for arson."

Sheriff Hank handed the can to a man standing behind him. "You see how close this can was to him, Stanley?"

"Yep, and no one else around? I'll testify to it."

Hank Underwood drew a pair of handcuffs from his coat pocket. He locked them about Trea's wrists.

A series of creaks came from the support frame on the bell tower. The wood suddenly snapped. The bell fell, clanging twice before it hit the earth.

Father Lindor had been unusually tired that evening, so Juliette prepared him for bed early. He'd fallen asleep right away, which was a blessing since no one else had.

"Lena," she crooned. "Go to sleep, my sweet girl.

Mommy would like to have some time alone with your new daddy when he gets here."

She could not help but wonder what Steven, looking down from heaven, would think about Juliette calling another man her baby's father. But Trea was the only one Lena would ever know. The only one Joe would know, too.

"I'll tell you about him one day when you are older, you and Joe both. And I think, knowing who he was, your first papa will not mind one little bit."

Juliette began to hum in the hopes that Lena would grow sleepy. But no, her big blue eyes stared up, apparently happy to be awake and not having to share her mother's attention with anyone.

"All right, then—"

A clang cut the night, harsh and jolting. Someone was ringing the school bell, urgently sounding an alarm.

Juliette hurried from her parlor to her dining room where she had a good view of the street.

People were running, shouting—some in their nightclothes, some carrying buckets, shovels and lanterns.

A wicked orange glow brightened the sky at the east end of town.

She hugged Lena tighter and sat down hard on a chair. The fire might be in the woods behind the school, but it was unlikely, not with snow and ice on the ground and in the branches.

Which could only mean—the school was on fire.

Trea was at the school!

As suddenly as it had begun, the school bell quit clanging. The silence was more alarming than the sudden ringing had been.

An agony of moments ticked by with the only noise being Warren's uniform snoring.

At last she thought she saw people returning, their vague shapes fading in and out of focus in the darkness.

She strained her eyes to see. Yes, a crowd, looking agitated, was coming down the middle of the road.

Sheriff Hank led the way. Steps behind him was Trea, head bent and hands cuffed.

The group rounded the corner, coming past her window, their churning voices excited, aroused.

Only the man under arrest appeared calm. He walked past without glancing up. With moonlight upon him, she saw that his clothes were wet, that he was shivering.

It took only moments to race upstairs, gather some of Trea's clothing and bundle up the babies.

She did not like leaving Warren alone, but she could hardly wake him out of a deep sleep to drag him out into the cold. No—he was better off here.

Besides, it would stress him to see Trea locked up. The men had formed a bond, living together as they did. There were moments lately when Warren confused Trea with his sons.

The last thing he needed was to see Trea in jail.

With three blankets draped over the buggy, she pushed it up the street. The moon cast their shadow in a long, distorted figure, which seemed as bizarre as everything else that was happening.

By now, only a few people remained outside. As frigid as it was, they had no doubt taken to their firesides to discuss the night's dire event.

How many believed the schoolteacher would set the school on fire? After how dedicated he'd been to the children's education, how many would?

Coming to the foot of the stairs of the sheriff's office, Juliette picked up the babies. With one in each arm she carried them up the steps.

Only two people were inside the office, the sheriff and Nannie.

Sheriff Hank sat at his desk, feet propped upon it while he grinned. Nannie, seated across from him, leaned forward, frowning but apparently intent on everything that hissed from the lawman's tongue.

Juliette did not know what evidence the sheriff had to make the arrest, but she did know it was false.

"Sheriff," she said. Hank Underwood looked up, clearly startled to see a woman holding two babies standing in his doorway. "If you would not mind bringing in my buggy?"

He hesitated. She readily interpreted the frown on his face to mean the chore was beneath his dignity as an enforcer of the law. He did look rather proud in the moment.

"I'd be ever so grateful. I'm sure you would not want the babies to take chill from it being frozen through."

"Why, not at all." All of a sudden his expression transformed. Evidently he liked the image of being a hero to her and the babies. Especially with a fledgling reporter, pencil in hand, watching him. "It's no trouble at all."

"What are you doing here?" Nannie asked once the sheriff had stepped outside.

"I don't imagine anyone thought of providing Trea with dry clothes?"

No one, she would bet, had bothered to light the stove in the cell area, either.

"No, I don't believe so." Nannie glanced toward the

closed door to the cells. She jotted something down on the notepad she held on her lap. "I'd have thought of it—honestly, I would have—if I weren't so taken up with writing the story for the paper."

The sheriff came back inside and set the buggy near the stove.

"Here." Juliette handed Lena to Nannie and Joe to Hank Underwood.

"Oh, no, I can't. I've never..." Nannie's expression looked stricken, as if Juliette had placed dynamite in her arms instead of a smiling child.

The sheriff looked down at Joe with a half-tender expression. How odd.

That just went to show that everyone, except maybe Nannie, had a soft spot for babies.

"I can hardly take her back there with me," Juliette explained.

"No one goes back there." The sheriff's soft expression vanished.

"Well, I do." Juliette snatched up the package she had stuffed into the buggy. "As I understand it, you have not provided dry clothes for the..." She could not get the word *prisoner* past her lips. "For the accused."

"Well, I—things were—go ahead, then. Don't be long and be sure and leave the door open."

Drat it! She had hoped for a few minutes alone with Trea.

Opening the door to the cell area, she found that it was, indeed, cold back there, and none too clean. Trea sat on a stained cot, shivering, his shoulders hunched.

Luckily the cell was in a spot that could not be seen from the open door.

She rushed forward, curled her fingers around bars

that felt more like icicles than iron. Seeing her, he stood, crossed the small space and wrapped his hands around her fingers.

"Charlie," he whispered. "I think it might have—"

A shadow fell across the hallway. Nannie, hovering just outside the door with Lena in her arms.

Trea dropped his hands, backed away from the bars.

"I've brought you some dry clothing, Mr. Culverson," Juliette declared loudly enough to be heard in the other room.

Half of her didn't care if they found out about her relationship with Trea. The other half, the prudent half, knew it would be folly to add more scandal to what he was already facing.

"I know you are innocent," she mouthed.

He nodded. "Charlie?" he mouthed back. The grief reflected in his eyes broke her heart.

"Are you certain?" she answered voicelessly.

He shrugged, whispered, "He was there—he looked stricken—I think he might have."

"You were there. You look stricken. Maybe he's as innocent as you are."

"You finished in there?" It sounded as if the sheriff's patience, such as it was, was near an end. She'd better take Joe out of his arms.

"I'll be back with breakfast," she called for him and Nannie to hear.

Turning, she blew Trea a kiss then returned to the office.

She swept past Nannie and snagged Joe out of Hank Underwood's arms. Then she took Lena and tucked her into the buggy beside her brother-cousin.

"Actually…" Nannie's gaze followed Juliette to the

stove where she paused to warm herself after being in the cells. "That was rather a half-pleasant experience."

"A child is not an experien—" This was not the time for a lecture on the joy of mothering. "Here is a story for you to put in the paper."

"I have one—about the fire."

"I'm sure you do, but I don't think you believe that Mr. Culverson is guilty any more than I do."

"What I think is not important. But what is your story?"

"That a visitor to the jail found conditions in the cell area to be abhorrent. That a prisoner was left back there to shake his health away in wet clothes without a fire to dry them while—" she fixed her gaze upon Hank Underwood "—the upholder of the law sat in toasty comfort in his office."

Nannie sat down, picked up her pencil and began to write.

"You can also report how said visitor refused to leave until said sheriff corrected the situation and lit the stove in the cell area."

"May I write that you corrected the neglect, Mr. Underwood? Because it would be unfortunate to have to report that the visitor sat here all night along with her two infants."

"And that her father-in-law was at home by himself," Juliette pointed out. "That perhaps he awoke, found himself alone and wandered over to the saloon where he became drunk as a magpie, fell and broke his hip."

"That would make for a story." Nannie tapped the tip of her pencil on the page. "One which would find our lawman looking for a new job, I fear."

"But the wood is all the way out back in the shed."

"Oh, yes! That is even better, don't you think so, Juliette? That the schoolmaster was sickened by the sheriff's fear of venturing into the dark?"

"I think that would make headlines as far as Smith's Ridge."

With a grunt, Sheriff Hank snatched his coat off a hook, shoved his arms in. He went outside while pulling on his gloves and cursing under his breath.

"It was kind of you to go to the trouble of seeing to Trea's welfare." Nannie sagged back in her chair. "I'm ashamed that I did not think of it myself. I'll have to think of a way to make it up to him."

As much as Juliette wanted to point out that it was not her place to make anything up to Trea, she held her tongue.

The very last thing she was going to do was give fuel to gossips.

Not that, in ordinary circumstances, an engagement would be scandalous, but given the fact that she and Trea were living under the same roof, that he was the disgraced schoolmaster and that his last name was Culverson?

It would be the horror of the decade.

Trea was a shamed man.

Especially given that he had chosen to remain silent in the face of the accusations the sheriff hurled at him.

There was no proof of any of it. Still, when he listened to some of the arguments, they did make sense.

He did have a reputation for setting fires. It had only been bad luck that on that long-ago night, when the livery burned, he'd been there, hiding from his father's foul mood in a stall. Worse luck that the peg holding a hanging lantern broke. The lantern had fallen into and ignited a pile of straw before he could do anything to prevent it.

It would appear that someone who knew his past—which was nearly everyone—wanted him gone badly enough to commit arson. Hell, apparently they had begun by burning his house.

Charlie? It seemed so. The thought made his gut sour.

A few people he'd overheard did wonder how he'd managed to burn his own house before he ever returned to town and why he would set a torch to the school he had worked so hard for.

Others remembered who he was, whose he was, and found him guilty as charged.

One man had seen him sprinting from the fire. He could not know that Trea was not running from something but to something. All he'd had in mind last night was spending a cozy night in close company with his bride-to-be.

If he hadn't been running, he might not be sitting here now. Still, there had been the empty can of kerosene that the sheriff believed he had used to ignite the flames. Hell, just because the can was found steps from him didn't mean he'd used it to set a fire.

Hearing the rattle of a tray, he stood up from his cot.

The thought of eating the breakfast Juliette was delivering didn't set right.

He was glad the sheriff was out of the office. What he had to say needed privacy.

"You don't look good," Juliette said, sliding the tray under the cell door.

She reached for his hand through the bars but he

backed up. This was going to be misery enough. If he was touching her, he wouldn't go through with it.

"I can't marry you." There it was, quickly said and to the damned point.

She stared silently at him, shaking her head.

"Of course you can." She waved her hand at the bars dismissively. "This changes nothing."

"It changes everything." He sat back down on the cot with a thud. The farther away he was from the scent of her, the unique combination of ham, eggs and infants, the easier it would be to have this conversation, maybe. "I'm a ruined man."

"But you aren't guilty."

"No, but it doesn't matter. My reputation is worse than it ever was. Everything you are working for will fail if you are involved with me. I won't be responsible for shattering your dream."

"Do you love me?"

He leaped from the cot, dashed to the bars and cupped her face in his hands.

"You know I do!" He had to make her understand. "That's why I won't marry you. I refuse to ruin your future."

She patted his hand, smiled as if what he'd just told her was not earth-shattering.

"I've had my future taken from me once before in an irrevocable way. You are alive and breathing. I will not have you taken from me, Trea. So, yes, we will be married tomorrow, just like we planned it."

"We won't. You have a future. I might not. You have got to accept my decision."

The kiss she blew him, and the wink she flashed in

spinning away, cut him off at the knees. He barely made it back to the cot.

"I'm going to prison!" he called after her.

If it came down to him or Charlie, it would be him.

"Tomorrow!" she called back.

What the blazes?

Juliette met the train and escorted her group of guests to the hotel.

Coming in the front door, she had the pleasure of hearing them gasp in delight over the twelve trees. One of them exclaimed that this was the most inviting establishment she had ever stayed in. Another declared loudly that he might book his stay for a day longer.

While Juliette was thrilled by this, the joy did not sink in as deeply as it might have, given the sharp turn her wedding plans had taken.

She had put on a show of confidence in front of Trea, but in the end he was in jail. Not only that, he had been right about her intimate connection with him being at odds with making a success of her business and her town.

If she was going to succeed financially, and she had to with a family to support, her hotel had to prosper.

Did this mean she had to choose between Trea and success?

Well, she would think of something. Making a choice was not something she could do.

In the spirit of courage, she smiled and thanked her guests before leaving them in the capable hands of Mrs. Cromby.

Thank goodness for the woman. Juliette would never have been ready for the grand opening without her help.

Bless her heart, not only had she made every room clean and inviting, but she'd welcomed the guests and volunteered to watch Warren and the children while Juliette paid a visit to Charlie Gumm.

Bunching the hood of her cloak close to her face, she walked into the wind, all the while thinking about the child.

His house was in the woods, but luckily not far out of town. She spotted the roof through a break in the tree branches.

Oh, my! The place looked cold, perhaps even deserted.

She knocked on the door. No one answered, but a cat strolled across the porch and brushed her skirt.

"Hello, friend," she said to the furry creature, its tail swaying proudly in the air as it breezed past. "Where is Charlie?"

"Here, Mrs. Lindor." Charlie's voice came from behind her.

Turning, her heart sank.

The child stood halfway between the house and a decrepit barn, his appearance ragged. There were shadows under his eyes that a boy his age should not have.

"Is your mother at home?"

"Sure. She's here. She's only just asleep."

Juliette glanced back at the dark house, unable to hide a frown.

"Mam's a real deep sleeper."

"I see," Juliette said, even though she did not completely. How could a body dwell in such a dreary place? "Well, I've come to see you, anyway."

"Is Mr. Culverson still in jail?"

Now that she looked closely, she noticed that his eyes were puffy, his nose red.

Had he been crying because of a guilty conscience? Weeping did not necessarily make that the case. Cora had also been weeping, along with many other students.

Having a beloved teacher accused of such a crime against them had to be devastating.

Especially for Charlie, whose bond with Trea had been deepening by the day.

"Yes, he is. But I'm sure they will let him out as soon as the truth of what really happened comes out."

Charlie's gaze shot to the ground.

"Sweetheart," she said, gently placing her hand on his shoulder. "Was it you—"

"Weren't me!" He jerked backward, but still would not look at her.

"I was not asking if you burned the school, Charlie. I don't believe you did and neither does Mr. Culverson."

At least, she did not believe the boy had done it on purpose. In her opinion, one that she knew Trea shared, Charlie would not have intentionally done damage to his school. Accidental fires were a common thing, after all.

"He doesn't?" the boy sniffed.

"No. He thinks the world of you."

Juliette pretended not to notice that Charlie had begun to cry again.

"What I was going to ask is, are you the one who is the leader for the singing—for the pageant?"

"Naw, it's Mr. Culverson."

"Oh, but—well—he wants me to ask you if you will take his place." This was not actually true, but she was confident that it would be true, if Trea had been here to do the asking. "With getting the students organized."

"We're still going to do it?" He blinked his wide, damp eyes, wiped them on his sleeve.

"Yes, of course. You will be performing at the hotel, instead. Mr. Culverson wants you to let the other children know, because there is no one he trusts more to get it done."

"For a fact?"

Probably… So she said, "For a fact. You won't let him down, will you?"

"No, Mrs. Lindor, I won't."

"Good, then. Give my regards to your mother when she wakes up."

Charlie glanced at the house, nodding and silent.

"I was just thinking." The thought of him having to go into that place left her chilled. "Cora is at the café. Why don't you come back with me and you can tell her first, while you have lunch."

"I'd like that, Mrs. Lindor. I wouldn't want to let Mr. Culverson down."

They walked together, neither one of them speaking. She didn't know why Charlie was silent, but her own silence was due to the fact that she was praying he was not living with the guilt of the crime—the shame of nearly injuring his mother and putting his teacher in jail.

This would be too much of a burden for anyone, let alone this needy boy.

Chapter Fourteen

Juliette opened the door to go out of the café carrying two lunch trays, one stacked upon the other. Yes, she did mean to butter up the sheriff and was not ashamed to do so if it would help get her what she wanted.

Glancing back over her shoulder, she saw Charlie and Cora at a rear table, huddled in deep conversation. Well, Cora was speaking while Charlie ate.

She had been in this business long enough to know a hungry person when she saw one. While it was not unusual for growing boys to be ravenous, Charlie was half famished.

As soon as she visited the sheriff, Juliette had half a mind to go back to the Gumm home, this time to confront Charlie's mother.

His condition wore on her heart all the way to the sheriff's office.

She was not in the best of moods when she entered and found the lawman sitting at his desk with a small piece of wood in one hand and a whittling knife in the other.

Seeing her, he put the knife and the half-formed shape of a bear into the top desk drawer.

He blew the shavings onto the floor, which made Juliette itch to—no, never mind that! The last thing she was going to do was clean up after this man.

She set one of the food trays on his desk.

He grinned at her in appreciation.

"Thank you, Mrs. Lindor." He rubbed his hands together, looking eager to eat. "Can't get out like I used to, now that I've got a criminal behind bars."

The scent of fried chicken drifting out from under the napkins reminded her that she hadn't eaten since—well—when was it? A good long time ago, anyway.

"I'd like to point out, Mr. Underwood, that you do not have a criminal in your cell, you have an accused man. Until the time Mr. Culverson goes to trial, and in the unlikely event he is found guilty, he remains innocent."

"So they like to go on about. But when you catch a fellow red-handed, makes you think something different."

"Who was it who caught him holding the can, exactly?"

"S'pose no one found it in his hand. But it was there and so was he."

"There were many people present. Most of them close to the can, I'm sure, even you. And, you were the only one actually touching the can. What's to say you—"

"I'm the upholder of law and order, that's what's to say."

A few things came to mind that she wanted to point out about that statement, but she settled for, "And Mr. Culverson is the educator of the children. Why would he burn down their school?"

"Can't say why, but he's got a reputation for that sort of mischief."

"And you have a reputation for—" Accusing him of being slipshod in his duties would not get her what she wanted. "For being fair and above prejudice."

"Folks think that, do they?" He drummed his fingers on the napkin he had not yet removed from the tray.

She nodded because she could not utter such an obvious fib out loud a second time.

"We both know I'm one wrong step away from losing this job." He drew the napkin off the food, inhaled the aroma of freshly baked bread. "Get to the point of why you're flattering me."

"Bail. I want to post bail for Mr. Culverson."

"Request denied," he said while biting off a hunk of bread.

"He has a right to it."

He pointed the end of the roll at her. "Only if I think he's not going to up and run off."

"Run off? He would never set that example for the children."

"So you say. Others will say I'm letting an arsonist loose on the town, one who might burn their homes down around them while they sleep."

"How much do you want? Aside from what the bail ought to be. How much do you want for yourself?" Oh, dear. She ought not to have said that. Most of her money was invested in the hotel.

"That's a downright insulting offer, Mrs. Lindor."

"Trea Culverson is an innocent man."

"That's for the judge to decide."

"And until he gets here, the accused has a right to bail."

"And I have a right to tell you to get out of my jailhouse. Get along now unless you want to get locked up, too. There's an empty cell back there."

"You can't just lock someone up!"

"Can if they're behaving in a disorderly manner." He opened the desk drawer and withdrew a pair of handcuffs, slammed them down. "Scoot on out of here and stop attempting to influence the just course of law and order."

Something in the narrow glint of Hank Underwood's eyes told her he did mean what he threatened.

Since she would do no one any good by being locked up, she set Trea's lunch down on the desk.

Spinning about, she walked toward the door, kicking wood shavings every which way—on purpose.

Juliette was getting married tomorrow.

Cold, hard facts did not indicate that to be the truth, but tomorrow was Christmas Eve. If any time of the year was ripe for wonder and unexpected miracles, it was this one.

Hadn't she given up hope of having a dozen Christmas trees in her lobby? Yet there they were.

She had despaired of seeing her town turn around, and now one of the saloons had closed, a doctor was setting up shop and there were guests in her beautiful new hotel.

Years ago she had tearfully given up her adolescent passion for a boy, stuffed it away the same as she had her dolls and games. Now the seeds of love that she had buried were blooming, too beautiful to even think of without emotions bringing her to the point of tears.

Although she could not see how, she did have faith

that Christmas Eve would see her a married woman. It might be a wavering faith, but it was faith nonetheless.

Which meant she had a lot of work to get done before then.

She'd meant to go straight to the hotel, but when she passed the café, she saw a crowd through the window.

No doubt Rose would need her help.

As it turned out, the dining room was not filled with paying customers but with schoolchildren.

"Mrs. Lindor!" cried out young Maxwell, rushing forward to wrap his arms around her skirt. "We is going to jail!"

"I certainly hope not, Maxwell." She patted his head, looked about to see several students nodding.

"It's true," Cora announced. "It's where our teacher is and so it's where we are going to rehearse."

"Your parents don't mind?"

"Most don't." She shrugged, apparently dismissing the objections of the ones who did.

"Well then, I'll bring the cookies and the hot chocolate."

Just see if Sheriff Hank had the audacity to turn children away!

In high spirits, they put on coats, scarves and gloves against the wind. Catching the spirit of adventure, Juliette smiled while she loaded the baby buggy with treats.

Even though this was not what the children had had in mind for their last rehearsal, it would be something they never forgot.

Juliette went to the kitchen to kiss Lena, Joe and Warren goodbye. Luckily the gesture did not wake them from their afternoon naps.

Hurrying back into the dining room, she pushed the stroller after the children.

A well-dressed stranger coming through the doorway stood aside to let them pass.

"Good day," he greeted them with a tip of his expensive-looking bowler hat. "I imagine you are Mrs. Lindor?"

"I am, yes."

"It appears you're in a hurry. If you don't mind I'll walk with you, introduce myself along the way."

"I ought to warn you that we are going to the jailhouse, but feel free to join us."

The fellow was dressed in fine clothing. A gold pocket watch peeked from under his open coat as they hustled along.

She was half winded from trying to keep up with the excited, chattering group of students. Even Charlie was close to smiling.

"I'm Dr. Fulsom. Suzie Fulsom's son."

That was very good news. From now on she would have fewer sleepless nights.

"I can't tell you how happy we are that you've come."

From across the street, she saw Nannie stroll out of the dress shop, three boxes loaded in her arms. Her gaze fastened on Dr. Fulsom. She nearly dropped her packages in her rush to cross the road.

"And I'm happy to be here," he answered, not seeming to be aware that Nannie was suddenly standing at his elbow. "From what my mother tells me, you have twin babies. I just wanted to introduce myself, let you know that I'm available night or day if you need me."

"I can't even say how grateful I am for that! Believe me—"

"Hello. I'm Nannie Breene." Nannie loosened her fingers from the packages she carried, apparently trying to shake his hand without dropping everything. "You must be our new doctor. I'm so very pleased to make your acquaintance."

"I'm pleased to make yours, as well." A package tipped from the stack. Dr. Fulsom caught it. "May I carry these for you, Mrs. Breene?"

"Oh! Thank you." Nannie smoothed a curl that had popped from its well-coiffed nest during her dash across the street. "And it's Miss Breene. I'm not a married lady yet. In fact, I'm the town's newspaperwoman. I wrote the article announcing your arrival."

"Did you? I thought it was very well done."

"You did?" Nannie looked equal parts astonished and pleased. "I'm new to the position, actually, but I feel it might be my calling—at least until I marry and make a home for my husband."

"We are just on our way to Sheriff Hank's office."

Somehow, Juliette felt that she had disappeared from the conversation. As usual, Nannie commandeered the attention. Juliette only hoped that the new town reporter didn't say something to make the doctor reconsider settling here.

"If you'd like to come along," Juliette said.

The odd thing was, the way the doctor gazed at Nannie looked anything but put off. And Nannie glowed with the attention.

"I'd adore to come along. But why are we going there?"

"The children are having their last rehearsal before the pageant. They want to do it with their teacher. I'd better hurry and catch up with them."

"It's the most awful thing. Our teacher has been arrested for arson. I, for one, do not think…"

The sound of Nannie's voice faded as Juliette half ran to catch up with the students.

"Charlie," she called. "Help me carry the buggy up the steps, won't you?"

If the sheriff resisted allowing the children into his office, she would offer him cookies and hot chocolate.

"Good day, Sheriff Hank," Cora said. "We've come to rehearse for our program and we cannot possibly do it without our teacher."

"I don't—"

"I told everyone that you would have invited us on your own accord if you hadn't been so busy protecting your town to have thought of it. A few of them thought not, but here we are and I, for one, know you are glad of it."

"All right, then—go ahead." He waved his hand toward the cell area, but reluctantly.

Juliette poured hot chocolate and placed it on his desk.

"Oh, but you'll need to bring Mr. Culverson out here. Our parents would never allow us to go back there."

"I don't want to get a whipping!" Maxwell cried.

"I'm convinced you don't want that, either, sheriff. But Tom…" Cora indicated a boy near the back of the group with an inclination of her head. "He thinks you would, but I guess we'll see."

Was that a chuckle coming from Dr. Fulsom?

"I can't figure what would be the more interesting story, Dr. Fulsom," Nannie said in a whisper meant to carry. "How the sheriff turned the children away or how he forced them to practice among the cells."

The sheriff snatched up a cookie Juliette had placed beside the hot chocolate, then he grabbed the cell keys from the desk drawer.

They jingled when he stomped away, then again when he came back with Trea, wrists bound in the cuffs.

Juliette glanced at Charlie. The child looked completely stricken. She was not sure he'd be able to sing.

Small Maxwell rushed forward and wrapped himself around Trea's thigh, sobbing.

"You is a mean man!" he hiccuped, pointing his finger at the sheriff.

"Let's just sing." Charlie clapped his hands when another child began to sob. Juliette thought if he hadn't done that, he would have been the next one crying.

Or Trea.

It broke her heart in a thousand ways to see the pride in his smile as he watched his students form their lines, lift their voices in song. Did anyone else notice that his eyes glittered ever so slightly?

Juliette stood near a window beside Nannie and the doctor listening to the children practice "Jingle Bells."

Glancing out the window, she saw an elderly man and woman stop on the boardwalk. She opened the door in order for the lovely sound to better carry outside.

By the time they sang "Hark the Herald Angels Sing" and "We Wish You a Merry Christmas," several passersby stood on the steps, smiles on their faces while they clapped their hats to their heads to keep them from flying away in the wind.

She held her breath while Charlie performed his solo. At times she thought he might not make it through the piece. Glancing at Trea, she wondered the same of him.

Cora must have noticed the gathering crowd, too. She motioned for folks to come closer.

"I would just like to let you know that even though the schoolhouse burned, we will be performing at the hotel tomorrow evening. Also, all of us want to say thank you to our schoolmaster for everything he's done. He is the best teacher in the universe and we cannot wait to begin school again after the Christmas holiday is finished."

The applause from outside carried easily into the office. Trea hung his head. Juliette knew he did not want his students to realize that they had brought him to tears.

"And," Cora continued, "we want to also thank Sheriff Hank for allowing us to practice here. It was a kind and generous thing for him to do."

The sheriff's face flushed the shade of a beet. It was hard to know if the emotion came from pleasure at the child's praise—or anger at having his will being neatly thwarted by a clever wisp of a girl.

Trea awoke from a half doze when he heard the jingle of keys.

At the sound of boots thudding in the hallway, he slowly opened one eye and then the other.

He expected the sheriff would have gone home for the night. What time was it, anyway? Stuck in this isolated space, it was easy to lose track of the hours. One blended into another.

The only relief he got from the boredom of these brick walls were the moments when Juliette brought his meals. Unless one counted the times when a small mouse came visiting after dark.

Hell, he'd even set aside a store of crumbs to encourage the four-footed visitor to come calling. Not that he'd ever admit the odd kinship he'd formed with the rodent. The eviction of four-legged pests was Juliette's crusade.

Keys rattled in the lock. Hinges squealed when the sheriff drew the cell door open wide.

Odd—since the chamber pot would not need emptying until morning.

"Thought you'd have gone home by now, sheriff."

"Can't. Not when I've got to babysit you." Hank Underwood tossed the keys on the floor inside the cell. "Besides, it's wicked cold outside and the fool wind's come up again."

"Don't think you have to hang around here and keep me company."

The sheriff scratched his head, frowning.

"Here's my problem, Culverson. It's hard to know when someone's going to show up. Won't look good if I'm not here."

"I won't tell anyone."

"Maybe not, maybe so. But let's just say for a minute that another fire starts, and what if it's here? If I'm at home and you're trapped in the cell, there'd be the dickens to pay. I'd be called negligent."

"You're expecting another blaze? Makes me think you know I'm innocent. How is a fire going to start with the arsonist behind bars? Looks to me like you need someone in jail to make it seem that you're doing your job."

"Could be an accidental fire. Stoves go wrong all the time. And Mrs. Lindor is always checking to make sure it's lit."

Trea sat up on the cot, stared silently at the sheriff.

"Why is the door open?"

"So you can escape."

"You want me to walk out of here?"

"Wouldn't leave the door open if I didn't."

Whatever the lawman was up to, he didn't have Trea's best interests in mind.

"It won't look good if you let a prisoner escape."

"Doesn't look good anyway. You wouldn't know it, but folks in town are real divided over you being here. Especially since those kids came in here singing Christmas carols. Don't know what you did to make them like you the way they do. Schoolteachers and the bogeyman were all the same to me."

Trea got up from the cot, feeling stiff from inactivity. He picked the keys up off the floor.

"You want me to escape because it's a better alternative than incarcerating a schoolteacher? You don't care about the right or wrong of the situation—only how it makes you look?"

Underwood nodded. "Also because I'd rather spend my nights at home. I'm done with being your nursemaid."

"Why didn't you give me bail when Mrs. Lindor wanted to pay it? Seems like bail would solve all your problems, sheriff."

"Now, I'm surprised a fine, educated man like yourself doesn't know why. If you skip town, then I'm the fool for granting bail. But if you knock me out, then escape, folks will just feel bad about the injury I got during our fisticuffs."

"You can save yourself the injury. I'm not going anywhere."

"You ran once before. No one will expect any different now."

That wasn't true. Someone would.

Years ago he'd been a frightened boy. The fact that he had been innocent hadn't meant a thing to anyone but Juliette. He'd run scared back then, but he wouldn't do it now.

Juliette trusted him, his students looked up to him—escaping would betray them all.

Right was right and wrong was not. This lesson in responsibility was something he could teach his students, even from here.

If someone had taught him that as a child, his life would have played out differently.

When he thought about it, though, he knew he would not change the past. Not if it kept him from being where he was today. Not this moment, standing accused, but having Juliette's love.

The fact that he could not now marry her didn't change anything.

"You'll have to find another way to look good. I'm staying put."

"That's blamed foolish. You can walk free."

"You ought to know better, sheriff—walking is the one thing to guarantee that I would never be free."

"You turn down this chance and I'll do my best to see you convicted, Culverson."

Blamed if it didn't feel good to close the door, lock it and toss the keys back at Underwood.

Wind howling about the eaves woke Juliette early in the morning. Gusts rattled the windows and sent unseen things skittering across the yard.

The fact that it was Christmas Eve and her wedding day did not give her the thrill it ought to have.

Whispering snow would be merrier than blustery wind. So would a groom standing by her side and reciting wedding vows.

But, nevertheless, this was Christmas and she was going to rejoice. Putting on a festive plaid dress and braiding a matching ribbon in her hair, she reminded herself that this was the babies' first Christmas and she was determined to make it wondrous.

"Where have you put the boy's cat?" She turned to see Warren standing in the doorway frowning at her.

"I believe it's in the lobby sniffing the trees," she answered, hoping that Dixie would do as well.

On the way out of the room, she paused to kiss his wrinkled cheek. "Merry Christmas, Father Lindor."

She would make the day happy for him, too, as much as she could.

On the day after Christmas she thought a visit to Dr. Fulsom would be in order.

To her surprise, he smiled. "Christmas? Why, Merry Christmas to you, Juliette."

On her way to feed the babies, she had to blink away tears. That one smile was all the gift she would need today.

After feeding and dressing the babies, Lena in red and Joe in green, she took them, along with her father-in-law, across the street to the café.

"I'm glad to be closing after breakfast is all I have to say!" Rose declared, turning from the stove and waving a spatula in her hand. "Oh, Merry Christmas!"

"Merry Christmas, Rose, and why?" Juliette asked

while putting the children into their cradles and tucking a blanket around Father Lindor's knees.

"It ought to be merry but everyone is in such a tizzy! Some arguing one way and some another. With all the vitriol being spewed about..." Rose sighed then turned back to flip a pancake. "It might just as well be any other day. Mr. Culverson's breakfast is almost ready."

"What are they arguing over?"

"I haven't wanted to say, since you are so busy with everything and you being Mr. Culverson's particular friend, but there's been a lot of conversation going on about dismissing him from his position."

"They can't do that! He hasn't even been proven guilty of a crime."

"Yes, and Cora has a good bit to say about that to nearly everyone who walks past her." Rose piled pancakes on a plate. "These are going to be cold by the time you get them there, I'm afraid."

Juliette felt her holiday smile slipping. "How many want him dismissed?"

"Oh, as many don't as do." Rose covered the plate with a napkin, tucking the ends neatly under. "But the blessing is that not as many are in favor of it as there were yesterday, before the children went to the jail to sing."

Rose handed her the plate. "In fact, did you notice Cora at the table in the corner when you came in?"

No, she hadn't, not with the bustle of getting everyone in the front door.

"She's painting a poster demanding freedom for her teacher. She is going to march all over town with it before the town meeting today."

"There can't be a meeting today!" Some things did not happen on Christmas Eve. "I didn't hear of it."

"No, you wouldn't. The council members are being tight-lipped. Even Nannie doesn't know."

"It would be all over town if she did."

"I believe she'd have sniffed it out anyway if she wasn't so head over heels for Dr. Fulsom all of a sudden. But everyone will find out as soon as my sister takes to the streets. Do you know—I think that one day, all on her own, that girl will win us women the right to vote."

No doubt that was true. She and other girls like her would one day rule the land.

With a quick goodbye, Juliette hurried toward the sheriff's office, struggling all the way against the wind and herself.

Ought she to tell Trea about the upheaval over the future of his career? Or not?

Spending Christmas Eve in jail would be a dreary prospect as it was. No need to add new angst to his day.

Of course, she did not believe he would spend all day in a cell.

A niggling voice at the back of her mind asked why not.

Her only answer was that it was Christmas.

Christmas would set everything to rights.

Chapter Fifteen

Cora had done her job so well that there were too many people attending the committee meeting to fit inside the sheriff's office, so Suzie Fulsom offered the former Suzie Gal as a meeting place.

This turned out to be a lucky thing for Juliette, given that Warren balked at being dragged out into the cold.

She had been trying to lift him from his chair at the dining room table when she saw people going into the former saloon with Trea and the sheriff in the lead.

"Look, Father Lindor, The Suzie Gal is open again. See all the people going inside?"

"Well, then, what are we waiting for, girl?"

"For you to let me put your coat on."

Standing, he stuck his arms out in a scarecrow stance. She slid a sleeve over one arm, then the other, all the while watching out the window.

There must have been thirty people wanting to have a voice in the schoolmaster's fate. Some hoped to see him vindicated; others hoped to see him condemned, but this was Trea Culverson so there would be plenty of opinions.

Only the first twenty or so people to arrive were able to get chairs. Juliette and her family were not among them. They took a spot in the back of the room with the others who were standing. At least it was warm inside.

That was something to be grateful for, because even if she'd had to peer through a window she would have. Whatever happened here would have a great influence on her town and on her life!

Here was where the man she loved—the one she was going to join her future with whether he thought so or not—would have his fate determined.

Trea sat beside the sheriff several feet from a long table where six stern-looking council members stared at him. Judging by the stony looks on their faces, she'd bet Trea was already condemned.

He must have sensed when she came in because he turned, shot her a crooked smile.

Funny that Nannie, standing a few feet from the door, saw the smile directed at Juliette but did not react to it. How interesting. Was it because she was standing beside Dr. Fulsom?

Perhaps Rose was correct and Nannie's affections had shifted.

As much as the smile she'd received from Warren earlier, this would be a Christmas gift that money could not buy.

For the first ten minutes of the meeting, discussion went back and forth in a civilized way, ideas presented respectfully on both sides.

But when Stella Green bolted up from her chair, accusing Trea of being a scoundrel, causing Adelaide Jones to leap from her chair and with a wagging finger call Stella an idiot, and then Mr. Jones told Mrs. Jones to sit back down, it all fell apart.

Shouts pinged about the room like stones flung from a slingshot until one man raised his rough voice and barked, "Sit down, the lot of you!"

Ephraim Culverson's glare sliced across the room. Voices fell silent.

When everyone was seated, staring wide-eyed, he shook his fist at them.

"You pack of moralizing hypocrites, accusing my boy?" Folks glanced around at each other, stunned and offended, but no one spoke. "Ned Jones, where were you last night? Maybe you ought to tell your wife that, instead of telling her to sit down."

Someone laughed, but only until Ephraim stung him with a frown. "I know your secrets, too."

"What you do or don't know about a few folks has no bearing on what is going on here," one of the council members found the nerve to say. "You, of all people, are not able to judge."

"What a bunch of fools you are if you think my boy set those fires any more than he set the livery to flame years ago. It's a plumb fact that he doesn't have it in him."

Trea stood up, turned around to face his father. No wonder he looked so astonished. He would not have expected the man to be here, let alone speak in his defense.

Herbert Cleary stood up. "Then why did he run?"

Juliette wished Herbert was not a council member. He would not be unbiased, given his shed had burned. "If he wasn't guilty he wouldn't have."

"You sober enough to hear what I'm going to tell you, Cleary? You sure weren't the other night."

The newest citizen in town, Dr. Fulsom, appeared to be fascinated by the shouts suddenly fired from around the room.

Ephraim Culverson gazed silently at his handcuffed son until folks wore their voices out and became quiet again.

"The reason my boy didn't stay had to do with me, not anything he did. You know good and well it wasn't him you were judging that night—it was my damned soul. How many times have I heard you good folks say, *like father, like son*?"

"Too many, I'm quite sure," Adelaide Jones put in. "I didn't live here then, but even I've heard it. You should all be ashamed."

She spoke to everyone but flipped her finger at her husband's ear, a clear message that he was guilty of this and other moral crimes.

"I always wanted my boy to be like me. For a long time I resented it that he took after his ma, instead. I wished he'd done all those things you accused him of—would have made me proud at the time. All you fine ladies sitting here judging—you weren't so fine back then—and some of you upstanding gentlemen? What mischief did you do and blame it on my boy? Hell, as much as I wanted him to have done those things, it wasn't in him and still isn't. It shouldn't be so hard for you fools to figure out that if it was, he'd have come back an outlaw, not a schoolmarm."

Wind shook the door, a fitting exclamation point to Ephraim's remarks.

"And that's what I have to say." With a nod at Trea, he stomped to the back of the room, flung the door open wide and left without bothering to close it.

"You sure you brought me to The Suzie Gal?" Warren stated into the silence that followed Ephraim's departure. "When's the bar going to open?"

When, indeed? A calming glass of wine might help everyone.

It was a crime in itself the way people were behaving in front of the youngsters sitting on the floor near their teacher.

If the children learned a lesson in carrying on a civil debate, it would not be from some of their council members.

One child sat apart from the others.

Charlie.

All of a sudden he bolted from the chair he slouched in.

"I—" he said, his gaze fastened on Trea's face.

Juliette went cold inside. Was he about to admit starting the fire?

But no, he sat back down, slouched in the chair, hands pressed between his knees while he stared at the floor.

Warren took a step away from her side, as though he would wind a path through the chairs to get to the bar. She snatched his sleeve, drew him back. The sudden movement knocked the buggy. Joe started to whimper.

"I believe Ephraim Culverson's outburst, his accusations against our fine citizens, only points out that what we've always believed is true," declared the banker, Lee Bonds. "In this case, it is like father like son."

"Ha!" Cora vaulted from her chair, stood in front of Trea, waving her arms as if to shield her instructor from the judgmental glares coming from the council members. "He's the best teacher we ever had. He's kind and he cares about us and he's a million times better than the one you hired last year. If any of us ever succeed in life, it will be because of what Mr. Culverson is teaching us."

Charlie drew his hands from between his knees, dug them into his hair. She would have gone to him if it not for the density of the crowd blocking her way and Warren's continued effort to go to the bar.

"What do you have to say for yourself, Mr. Culverson? Where were you on the night of the fire?" With her attention distracted, Juliette was not sure who asked that.

Trea glanced at Charlie, then quickly away. His silence spoke louder than an admission of guilt.

Joe's fussing became increasingly fretful. He woke Lena.

"He—" Nannie's voice cracked, her glance shifting between the doctor and Trea. It settled on the doctor. "He was with me. We spent the evening together—we saw the fire at the same time."

"Can anyone verify this?"

"No," she half whispered. People shifted in their chairs, pivoted where they stood, eager to hear the softly spoken words. "We were quite alone."

If an ax had suddenly slammed Trea in the gut, he could not have looked more stricken.

Apparently robbed of speech, he shook his head in silent denial. Holding Juliette's gaze, she knew he pleaded for her not to believe it.

"Suzie Gal! Bring me a beer!"

Juliette would have shushed her father-in-law if she had not been so stunned. If Lena hadn't chosen to react to Joe's fussing with a long, high-pitched screech.

* * *

Nothing in Trea's life had been worse than seeing Juliette's gaze turn to him, stricken. Clearly she had been rocked to her core by what Nannie revealed.

Not a single thing that anyone had ever thought of him was worse than this.

If the one person who had always trusted him no longer did, what would anything be worth?

But Nannie! Why had she done it?

Voices buzzed around his ears like angry bees while he tried to figure it out. All the while Joe and Lena cried, as if in competition with each other.

Juliette looked like an ice statue, standing there stiff and pale.

Nannie, red-faced and wringing her hands, stared at the floor. Why would she sacrifice her reputation to give Trea an alibi? It made no sense at all.

Oh, he could play along with her and go free—lose Juliette and then have the investigation implicate someone else—Charlie, perhaps.

But no. He could not claim to love Juliette and break her heart in order to gain his freedom—in case he hadn't already broken it by refusing to marry her.

He hadn't run when the sheriff gave him the chance and he would not do it now.

"Why would you say that, Miss Breene? It's not true. I was at the schoolhouse all evening."

That admission ought to seal his doom, but the truth was the truth.

"Like I said," declared a faceless voice from the crowd. "I saw him running away."

He wanted to tell Juliette that he had not been running away, but had been hurrying to her. But the last thing he was going to do was implicate her in this nasty bit of business and ruin her chance of making a success of her hotel and her life.

"I make a motion that Mr. Culverson be dismissed as schoolmaster on grounds of being morally depraved." Who'd said that? Trea lost track of who was accusing him, with so many voices at once it was impossible to say.

"He's not!" Cora added her high-pitched voice to the din. "He's wonderful."

"Miss Breene?" When Sheriff Hank stood to speak, silence seemed to suck the voices out of everyone. "Was the prisoner with you or wasn't he?"

Nannie shook her head. "Wasn't."

"Then why would you say he was? And why shouldn't I lock you in a cell for perjury?"

"Because she's not under oath." This composed statement came from the doctor.

"Sheriff!" Trea said. "You have your man. Leave Miss Breene alone."

"I'm sorry." Tears dampened the corners of Nannie's eyes. "I didn't mean any harm. I only thought to help."

Nannie pivoted away from Trea, toward the doctor, her face hidden behind her hands.

With a screaming baby in each arm, Juliette held his gaze. Did folks wonder why they looked at each other so intensely? Probably did, because they were growing silent, all of a sudden clearly suspicious of what went on between Juliette and her boarder.

Please don't let them judge her for who he was! Or, more rightly, who he had been.

She set the babies in the stroller, snagged Warren by the coat sleeve and made her way toward the door.

All the while she held Trea's gaze. Then, framed in the doorway with wind tossing her hair, yanking at the hem of her dress…

"I love you." Her voice carried clearly to the four corners of the room.

And tonight we are getting married—it's what her eyes vowed, even in the face of the impossible.

Before he called out that he loved her, too—because now that everyone knew, why deny it?—she was gone.

The most intense silence he'd ever heard lay heavy on the room until the sheriff spoke.

"As touching as that was, let's go, Culverson." Underwood took him by his handcuffed arm. "Looks like we'll be spending Christmas in jail."

"Noooo!" Charlie launched off his chair, ran for Trea so fast that folks had to get out of his way or be bowled over. "No!"

He flung his arms around Trea's middle, making the sheriff loose his hold.

The child's face was red, streaked with hot tears.

"Wasn't him!"

Charlie took a swing at the sheriff. Trea caught his hand.

"Son." He hugged the boy tight, patted his back as best he could with the restraints. "Don't say anything else."

"But it wasn't me, either, Mr. Culverson. I'd never burn down our school."

"If you know something, you'd better tell us now," Sheriff Hank demanded.

Trembling, Charlie spoke to Trea, not the sheriff.

A shudder shook him head to toe.

"It was Mam—she set all the fires."

"Why, Charlie? Why would she do that?" Trea asked.

"She didn't want me going to school—didn't want me to have anything good 'cause I might get full of myself and leave like my pa did. She thought if I sang my song..."

Cora took Charlie by the hands, squeezed them and looked him in the eye.

"It's all right," she said. "No one blames you for her."

"But I knew about the other fires she set. I couldn't say anything. She's all I had and I never thought she'd burn our school. I'm sorry, Mr. Culverson. It was wicked of me to let you stay in jail. I'm so powerful sorry."

"Then why'd you do it, boy? Why'd you let an innocent man stay locked up?"

Trea took Charlie, tucked him away behind his back. Sweet, brave Cora flanked him.

"Leave him be, sheriff. You know he kept quiet to protect his mother. Any child would do the same."

"Where is your mother?"

"Gone." Charlie covered his face. Sobbing he sat down hard on the floor. Cora went down beside him and wrapped her arms around his heaving shoulders.

"Gone where?" Hank Underwood's voice softened as he looked down upon the broken youngster.

"I don't know. She's just gone. She's been gone since she burned the school. I didn't mean you harm, Mr. Culverson. No matter what anyone comes to say about it, I didn't! I'll accept the blame for what she did."

"Oh, no, Charlie," Cora said. "Don't ever do that! Our teacher knows. You aren't your mother, you are you. It's not like parent, like child. It's ignorant to say so. I like you. And as long as you don't pull my braid again, I'll be your fast friend forever."

"Ah! Out if the mouths of babes." Adelaide Jones broke the silence that had gripped everyone since Nannie made her false confession. "All you good people need to put away the ill feelings that have turned this town sour. It's Christmas and I suggest we all act like it is. I, for one, will go merrily to the hotel's opening tonight to hear this brave child sing."

"Looks like you're free to go, Culverson." The sheriff took off the handcuffs then spun about, walked toward the door that remained wide open.

From where Trea stood, it looked like the wind had suddenly stopped, giving way to a bank of dark clouds that swept down upon the town.

Sheriff Hank halted in the doorway, blocking the way of people going out. He spun about. "I've got something to say to you, Culverson."

Anyone who had considered leaving The Suzie Gal must have changed their minds because their rapt stares fixed on the sheriff without pretending to disguise their curiosity.

Couldn't say he blamed them. It had been an interesting few days in Beaumont Spur and apparently it was about to get more interesting.

"Stay a minute, won't you, folks? After I speak with Sheriff Hank, I've got something to say to you."

A few of them, he figured, thought a rebuke was coming, given the way their gazes suddenly slid away. But they didn't leave.

The sheriff nodded his head, indicating the corner of the room.

People would be disappointed, but it looked like this would be a private conversation.

"I reckon I owe you an apology, Culverson."

"Maybe so, for a few things. But not for arresting me. You had a duty to perform. It was your job to take me into custody."

"Yes, and I'd do it again. But the thing is—I wanted you to be guilty. Would have given me respect in this town if I'd apprehended an arsonist. I know I'm on thin ice with my job, what with my criminal cousins causing trouble and some other mistakes I've made. If I could have gotten you convicted—hell, I'd have looked better. I want you to know, I do regret how I closed my eyes to the fact that you might have been innocent."

"Have you noticed that we've got a couple of things in common, Underwood?"

"Don't know about that. From all I can see, your students think highly of you. The folks of Beaumont Spur don't think much of me."

"Some of them don't think much of me, either. It occurs to me that's for a bit of the same reason. You've been fighting your family's reputation for a long time, same as I've been fighting my father's."

"Reckon that's so. Never saw the similarity before." The sheriff nodded, grimaced. "I've said my piece, now I'll be on my way."

"Hold up a minute. What I've got to say goes for you, too."

"Man's got something to say, folks!" the sheriff called, as if he needed to get anyone's attention.

"You know that Juliette Lindor is planning Christmas dinner for you all at the hotel tonight. That's still going to happen. So is the pageant. And so is my wedding to Juliette. You are all invited."

"Wedding!" He heard gasps all over the room.

After everything, he would not have minded it being

a private affair, but he needed to make it clear that he and Juliette were engaged so folks would not think they had been carrying on a tawdry affair under the noses of them all.

Yes, a part of him did not want to invite them, but he did it anyway. If there was ever an event to mend a rift, it was a Christmas Eve wedding.

What Juliette wanted to do was watch out her dining room window for Trea to return to the hotel.

According to Rose, he had been set free when Charlie revealed the truth about his mother.

But once again, Father Lindor was stressed over his children's missing cat and no matter how she tried to convince him that Dixie was the absent animal, he would not believe it.

Truth be told, she was grateful that he did not. As surly as he often was, he was hers and it broke her heart to watch him fade.

In the end, they spent an hour looking under the lobby trees and the beds, and in dim closets before he forgot what they were searching for and decided to take a nap, instead.

As soon as Warren fell asleep, Lena wanted to be fed. Juliette didn't mind that, since it would give her a few moments to sit beside the window and watch for Trea's return.

But would he return? She had gone against his desire to protect her by making a very public declaration.

She had betrayed him, even though in her eyes it had been the right thing to do. Perhaps her disregard of his wishes had caused a wound too painful to heal. A dark place in her heart suggested that he'd left town without a backward glance.

Of course he hadn't! To think so was yet another betrayal.

What she needed to do was focus on the depth of her love for Trea and have faith in his love for her—believe that nothing could shake that.

"Look at that, Lena," she murmured to the baby, even though she had fallen asleep. "All of a sudden it's snowing. I would have bet money that it wouldn't. So, in the spirit of wondrous happenings, I am getting married tonight, and you, my sweet girl, are getting a father."

In an hour she was going to her room, where she would prepare for her wedding.

She would put up her hair in simple but pretty whirls and attach the ribbons, berries and flowers that took the place of a veil. In high spirits, she would shimmy into her lacy underwear. With a rejoicing, grateful heart, she would step into her wedding gown.

After that, she would go to the lobby and greet her guests…however many showed up after today's drama.

All she needed was one more gift for Christmas—if she got it, she would never need another.

She rallied her spirits with a vision of Trea and the preacher, wrapped up in a huge red bow, standing in front of the biggest and most dazzling of her Christmas trees.

Lighting the hundreds of candles on that tree and the others would have been impossible without Rose's help. Everything she'd done to get ready for this night would have been, as well.

How Trea had managed to do it all on his own, she

could not imagine. She fell in love with him all over again for going to the effort.

But where was he?

At last, she stood among her trees in her green wedding gown with candlelight winking merrily on the satin, believing in Christmas and that all would be well.

Looking up at the angel Trea and Charlie had fashioned from straw, she felt confidence rise. Love was, after all, more powerful than life, death or betrayal. She made this thought her anchor.

Since the guests were not due to begin arriving for another twenty minutes, she had a bit of spare time to wander about the lobby, appreciating the magic caused by candlelight shimmering off walls, floor and ceiling.

She half thought Santa's elves had checked into the hotel.

Remembering how the place had been and seeing how it was now, she was proud of what she had done. But more than that, she was grateful. Had Laura Lee not given her such an unheard-of gift, this might still be a home for vermin and fleas.

The thing was, without Trea, none of it mattered.

Yes, she could live without him. Life had taught her that lesson.

But the sad fact was that her days without him would be much like this lobby had been before the addition of the Christmas trees. Adequate, comfortable, but without magic.

Making her way back to the big tree by the stairs, she looked up, past flickering candles. She gazed upon the handcrafted angel, let the loving spirit of Christmas swirl around and through her.

"Where are you, Trea Culverson?"

A hand, firm and familiar, touched her shoulder from behind. “Hello, Beautiful.”

She spun about, launched herself against him.

It took a moment of squeezing to believe he was really here and not one of the fantasies that had lived in her mind all day long.

“You’re here!”

“It’s our wedding day. Where else would I be?”

She cupped his freshly shaven cheeks in her palms, breathed deeply of his clean masculine scent.

“I’m sorry, Trea, I only said what I did because—” He kissed her words away, made her half dizzy for want of breath.

“You were right to do it. I’m sorry for—”

This time she kissed him, felt the quick thud of his heart. “You don’t have a single thing to be—”

They kissed each other, lips colliding and hearts rejoicing.

“You’re really free?” Of course he was; she was touching the curve of his cheek, the line of his jaw, and the moisture from their kisses lingered on her lips.

“Only until you tangle me up in wedding vows. Let’s quit being sorry and get married,” he said.

“Not much time, then, until you feel those shackles and chains.”

He shook his head, his hair glinting deep brown in the candle glow.

“Better value your own freedom while you can. The preacher should be here soon.” And there was that teasing half smile she loved. Her heart was overwhelmed, knowing she could freely announce that she loved him whenever the urge came upon her.

"But I don't value it." Not one little bit. "Where have you been?"

He stepped away from her, tilting his head at a jaunty angle and showing off his fancy black suit.

"Can't you tell? Getting spiffed up for our vows. Me and my best man."

"Who is that?"

"Charlie."

"I heard what happened! Was his mother arrested? I didn't hear what happened to her."

"No. The woman ran off without a word."

"What a wicked thing to do to him. Poor Charlie. I should have guessed as much when I visited him. That house was so dark and cold."

"I imagine it was even worse when she was there. In the end, Charlie will be better off with her gone."

"I could not be happier that you chose him for your best man. How is he holding up? It's an awful lot for a boy to handle."

"He's strong, and Cora has taken him under her wing. But the thing is, I don't want him for just my best man. He'll need a home. I'd like to offer ours."

"Yes!" What a wonderful and generous man she was about to marry. "Yes! Yes and yes! All of a sudden I can't picture our family without him."

"No wonder I love you." He wrapped her up tight and squeezed.

"Where is he now?"

"Across the street with the other students, getting ready for the performance." He held her at arm's length. His gaze passed over her, lingering, intimate on the places that tended to flare and curve. "You look like a Christmas angel all dressed in green."

"Oh, well." She lowered her voice even though no one was nearby. "I'm wearing white underneath, but I don't think there's anything angelic about it. You'll have to let me know later."

"It's a very good thing the wedding is right after the performance."

"More than you know. I've already moved your clothes into my closet."

His clothes in her closet?

He hadn't thought of that before now, his pants hanging beside her skirts. He'd imagined plenty of other things, but the image of his ties tangled in a drawer with her garters was all kinds of erotic.

"I nearly wish we could skip the performance, say the vows quick and run to the bedroom." And get as tangled up as ties and garters.

"Tempting. But I want to look at my handsome groom for a while first." She stroked the fabric of the black vest showing under his coat.

"You like it? I've got Sheriff Hank to thank for these fine threads."

He heard voices on the porch. In only a moment the event Juliette had worked so hard for would begin.

"What?"

"He rousted Leif from his apartment over the store and got him to sell me this suit." Trea posed, turned this way and that, showing off the fine cut of the garments. "He's the one who bought Charlie's suit. Then he took us back to his house to let us bathe and get ready."

"I hardly know what to say. Will he be here tonight?"

Trea shook his head. "I tried to convince him to come, but he thinks his presence will cast a shadow.

Besides, he says he's got a lot of thinking to do, looking deep down to see if he's cut out for being a lawman. And just so you know—our wedding isn't going to be a surprise, after all. I made the announcement so there ought to be a big crowd tonight."

"It's what I wanted and there is plenty of food. Thank goodness and Rose."

While she appeared to fall deep into thought, probably reviewing seating and wedding cake, the front door opened.

She hurried forward. So did Trea. Everyone here was his guest as well as his bride-to-be's—bride-to-be for a very brief time, that was.

Adelaide Jones swept inside, laughing, taking the room in with a glance. Her children followed, dressed in Christmas finery.

The youngest, a girl, clung to her mother's skirt, but her eyes and her mouth opened in astonished circles at the sight of so many candles.

"Santa already comed here!" she gasped.

"Not yet, Pauline." Adelaide picked up the child and walked through the trees, exclaiming at this and that.

The other three children trailed after. Adelaide looked like a hen leading her chicks from wonder to wonder.

"Santa won't come until later tonight when we're all abed," Adelaide reminded them.

Abed seemed a fine place to be, in Trea's soon-to-be-wed opinion.

"And Papa's getting coal?" the little one asked.

"Oh, yes, my sweet one. He certainly is."

Trea slipped his arm around Juliette's waist, tugged her in tight then whispered, "Ho-ho-ho."

She turned in his arms, kissed him deeply.

"Merry Christmas, indeed," she whispered against his ear then lightly nipped the soft, fleshy lobe.

"Just so I'm not surprised, what color are those garters in your drawer?"

"Hell." The raspy voice of his father jolted him back to the here and now, reminding him that he was not yet a married man, not quite free to act on his every impulse. "I recall a time when your mother—"

Felix stood beside Ephraim, a broad grin stretching the wrinkles bracketing his mouth.

"What is it you recall?" Trea asked. Could his father be about to say something good about his mother?

"Most of it, you don't want to know—but she was nearly as pretty as your gal is—and a long time ago she looked at me the same way. Still, you won't get me to say sweet, flowery things about her."

That would have to do, and it was more than Trea had gotten in the past.

Plus, it was nice to note that both men had cleaned up before coming from next door.

"Tell him why you came, then," Felix said.

"Wouldn't you like to stay?" Juliette asked, including both men in the invitation.

"All this fancy—" Ephraim indicated the room with a jab of one finger "—decor. It makes me itch."

"I'd be pleased to stay, Mrs. Lindor." Felix tipped his hat, then went to join some other guests who had come in.

"I appreciate you speaking up for me earlier, Pa."

"It was the blamed truth, bore saying is all." He put one finger between his neck and his shirt, yanked it as if it were choking him. "I'll have my say, then get on back. The thing is, with Mrs. Lindor on her crusade to make this town respectable, don't see how I'll be able to support two saloons—even with Suzie Folsom closing up. So I figure you might as well have The Saucy Goose for your schoolhouse."

"That's very kind of you, Mr. Culverson!" Juliette spoke up when Trea stood silent as a stone. "The children will be grateful."

His pa nodded his head once, firmly, then turned and took four steps toward the door.

"Pa! Wait!" Trea dashed after him, halted his father with a tug on his elbow. "I'd like for you to stay, for my wedding, right after the children sing."

"Son, you—" Ephraim placed his big rough hand on Trea's shoulder, squeezed, then seemed to be searching for words. "That boy's going to sing again, you say?"

"He is." Trea placed his hand on top of his father's, squeezed back.

"Where'd Felix get off to?"

A second later she and Trea both stared through the trees, seeing the big silhouette lumbering in and out of sight.

"I think he just gave us his blessing," Trea murmured.

"Yes, I'm sure that's what that was."

Trea kissed her cheek. "I better bring the children over. The sooner they sing, the sooner you become my wife."

"I'll be here greeting guests and checking on the food."

Juliette felt compelled to watch Trea in the distance while he spoke to his father, just to make sure he was really there and that she had not dreamed the gift of the new schoolhouse.

She hoped that Trea would make a public announcement of it so people would quit looking at Ephraim and Felix as if they had accidently wandered into the wrong building.

"There you are!"

"Hello, Nannie."

"You won't believe it!" As always, when she had something to reveal, Nannie's eyes glowed bright blue, her chin jutted forward.

"I might. Let me guess. Dr. Fulsom is sweet on you and plans to begin courting?"

Of all things, Nannie blushed. Juliette could not recall seeing that happen in the past.

"I hope that's true, but it isn't my news." She snatched up Juliette's hands, held on to them as if she might float off the floor if she did not. "Papa is retiring and leaving the newspaper to me. Can you believe it? We are both career women. Of course, you'll need to tell me how to balance babies and work just in case the doctor—but I've vowed that I will not get ahead of myself like I did with Trea."

Nannie dropped her hands, put them behind her back. "I see now that he only ever wanted you, even when we were young. I'm sorry for everything, Juliette, and especially what I said to everyone earlier today. I don't know what got into me, except that I wanted to make up for—"

"It's all right," Juliette rushed to say, because it was. Everything was working out as it should. "I know you meant well."

"Yes, I did. But I haven't always, and you know it.

I think, though, you forgive me and I'm grateful. And wait until you see my headline for the next edition of the paper. It's all about how you pulled Beaumont Spur back from the edge of desolation. Made it a promising place to live."

The article might be the very thing to make families intending to move reconsider! Having Nannie Breene running the paper might be a very good thing.

Nannie looked as if she was about to walk away, but didn't.

"You know, Juliette, you might have done something more elegant with your hair, given that it's your wedding day. But—" the newspaperwoman cocked her head to one side, studying her appearance "—it would not have looked half as lovely. You are a simply stunning bride and I will say so in the paper for everyone to read."

"There's one thing I don't have. Perhaps you can help me with it."

"Of course. I'll try."

"I don't have anyone to stand up with me. Would you do me the honor?"

"We were fast friends once upon a time. And I suppose I am dressed for it, so, yes, I would be thrilled to." She squeezed Juliette's hand.

Half stunned by what she and her former fast friend had said to each other, Juliette squeezed back. Perhaps their friendship was not so "former" as she had long believed.

Christmas was a time for wonder! Through everything, she had held fast to that conviction. So far her faith had not been misplaced.

"Mrs. Lindor." Juliette's gaze turned from watching Nannie hurrying off to freshen her appearance to Charlie, who stood twisting his fingers in front of him.

He looked nervous and the sight wrenched her heart.

"You look very handsome, Charlie. You will bring our guests to their feet with applause."

"I'll do my best, ma'am. I just—well, Mr. Culverson—he told me about coming to live with you."

"Is it what you want? You know that you will be the big brother of two noisy, leaky babies and they will look to you to teach them things."

"I want it more than anything!"

"Good." She touched his shoulder. "So do I. But you can't call me Mrs. Lindor any longer, of course."

"What should I call you?"

"Ma, if you like. But you do have a mother, so if you'd rather not—"

"No, she was only ever Mam. I reckon you and, and Pa, care for me more than she ever did, so I'll call you Ma."

"Thank you, Charlie—son." She bent down and kissed his cheek. "Better hurry along to your friends. The singing is going to start."

She was weeping for joy. Two sons had come to her, straight from heaven. God willing, there would be more.

She watched her newest, all long legs and gangly arms, rush to meet Cora, who stood in the dining room doorway.

Grateful did not begin to describe how she felt—about everything. Trea, Charlie, her hotel and the beginning of new life for Beaumont Spur were all things she could never have imagined only weeks ago.

Merry Christmas was all she had to say about that.

An hour later, the children performed their last song.

It was time for her wedding.

Given the way news spread in Beaumont Spur, no one was surprised at the nuptials about to take place.

In all the upheaval of late, she hadn't given a thought to who would walk her down the aisle.

She could ask Ephraim. He was standing in a corner with a half-tender look in his eye. In moments he would be her father-in-law, so it would be fitting.

But no. It had to be Warren. He might not understand, but it would be very meaningful to Juliette. In some way, she would feel it was Steven walking beside her, handing her over to her future.

Warren looked at her in confusion for a moment when she asked him, but then his expression brightened. "This mean you'll finally stay home and take care of your family?"

"Perhaps it does, Father Lindor," she told him. It was partly true, since she would be living and working in the same place, at least until Trea rebuilt his house.

"I reckon Steven won't mind." For an instant, the man he used to be gazed at her, clarity and remembrance in his eyes, then… "Maybe that new man of yours will find the cat."

"I love you," she whispered. No matter who he was or was not in any given moment, she did.

"I love you, too, Juliette."

And then there she was, standing beside the man she had waited her whole life for.

The vows didn't take long to recite, but they bound her to Trea for a lifetime, and him to her, same as the ring that he put on her finger.

Same as the kiss he placed on her lips—for everyone to see and cheer over.

After a time of accepting congratulations, her new husband whispered in her ear. "Think they can get by on their own for a while?"

"All night, I don't doubt. Rose made enough food to last until the New Year."

Not at all discreetly, he snatched up her hand and hustled her out of the dining room.

Once out in the lobby he kissed her then scooped her up, twirling her through the trees. Hundreds of candles swirled past, a vision of sparkle and enchantment.

Trea carried her into their private quarters, kicked the door closed with his boot.

He laid her down gently on the bed and lowered himself beside her.

"I'll love you all my life, Beautiful…my wife."

Slowly, with laughter, with tears, with reverence and lust, he took her the way that made them one in the eyes of heaven and man.

Then he did it over again.

"I like them," he said at last, breathing hard while he stared at the ceiling, sweat gleaming on his chest.

"Like what?"

"Those pretty white underclothes. Put them on. We'll start all over again."

"We ought to get back. Folks will wonder what happened to us."

"No, they won't." He reached over the edge of the bed, snatched up her sheer camisole and drew the delicate fabric across her chest, making her shiver. "They'll know."

Shifting his weight, he came over her, moved so that the chemise slid between his hard body and her soft one.

"Merry Christmas, Mrs. Culverson." His breath fell

upon her lips, gently drifting like the snow tumbling past the window.

"Merry Christmas, husband."

She may have heard a baby fussing in another room, Mrs. Cromby soothing it with a lullaby. She might have heard a dog barking and Warren searching for the cat.

She didn't mind any of that. It was the song of her life.

It came to her as the loveliest of carols.

A song of joy to fill her up forever.

Epilogue

Christmas Eve, one year later...

You are cordially invited to the wedding of
Nannie Breene and Dr. James Fulsom
on Christmas Eve
at the Beaumont Spur Hotel.
Vows will be recited at noon
with the school pageant
then a reception to follow.

"No need to be nervous." Trea watched Juliette hurry toward the lobby ahead of him.

She twined a red satin ribbon in her braid. The motion lifted her elbows, somehow accentuating the sway of her hips.

"I'm not nervous, I'm late." She cast him a wink. "And it's all your fault, dragging me to the bedroom in the middle of the morning as if I hadn't a thing to do."

"Guilty as charged and unrepentant."

She stopped, whirled about, kissed him quickly. "Happy anniversary."

"It's been a blessed year, honey. I'm a grateful man. Sometimes I need to show you just how grateful." He tied up the bow at the end of her braid. "I only hope Nannie and Dr. Fulsom are as happy."

"Well, they will begin that way. The lobby may not have as many trees as it did last year, but the four you brought home are huge and beautiful."

"Father Lindor seems to like them. He sat for three hours yesterday in his chair just staring up at them."

Following Juliette into the lobby, Trea saw Cora dashing here and there after the babies. She picked up Lena, who had taken a tumble, then noticed Joe about to close his fat little hand around the cat's tail. She dashed across the room, caught his fist and plucked out the fur he'd managed to snatch.

The animal hissed, then hopped onto Father Lindor's lap to join him in a nap.

When Charlie had come to live with them, his cat had come and a dog, too. Ever since, Warren seemed more at peace. Dr. Fulsom had told them that, sadly, he would not get any better, only worse. All they could do was make him as comfortable as possible and be grateful for the time they had been granted with him.

In spite of how unpredictable his moods might be, Juliette tried never to treat him with anything but kindness and humor.

"Has she come down yet?" Juliette asked Cora with a glance at the stairs.

"She's been in the kitchen for hours already."

"Shouldn't she be resting?" Trea thought so.

"I'd better go check on her."

"I'll come with you." He thought Juliette ought to be taking it easy, too. It was too soon to be completely certain that she was expecting, but Dr. Fulsom thought it very likely.

Given that school was not in session due to the Christmas break, out of caution, Trea tended to shadow her. And he would keep at it until the wedding was over and things returned to normal. Normal was busy enough on its own.

Nannie's wedding was no simple affair, as his and Juliette's had been. A kinder side to the woman's personality had emerged, but still, she was who she was.

It was in some part due to her efforts as newspaper owner that the town was prospering. Good news tended to make the front page, rather than bad.

"Laura Lee Creed!" Juliette exclaimed. "Get down off that stool!"

"I would, but it seems that I can't." Laura Lee stroked the huge curve of her belly, smiling.

Trea rushed forward, braced her under the arm and helped her down.

"Where's your husband? Seems to me he ought to be here keeping you out of trouble."

Laura Lee laughed, her eyes gone a-twinkle. "Aren't the two of you cut from the same cloth? I convinced him to go visit the sheriff since there's still a couple of hours until the wedding. When they last met it wasn't on the best of terms. He wanted to see for himself if what folks are saying is true, that he's turned over a new leaf."

"It does seem to be true," Juliette said. "Sit down, I'm going to make you some tea."

"Coffee and one of those pastries on the counter."

"Is it right that a lady in your condition gets whatever she wants to eat?"

"Of course."

"Yes, it's a rule, in fact," Juliette added, placing the coffee and cinnamon muffin on the table. "Laura Lee, did you know that Sheriff Hank testified against his own cousins and Johnny Ruiz at their trial?"

"I did not!" She patted the great bulge of her belly. Could a human being really be in there? "That does say something for him, then. That Underwood clan won't betray kin for the world."

Laura Lee frowned, stretched and rubbed her back.

"Are you well?" It made Trea a bit nervous to see her slight grimace.

"Being trapped on a stool will cause a few aches, but nothing to be alarmed about."

Maybe, but why was Juliette looking at her with that half-secret smile?

The three of them took coffee together.

"I know I've said this a dozen times, but I love what you have done here, Juliette. It's not the same place at all. I'd give you the money all over again."

"And I would accept it. Truly, this town would not have survived without your gift."

"Juliette!"

"Sounds like the bride has arrived," Trea said. "I'll leave you to your women talk."

"Hello, Trea." Nannie paused to kiss his cheek before she hustled into the kitchen, her wedding gown draped over her arm.

He figured his time could be put to best use by helping Cora pick up the babies, who, still new at walking, tended to topple over.

Coming into the lobby, he scooped up his baby girl, lifted her up and jostled her just to see her giggle.

The front door opened. Trea's father came in. As always his big voice crashed about the room.

"There's my girl!" Again, as always, Lena did not hear the deep rumble as a growl. She reached her small arms toward her grandfather. "This here might be the only female who ever took to me, 'sides maybe your wife, but could be she only tolerates me. Happy anniversary, son."

Having his father clap him on the shoulder still seemed strange.

"How are things at the Gentlemen's Club, Pa?" Trea's father had refused to give up his saloon, but for the betterment of the town his grandchildren would grow up in, he had made changes.

"Too refined for my taste, but Felix likes it well enough. Gets to play those hoity-toity classical tunes he's partial to. Hell, 'gentlemen' might come dressed in their fancy suits and act all dignified, but they drink and gamble same as anyone else."

"The wedding isn't for another hour. You're early."

His father handed Lena back to him. "Figured I'd try and win over that boy of yours. That him hiding behind Miss Cora's skirt?"

"Go slow with him, Pa. He's shy."

"Reckon I know that by now." Lena fussed to be returned to her gruff grandfather. "I'm going to say this just one time, so listen up, son. I'm proud of you for taking another man's children and loving them like they were your own, and I include Charlie in that. You know that I had the devil of a time feeling like that about the one who was mine, but I do now. I'm proud as spit of you."

"I'm proud as spit of you, too, Pa." Maybe the goodwill was brought on by Christmas, and the good feelings brought on by a wedding, but that didn't mean it wasn't true. "And I love you."

That was all they had to say on the subject, all they might ever say again, but it was enough.

His father tried to win Joe over until the guests began to arrive. Joe did warm to him enough to smile, but not enough to come out from behind Cora's skirt.

When all was in place for the wedding, Trea scooped up his busy one-year-olds, one in each arm.

A small orchestra was set up on the landing of the stairs. The beautiful strains of Pachelbel's Canon in D filled the lobby.

Trea was happy to see that the melody made Warren look up from where he sat, smile and seem aware. Charlie stood beside him, his strong young hand bracing the frail old shoulder.

Nannie stood close to her groom, glowing as a bride ought to, as he remembered his own bride glowing only one year ago today.

Juliette stood a few feet to the side of Nannie, serving as her witness.

Wedding magic mingled with Christmas magic while the couple recited their vows.

"Do you take this woman…" The preacher recited the sacred words.

Trea's heart swelled, tripped over itself when Juliette turned to wink at him.

"Do you take this—?"

All of a sudden Laura Lee gasped and looked at Jesse, shock making her eyes go round and wide.

"Sorry," she said to the bride. "Go on ahead. I'm—"

She groaned, held tight to her husband's arm.

"She's…" Jesse Creed gaped at the puddle that appeared on the floor beneath his wife's skirt. "Having a baby—now?"

"I take you, James Fulsom," Nannie said in a breathless rush. "Kiss me quick and get to work!"

The bride and groom hustled the soon-to-be parents away.

It was a lucky thing the doctor's office was only across the street.

"From the looks of things," Juliette said, lifting Joe from Trea's arms, "the new Fulsoms will be back in time for their reception."

"As I recall, we missed most of ours."

"I'm sure it was every bit as wonderful as this one."

"This is some Christmas!" Trea placed his hand over Juliette's belly. The guests were in such a joyous uproar over what had just happened that no one noticed.

"Fireworks, do you think, for us?"

She went up on her toes, kissed him. "Get out the sparklers, Trea."

* * * * *

If you enjoyed this story you won't want to miss these other great full-length reads by Carol Arens:

The Cowboy's Cinderella
The Rancher's Inconvenient Bride
A Ranch to Call Home

And check out her The Walker Twins duet, starting with

Wed to the Montana Cowboy